Inevitable

Tamara Hart Heiner

Also by Tamara Hart Heiner:

Perilous (WiDo Publishing 2010)

Altercation (WiDo Publishing 2012)

copyright 2013 Tamara Summer Heiner Print edition

All rights reserved

This is a work of fiction. The characters, names, places, incidents, and dialogue are products of the author's imagination and are not to be construed as real.

No part of this book my be reproduced in any form whatsoever without prior written permission of the publisher except in the case of brief passages embodied in critical reviews and articles.

ISBN-13: 978-0-9890888-0-0

Tamark Books
Bella Vista, AR http://tamarahartheiner.com

ASIN: B00B8TMI5C

cover art by Steve Novak

copyright 2013 Tamara Summer Heiner

Dedication

To my sweet children, who know that Mama writes books but don't understand what that means, other than when she's at the computer, it's quiet time.

You little people are the light in my world.

And to my husband, without whom none of this would be possible. Thank you for everything.

CHAPTER ONE

THE SMELL always hit me first.

I noticed it right when I opened the office door, and I paused. It was a lemony smell, like walking through a citrus grove. Growing up in New Jersey, I didn't know much about citrus groves, but I was sure that's what it would smell like. Every time I smelled the lemons, I knew death was in the air.

Mr. Harris looked up and gave me a smile over his dark brown glasses. I made eye-contact with his forehead, a survival technique I mastered years ago. The aroma rolled off him in waves, overpowering the scent of his black leather chair.

"Ms.—" he glanced down at my resume on the mahogany desk. "Lockwood. Please come in."

I swallowed and stepped inside, the wooden door behind me closing with a swish. *Don't look into his eyes.* My palms felt sweaty, and I was glad I wore a black blazer over my white button-up shirt.

Clutching my spiral notebook to my chest, I sat in the chair across from him. My eyes dropped to my polished black heels. I spent a lot of my time studying shoes. Looking at the ground was safer than looking at faces.

"Thank you for showing interest in our internship position, Ms. Lockwood." Mr. Harris's voice was kind, and I knew he thought I was nervous. Little did he know that if I met his eyes, I would See his death. Lucky me. "I notice from your resume that you write the sports column at your high school. You go to Lacey Township High?"

I gave a nod. "That's right." How could I escape this? There was no point in continuing. My interest in the internship position at Lacey Patch, the online news column for Lacey Township, had vanished. I examined his desk, determined to avoid eye contact. My gaze landed on a picture of Stephen, wearing his navy blue and white lacrosse jersey.

My stomach plummeted even further. Harris. Great. Not only was a vision of this man's death taunting me just out of eye contact, but he was the father of my ex.

He must've noticed my stare, because his fingers closed around the photograph. "You covered the lacrosse team extensively in your column. You even mentioned my son a few times. Do you know Stephen?"

Did I know Stephen? I was embarrassed he had to ask. I happened to know Mr. Harris had a small affinity to his Scotch, and that was probably why he didn't remember the night Stephen had brought me over after Jessica's pool party.

Not that I remembered much from that night, either. It was the same party where Stephen hooked up with Jessica—the little hoochie—and still had the gall to take me to his house afterwards. To Mr. Harris's credit, we'd only met briefly, saying hello as Stephen pulled me up the stairs to his room.

"Ms. Lockwood?"

Oh, right. He wanted to know if I knew his son. "Sure, sure." I looked over his shoulder, out the window. Clouds floated lazily by, and the branches of an oak tree with pink blossoms waved at me. "Everyone knows Stephen."

"I've looked over your writing samples, and they are very precise. Yet you manage to insert your voice nicely. Would you be comfortable venturing outside of sports?"

I jerked my head up. "Oh, no. I couldn't." *Stop talking. Stop talking. Drop your eyes.*

Too late.

The vision started as soon as our eyes met. I melted into his soul, becoming, for a brief moment, Ben Harris.

Images flashed through my head of Mr. Harris with his wife, photographing Stephen in front of the mantle with his prom date. Even locked in the vision, I couldn't help feeling a stab of jealousy at the sight of the beautiful blond.

Wait. That wasn't Jessica.

The vision continued, sucking me back into Ben's mind. An ambulance, a white hospital room. A funeral. My heart clenched with the pain of the death of Ben's wife, Abigail Harris. Abigail was dead, and Stephen blamed his father, turning into a moody, rebellious teenage boy. I couldn't bear the guilt, the anger, the sorrow that suffocated me.

Those weren't my emotions. *Hold on to yourself, Jayne.*

I struggled to maintain my own identity while Mr. Harris climbed onto the roof of the house and gave into his despair. He hit the pastel bricks head first, with a crack that threw me out of the vision.

The End.

I gasped and jumped to my feet. It took a moment for the pain in my head to dissipate. Mr. Harris frowned behind his desk. He was still alive. It hadn't happened yet. And the air was free of the oppressive lemon smell.

Maybe two seconds had passed. Time doesn't really move for them when I'm in a vision. I shook my head, trying to clear it away. My heart still pounded as if I stood on the roof, looking three stories down.

"Mr. Harris—" I began. I never knew how to tell them about their impending death. Especially since they never believed me. I swallowed hard. "You should—you shouldn't—"

My phone rattled next to me and I pulled it from my bag, grateful for the distraction, not caring how unprofessional it was.

It's bad enough that I can See their deaths. Experiencing them is even worse. My throat ached with unshed tears, as if it were my dying wife and my angry son.

"Are you all right?" Mr. Harris asked. "Do you need something to drink?"

The tears welled up, threatening to overflow. "Excuse me. I have to take this." I tried to keep my voice steady and rushed from his office, dragging my binder and purse with me.

I needed to warn him. But how? No way was I walking back in there. He'd call security for sure. Or was I just making excuses? *I'll send him a letter,* I consoled myself. *I'll remind him what he has to live for.*

Joshua's face flashed in my mind, a vivid reminder of the first time I'd tried to change a death and failed. The first of many, many times.

I stopped in the hallway and closed my eyes, forcing myself to breathe. I remembered his little red bike with the yellow training wheels, the one he always rode around the neighborhood. He couldn't have been more than six years old. I was only twelve when I met him, and new to the lemon smell.

Taking a deep breath, I pushed off the wall and lifted my eyes. Light streamed through a tall window at the end of the hallway nearest me. Curiosity overran my desire to get away from Mr. Harris's office. Was she there?

I stepped up to the window and peered outside. *She might not be here*, I reasoned. *Maybe she's on the other side of the building, where I can't see her.*

There she was. I spotted the tall, wiry blond, her billowy white dress blowing in the breeze. She stood regal and out of place on the busy New Jersey sidewalk. People moved next to her as if she didn't exist, oblivious to this odd, beautiful woman rooted to the concrete.

She turned her head toward me, and I ducked back, heart pounding. There were two things I could always expect with a vision: the lemon scent beforehand, and the woman afterward. She'd probably always been there, but I had only noticed her in the past year or so.

The visions were coming more often. I used to get them a few times a year, at most. Now I got them several times a week. It unnerved me, made me anxious about going out in public. And I was beginning to resent the woman in white, who surely knew what was going on and did nothing to stop it.

I ran all the way down the two flights of stairs, stopping only when I reached the first floor. Shoving open the bathroom door, I dropped into a stall and snapped my phone open. I had to be the only person left on earth without a smartphone.

"Dana?" I whispered, finally returning my best friend's phone call.

"Oh, Jayne!" Dana's bubbly, perky voice sang out from the small blue speaker. I winced, holding it away from my ear. "I totally forgot. You're in an interview, aren't you?"

"Was." I exhaled, feeling my blood pump a little slower. I hated Seeing. "It wasn't working out. So I left."

"Ugh." Dana gave a non-committal grunt. "How so? One of your feeling things?"

I paused, considering how to answer. I kept telling myself that I should tell Dana about my ability, but somehow I could never bring myself to do it. "Yeah. Just didn't feel right."

"Oh, well, sorry. So, what are you doing now? Want to come over?"

I could just picture Dana, blue eyes sparkling with mischief. Confident, not a care in the world. She wore her curly blond hair cut at the shoulders, where it always bobbed in perfect ringlets. "Well, I have some free time. I should probably get back to job hunting." I relaxed against the toilet seat. "What are you doing?"

"Oh, just organizing."

Emerging from the stall, I stopped in front of the mirror and examined my eyes. Just slightly red now. "Organizing what?"

"My closet. Why don't you come over?"

Really, I wanted to go home and light a candle. The pink one called "Sweet Pea." It was the only thing that could clear the visions from my head. But it could wait. Dana was a year older than me, and at graduation next month we would be parting ways. I didn't want to miss a chance to be with her. "Yeah. I'll be right there."

I slipped the phone into my purse and pushed open the bathroom door. The secretary sat behind the front desk, talking on the phone and writing a message. I brushed my short brown hair in front of my face, shouldered my purse, and marched by with as much confidence as I could muster. My heels clicked across the marble flooring, echoing in the silent lobby. Nobody called out to me and I walked through the revolving doors without a second look.

Fresh air. My shoulders relaxed, even though I knew at any moment I might turn the corner and be accosted by someone's death.

I didn't know what the official stats were, but I felt sure the majority of people in New Jersey die peacefully in their sleep, just like in the rest of the world. For some odd reason, I didn't get to See those people. The ones I Saw were dying before their time. And usually it's not a happy death.

Worry about something else, I told myself. *Like getting to the car before the parking meter runs out.*

Sunshine fought to get past the gray clouds in the New Jersey sky. I shoved on a pair of sunglasses, wishing they would keep me from Seeing. I took out a newspaper subscription for a month, just to check out the obituaries. Once I saw how many accidental deaths occurred every week, I realized I was bound to run into some of these people during my daily activities.

Somehow this knowledge didn't make me feel better.

I only had ten minutes left on the parking meter when I got to my decade-old white Honda Accord. Since I couldn't seem to hold a job, I couldn't afford anything nicer.

The thought made me scowl. I always froze up when I smelled that citrusy, lemon smell. I didn't want to know their lives, and especially not their deaths.

Even now, images of Mr. Harris's impending suicide danced before my eyes. The man with the kind voice and professional exterior was upstairs in his office, probably interviewing the next hopeful intern, blissfully unaware of the unhappy turn his future would take.

CHAPTER TWO

I TURNED THE CAR on and checked my CD player. *The Fray*. The dramatic, melancholy sound was exactly what I needed. Turning it up a few notches too loud, I merged with traffic and headed to Dana's house. She lived in a posh residential neighborhood of Forked River, overlooking Deer Head Lake. With the late afternoon traffic, it would take me at least half an hour to get there. I settled in for the drive.

The music washed over my mind. By the time I parked the car in the circle drive of Dana's white plantation-style mansion, the only worry left was if I had dirt on my shoes. The warm spring sunshine kissed my cheeks and I tossed my head, smelling the salt that carried inland on the breeze. I loved living close enough to the ocean to smell it.

I used my key to let myself in the front door. "Hello?" I could never remember Dana's housekeeper's schedule, and she didn't like to be caught unaware. No answer. I slipped my heels off and padded up the off-white carpet.

Stepping into Dana's room was like stepping into a fairy land. The bubble-gum pink carpeting interrupted the tranquil off-white at the door frame. She had finally replaced the twin canopy bed a few years ago with a full that had enough frills and lace on the comforter to be an advertisement for curtains. But the unicorn and fairy wall mural remained, a reminder of the care-free days of childhood, when we still dreamed of being princesses and hoped for happily-ever-afters.

Today, though, a mound of clothing grew outside the walk-in closet. Dana poked her head out, holding a phone to her ear. "Hey."

"Hey," I replied.

"Yeah, sounds fabulous." She nodded at me and snapped her gum, round blue eyes sparkling.

What sounded fabulous? I cocked my head before realizing she wasn't talking to me. I crawled over her mess and collapsed on the bed.

"Listen, Jayne's here. I'll call you later. Great. Bye." She tossed the phone on the covers next to me and pounced down, propping her chin up with her hands and flashing a smile. "Jaynie! If you really want a job, you're going to have to stop being so picky, you know."

"I know." I grabbed one of her pillows and hugged it to my chest. "But not that job."

She hopped off the bed and disappeared into her closet again. That was easy to do, since the closet was bigger than my bedroom. "You don't really want to work. You just like having job interviews."

"Whatever, Danes." I couldn't defend myself without telling her the truth, so I let her assumption slide. "What are you doing in there? Spring cleaning?"

Her head poked out, and she threw an empty suitcase on top of the clothes. "No. Packing."

"Again?" I tried to sound light but ducked my head before she could see my reaction.

We had always planned to stay close to home and go to Brookdale Community College, about an hour from here. But when Dana got accepted into Massachusetts Institute of Technology on a math scholarship, she didn't turn it down. Not only that, but she planned to exit Forked River as soon as graduation was over.

Not that I blamed her. Lacey Township and the towns that made it up had nothing new or interesting to offer. Which was exactly why I intended to stay put.

"I have to make sure I can fit everything." The bed sank a bit and I looked up as Dana sat cross-legged in front of me. "You're smart. Don't you want to do something exciting with your life?"

That was just it. I didn't. I faked a smile. "No. You think I'm boring or something?"

"Well, you were more fun before..." She looked up, her eyes widening. "I didn't mean to say that."

Before Stephen and I broke up. She didn't have to say it. We used to do things together. And not just normal things like dances and movies, but things like scuba-diving and hiking and going to Walmart at two a.m. To restock our candy supply. Now all of my focus was on surviving the school year.

I chewed the nail on my index finger. "Let's go do pizza-karaoke tonight."

Her eyes lit up. "Now you're talking. Karaoke! It's been forever." She tossed aside her suitcase. "You're on, girl."

"But I'm driving."

"No problem." Dana paused in front of her vanity, reapplying purple lipstick and fluffing her short blond hair. "I'm out of gas, anyway."

I narrowed my eyes and frowned. Her parents gave her a handsome gas budget. "Wherever have you been driving to?"

She gave me a sheepish grin. "I met this guy at the club last week. He invited me up to campus, and I've gone a few times. I'm not interested in him, you know. It's just...fun." Dana threw a scarf at me, which I caught. "Put that on, it matches what you're wearing."

I looked down at my short black skirt, white shirt, and black blazer, and thought how out of place the lime-green scarf would look.

"You need some color." Dana nodded. "Put it on."

"Fine." I wrapped it around my neck and knotted it.

My phone began to vibrate inside my bag. I got an uneasy feeling in the pit of my stomach when I saw the caller: Beth. My little sister.

With a four-year difference between the two of us, Beth and I had always had a comfortable relationship. But ever since she developed the lemon smell two months ago, I couldn't shake the fear I felt whenever I was around her. I had two choices: See the horrible way in which she'd die and live with the guilt of knowing I couldn't change it, or avoid her as much as possible.

I chose to avoid her. Not an easy task when you share a bathroom with someone.

The phone was on its last ring. I flipped it open. "Hello?"

"Sheesh, Jayne, I thought you weren't going to answer."

I wasn't. Out loud, I said, "Well, I did. What's up?"

"I just got done with my study group and need a ride home. Mom told me to call you. I'm at school. I'll wait at the curve by the flagpole."

"Wait!" I protested, but Beth had already hung up. I sighed.

"What's wrong?" Dana stood next to the bed, hands on her hips.

I cocked an eyebrow. "I'm on taxi duty."

"Figures. Want me to come?"

If Dana came along, the two of them could chat and I could just drive. "Actually, that sounds like a great idea. You can keep her entertained." I made no move to leave, however. Beth could wait a little longer.

As if reading my mind, Dana said, "Don't leave her by herself. You heard about that murder in Lanoka Harbor, right?"

"Yeah, creepy." Lacey Township was made up of several smaller communities, all considered quiet and boringly safe. A homicide made the headlines.

And I didn't know how Beth was going to die. Better not to take chances. "All right, let's go."

We took my car, heading out of town toward the middle school. I chewed on the sides of my finger, having run out of nail.

"Look." Dana pointed out the window. "JT's Bagel Hut is hiring. Maybe you could get a job there." She chuckled as if this were immensely funny.

I frowned. "That's an idea."

Dana widened her blue eyes and shot me a look. "Come on. You want to be a journalist."

"I need a job, Dana. Daddy's not paying for this gas."

"You *had* a job. A good one. You quit—again."

"Working at Camela's Fashion wasn't exactly furthering my career," I protested. "I just got lots of good discounts."

"Granted." Dana nodded her head. "So you quit that job because you wanted to start an internship as a journalist."

Something like that. "Right."

"And you walked out of today's interview because...?"

I scowled at her. "It wasn't right for me. I wasn't a good fit."

"And JT's Bagel Hut is what you're looking for?"

I didn't answer. I had no response.

"You're keeping something from me, Jayne. Why don't you tell me what's going on?"

I squirmed in my seat and focused on the road. The commercial district disappeared behind us. Ripe corn fields flanked us on either side, and I stared at the waving golden tassels.

There were so many times I'd almost told Dana my secret. But I didn't want her to think I was crazy. Like the therapist had. Crazy Jayne.

I pulled up at the middle school. Beth flounced over to the car, grinning at us. I put on my sunglasses and stared out the windshield. The essence of lemons wafted in the air around her. My heart rate increased out of habit, and I swallowed hard.

"Hi!" Beth called. "Are you guys going somewhere?" She paused outside the driver's side.

Why hadn't I rolled up my window? I could feel her eyes on me, waiting, watching to see if I would respond. I kept my gaze trained straight ahead. "Yeah, we're going out tonight. Hop on in, I'll take you home."

Beth slowly moved to the back door. I sneaked a peek in the rearview mirror and saw her eyes still on me, her lips drawn together. I rearranged the mirrors so we wouldn't accidentally make eye contact.

I put my foot on the gas and tried to ignore the guilty feeling in my chest. I would not allow myself to See her.

CHAPTER THREE

"THIS IS YOUR junior year of high school?" The manager of JT's Bagel Hut sat across from me at a little table, twiddling with the pen wedged between his ear and visor. The crooked nametag on his shirt spelled out, "Tom." His eyes scanned the one-page application I had filled out.

"Yes." My hands ran over my thighs, straightening any wrinkles in my pink skirt. I felt overdressed. Why hadn't I just worn jeans and a t-shirt? Because I couldn't get over the idea that an interview was professional, that's why.

"Hmm." He put down the application and met my gaze.

I flinched before relaxing. The only thing I smelled on him was garlic and butter.

"Well," he said, "you seem very qualified with customer service. You've never worked with food before?"

"No." I shook my head. "Not professionally. But I cook a lot." Spaghettios, anyway. I flashed what I hoped was a dazzling smile.

"Not a problem, we'll train you. We'll start you as an associate making minimum wage, but there's definitely room for advancement. Sound okay?"

"Yes." I nodded my head, trying not to appear too eager. "Of course."

He eyed me some more. "Great, then. Can you start tomorrow at four?"

"Hold on." I reached into my purse and pulled out a small pocket calendar. Tomorrow was Tuesday, and there were no games to cover. Spanish club met on Wednesday. "Sure. I'll be here tomorrow."

"You're a size small, right? We'll have a uniform ready when you come in."

Uniform? I had forgotten that tidbit. I worked hard to keep the smile on my face as I stood and shook his hand. My eyes surveyed his purple-and-turquoise-striped polo. "Medium. Thanks. See you tomorrow, then."

I turned around. My heels clunked across the gray linoleum as I walked toward the exit. I so didn't belong here.

My phone started vibrating before I even got to the car. I snatched it up and sighed. Dana wasn't going to be happy about this. "Hey, Danes, I can't really talk right now."

"Where are you?" she demanded. "I've got *news* and I've been trying to call you for the past hour! Why weren't you answering?"

"Um." I slid behind the wheel and fished around my CDs. Sarah Brightman caught my eye. A little operatic Soprano to soothe my nerves. Perfect. "I was busy. What's the news?"

"Stephen and Jessica broke up."

My thoughts flashed first to Jessica, the skinny cheerleader with long brown hair. My stomach always clenched at the thought of her. Stephen and I had been so happy until she set her sights on him. When had it happened, anyway? The night of the pool party, when Stephen threw me into the water and dived in after me? Or was it already going on before then?

My thoughts flashed next to the vision I'd seen, of Stephen with a blond at his house, getting ready for prom. I sucked in a breath. He was already on track with his destiny. He had to break up with Jessica so he could go out with the other girl.

"Oh, really?" I tried my best to sound appropriately shocked, while swerving out of the way of a car that almost ran me over. The driver honked, and I mouthed a "sorry." "How do you know?"

"Babe, it's all over school. She was—get this—making out with Blackard in the boy's locker room. Blackard! In the boy's locker room!"

I blanched. "She dumped Stephen for Blackard?" Corbin Blackard was captain of the football team, and fit the stereotype perfectly: big, handsome, popular, arrogant, rude, and ignorant. Not to mention, he changed girls every weekend. My face flushed with indignation. "That cow!"

"You need to come over here." Dana was practically purring now. "Get over here, put something nice on, and we'll head over to Bay Bookstore."

Stephen worked at Bay. I thought of all the lovely evenings where I had settled down in a chair, book in hand, and read contentedly while Stephen worked. Every once in awhile he would pass my chair and flash me a secret smile, like he and I were the only ones who knew I was there for him. My chest warmed at the memory.

And then the blond girl popped into my mind, and I sighed. "No good, Dana. It's over between us."

"What?" she screeched. "It only ended because of Jessica! I bet Stephen feels so stupid now! I know you're not over him."

Of course she knew. Everyone knew. But I'd seen the other girl. I wasn't who Stephen would end up with. "I don't want to be his rebound."

Dana groaned. "Then at least come with me to say hi. You never know what might happen, hey?"

Except I did know. It had been two months since Stephen and I broke up, and I missed him. Horribly. But I already knew the ending, and I wasn't going to put myself through that for no reason. "I'm almost home, Dana. You can go by and say hi if you want. Oh, by the way, I got a job. So tomorrow after school I have to work."

I could hear her getting ready to launch into another speech of some sort, but I didn't want to hear it right now. I hung up the phone and tossed it across the car, out of temptation's reach. It rang the rest of the way home, but I couldn't grab it even if I wanted to.

For a moment I indulged in a fantasy where Stephen and I got back together. He wept for leaving me and I forgave him, and we had a great relationship—for a week? Two? Prom was three weeks away. That didn't leave much time for Stephen to have a relationship with me and then meet Ms. Prom Date.

And besides, I knew something awful about Stephen's family now. How could I spend time with him with that between us? *No*, I realized. *If Stephen and I hadn't already broken up, I would have to break up with him now.*

I parked the car in the driveway and leaned across the transmission to grab my phone.

Four missed calls. Three from Dana and one from Stephen. Oh boy. It would be a long day in school tomorrow.

ଓ

Sure enough, the school day dragged by, with me doing my best to sidestep Dana every time she tried to drag me over to Stephen. As soon as it was over, I headed over to JT's. I was one of the first cars out of the school parking lot, evading Dana and her insistence that I speak with my ex.

"This is where you keep your stuff when you're working." Matt, a coworker and my designated tour guide, led me to the back of the restaurant and showed me a rack of hooks. I nodded and slipped my backpack on one of the pegs. "Here's your uniform. And your nametag. Jayne? Hope they spelled it right, looks funny to me."

"It's right." I picked up the magnetic tag and examined it. "My parents wanted a unique spelling."

"Okay. Anyway, there's a bathroom. You can change and then come up to the front. I'll show you how to work the register and that's all you'll do today. Oh, and I'm the shift manager. Which means, I'm in charge when Tom's not in." He gave me a grin that bordered on shyness, as if he didn't want to admit how cool it was to be a manager.

I nodded. Taking a deep breath, I stepped into the bathroom. A dirty mop stood in a corner and rust stained the white sink. Could be worse. At least I wouldn't be messing with food today. I pulled my wavy brown hair into a ponytail, but a few pieces still escaped around my face. Then I noticed the hairnet sitting on top of my uniform. A hairnet. I lifted it between my fingers and sniffed it. At least it didn't look used. I guess I couldn't expect to look *nice* at this job.

I suppressed a sigh and put the net on over my hair. Not even the wildest of curls could escape now.

Suitably dressed, I headed for the front of the store. Matt had shoved a baseball cap over his hair, which I guess passed for a hairnet around here. He grinned at me, his brown eyes sleepy.

"Hey, that looks cute on you. Come on."

He led me to the register and stood behind me, pointing to buttons and whispering hints while I tried to ring up customers. It unnerved me. "You know," I said, turning around to face him, "I think I might be able to do this better if you're not hanging over my shoulder."

Matt lifted both arms up in mock defense. "Just trying to help."

I took a deep breath and turned back around. I pushed at my forehead, but there was no hair to tuck behind my ear.

"I know it's the middle of the afternoon, but do you have any breakfast sandwiches left?"

I couldn't help but smile at Dana's voice. I lifted my eyes and saw her, giving me a quirky grin just in front of my register. "Sorry, we don't serve breakfast sandwiches after ten in the morning."

"Figures," she sighed. "You look great, babe. Love the hairdo."

"Ah." I fingered my hairnet. "You and me both." I was happy to see Dana. She had thrown an absolute fit when I told her about my job, a fit that was made even worse when I confessed to not returning Stephen's call. "What can I get for you?" Gabby, the girl working the register next to me, was moving customers at a much faster rate, but I could always play the "I'm new" card.

"A cream-cheese and cranberry sandwich on a honey bagel. And a blueberry muffin."

I scanned the register and found the items without difficulty. "Anything to drink?"

"Make me the latte of the day."

"Sure." I flashed her a smile.

Dana handed me her dad's credit card. "Get yourself something too, if you're hungry."

"I'm good." I swiped her card. This wasn't so different from ringing up clothes, after all. "There's tons to eat here."

"I bet." Dana smoothed her hands over her checked green and white sundress. Springtime was for dresses—we both agreed on that one. "Better watch your figure."

"I know you'll watch it for me."

She shrugged. "It's cuter than mine, so why not?"

Her food came up from the kitchen, and I put it on a tray. "Here you go. Thanks for eating at JT's." I smirked.

She slid the tray over and picked up the latte. "Call Stephen. It's not too late. Don't be such a scaredy-pants."

Before I could come up with an adequate reply, she was gone, sliding into a booth in the back.

The thought crossed my mind again that I should just tell her. Tell her everything, about my Sight, and the visions, and my attempts to thwart destiny.

But I knew I wouldn't. This was my burden to bear. My secret. She might think I was a chicken, but at least she didn't think I was insane.

Crazy Jayne, Crazy Jayne.

The after-school crowd shuffled in and kept me busy for awhile. Dana slipped out with a wave and a motion for me to call her when I got off work. I waved back.

"Hey." Coworker Matt joined me at the register. "Any problems?"

"Nope." I shook my head. "So far, pretty easy."

"Great." He pulled a wet rag off his shoulder, leaving streaks of water on his purple/turquoise shirt. "Orange juice spill in the left corner. You're up."

"I'm up?" I echoed, taking the rag. "What, we take turns doing this?"

"No." He grinned. "You're the new girl. You'll be up a lot today. Have at it!"

Funny guy. I could tell this job was going to be interesting. I stepped through the counter and began wiping up the orange juice. Still better than being stuck in the hot kitchen making food.

I surveyed my work and went back to the kitchen. "Where do dirty rags go, Matt?"

"Laundry basket in the back," he yelled from the drive-thru window. I dumped the rag and hurried to the front.

The smell of lemons hit me two feet from the counter, and I staggered. *No.* I cast my eyes sideways and saw Gabby making quick work of the people in her line. The lemony-smelling customer could go over there. I turned around, knocking my thigh against the prep station in my rush to escape.

"Hey, Jayne?" Gabby called. "I need a bathroom break. Cover, please?"

Before I could even think of an excuse, Gabby hurried past me. Fine. I went over to her line, taking a deep breath. Lemon-person was in my line, and Gabby could handle him when she got back.

"What are you doing?" Matt came over before I even started taking the first customer's order. "You've got someone waiting at your register."

"My register?" I didn't know the registers were assigned. "Gabby had a longer line and she asked me to cover for her."

"You don't ever leave your register." He turned to the customer in front of me, dismissing me without another glance. "What can I get for you?"

I stood there, debating my options. I could run out the door, and lose this job on my first day. Or I could keep my eyes down, pretend to be shy, take this person's order and be done with it.

Matt shot me a dirty look, and I backed away. Option number two it would be.

I shuffled back to my register, not lifting my eyes. I knew from the citrus scent that pervaded the air around me that the person hadn't left. "What can I get for you?" I stared at the plastic covering the register keys.

"Can I have a grilled Swiss sandwich on a cheese bagel and some potato wedges, please?" The customer's tenor voice and rich English accent washed over me, melting me to the front of the register. I gripped the sides, using all my will power not to look up. Someone with a voice that beautiful had to be incredibly handsome.

"Anything to drink?" I hoped he didn't notice how my voice trembled.

"Orange Fanta. Thank you." Even the way he pronounced 'Fanta' tasted like a delicacy in my mind.

I rang up his order and handed him the receipt, not trusting myself to speak again. I stared at his tanned hands as he took the paper and then handed me a credit card. Aaron Chambers. Curiosity got the better of me—that, and the desire to hear his voice again. "Are you visiting New Jersey, Aaron?"

"No." I heard a smile in his voice. "My parents just moved here from Herefordshire. That's in England, if you didn't know."

His parents. How old was he? My hand lingered with his card between my fingers. I was desperate to look at him. Almost desperate enough to accept whatever I might See. "And what are you going to do now that you're here?"

"Jayne? That's your name, right?"

Betrayed by the nametag. I nodded, staring at the letters embossed on his card.

"I bet you have pretty eyes."

I felt my face grow warm. He was flirting with me! Oh, Satan, get thee behind me! I handed him back his card, then gathered up his food items and put them on a tray. "Thank you for choosing JT's."

"Thank you for serving me, Jayne." My name sighed off his tongue, molding itself to the timbres of his voice. I listened to his footsteps die away, but only when the smell was gone did I look up.

Aaron from England sat facing me, his eyes down on his bagel as he unwrapped it. And yes, he was hot. I couldn't see his eyes, of course, but his sharp cheekbones accentuated his strong jaw. He'd tamed his dark brown hair with gel, but a piece of it still swung in front of his chiseled features. I averted my eyes in case he should look my direction and instead admired his muscled physique. The short-sleeved blue polo showed off his biceps and golden hue. A soft sigh escaped my lips, and I shook my head. What a pity. He was definitely adorable.

I picked up my rag and wiped down the counter, waiting for Aaron to leave.

CHAPTER FOUR

"JAYNE! JA-AYNE! JAYNE!"

I rolled my eyes and slammed my locker shut as Dana slid into the spot next to me. "What, Dana?"

Dana took a deep breath, her cheeks flushed under her sparkling blue eyes.

I raised an eyebrow, wondering what could have gotten her so riled. I'd seen her just before school started, and the only thing on her mind had been passing her statistics test. "I take it stats went well?"

She furrowed her brows. "What? Oh, that. Who cares? This is way more important. It involves a boy—more specifically, a *man*."

"Oh." I opened my bag, checking to make sure I had my calculus book. "Don't you have enough men? What's going on with college dude, anyway?"

She shrugged. "He introduced me to a friend of his. Haven't heard from him since." Dana didn't sound too let down.

"Is friend cute?"

"Jayne! You're so not listening to me!"

"Sorry." I started pushing my way through the hall. Dana kept step with me. "I'm not into guys right now, Dana."

"Please don't tell me this is about Stephen," she groaned. "You've been heartbroken over him since he broke up with you. And then you don't return his call? I don't think you have room to complain."

For a moment I paused, my thoughts torn between the green-eyed lacrosse player and the mysterious boy from yesterday. Thinking of the former brought a tangible ache to my chest, while thinking of the latter brought such a tingle of excitement that it very nearly drowned out the ache.

"I knew it." Dana's voice was soft in my ear. "You're just pretending to be over him. Because you're afraid of getting hurt again."

Afraid. Scared. Chicken. Dana knew me too well. I started walking again.

"Okay, so you don't care about guys. I still do. Don't make me suffer, Jayne! I'm dying to share details with you!"

I let a smile touch my lips. "All right, fine. What boy in our school has suddenly turned into a mature adult and become worthy of your attention?"

Dana hooked her arm through mine and let out a contented sigh. "No, Jayne. There's a Benny at our school. And he is divine."

"Benny" was the local term for an outsider, someone not from Forked River. I stopped and drew back, studying her face. "He just moved here?"

"Yes." Dana gave a dreamy sigh. "And he looks exactly like Christopher Reeve—you know, in the Superman days."

It couldn't be him. I felt my heart tumble under my ribcage, and I didn't know which emotion hit me stronger: fear or anticipation. "O-oh yeah?"

"And Jayne, he has an accent." Dana closed her eyes and snuggled close to me. "The sexiest accent you ever heard. He's definitely not American."

"What color were his eyes?"

Dana's eyes popped open. "What do you care? You don't even like boys." She slid into her spot at our shared calculus table.

I pulled my chair up next to her. "I'm just curious. I mean, how much like Christopher Reeve does he look?"

"Oh, like exactly. Only younger. He's got those crystal blue eyes, if that's what you want to know."

I nodded and opened my book, pretending to have lost interest.

But inside a storm raged. I was jealous. Jealous that Dana could look into those eyes and have nothing happen, other than a swoon of ecstasy. I had to admit this guy had captured my interest.

Mr. Keuhl called the class to attention, and Dana whispered, "I'll point him out to you if I see him."

I gave a bob of my head, eyes still on the book. That wouldn't happen. If I even smelled lemons, I ran the other way. I had my classes set up carefully; only two of them had people who triggered my Sight, and I sat as far away from those people as possible. The first week of school had been a bit crazy as I tried to rearrange my classes, but at least the office had cooperated with me.

Dana leaned toward me, about to whisper something else, when Mr. Keuhl turned around and glared at her. Slumping back in her seat, Dana hissed, "We'll talk more at lunch."

I didn't bother answering. It was second period, and I still had to get through two more periods before lunch. Not that I minded. I enjoyed English, and my teachers treated me like a prodigy because I actually did the homework.

The bell rang, and Dana and I joined the throng of anxious students trying to get out of the classroom.

"See ya at lunch," Dana said, popping a Dum-Dum into her mouth. "Wonder where Hottie is now?"

Several girls in the hall glanced back at Dana before whispering together and moving on.

"Looks like you're not the only one who's noticed him. Watch out," I warned.

"From those girls?" Dana glanced over her shoulder. "They're more likely to be the Lacey Township murderer than boy competition."

"What?" I wrinkled my nose at her, perplexed. "Where did that come from?" The afore-mentioned girls might have claws under their manicures, but they sure weren't murderers.

"Oh, you must not've heard. There was another murder last night. In the Pine Barrens."

"Another murder?" I shook my head. "People get lost out in the Pine Barrens all the time." I pictured the dense cedar forest just west of us. "Probably got dehydrated or something."

"Right. And then slit her own throat?"

I couldn't wrap my mind around it. I knew death, and I knew people went before their time. But murders? "That doesn't happen around here."

"Of course not. We don't get cute guys from foreign countries either, and yet... there's one here."

I shifted gears with Dana, my mind already on the new kid. "Well, good to know you're interested. I'll steer clear."

"Who even said I was interested?" She shrugged. "I just like looking."

We both laughed and then turned down different hallways. I ran my fingers along the painted white brick. Dana had no idea how easy her life was. This whole Sight thing totally ran mine. How unfair.

I daydreamed my way through history, a class that didn't require any more of my attention than a few devoted hours right before exams.

I opened my English folder on the way to fourth hour, just to make sure my outline was there for our final research project. I'd already started researching and nearly had my first draft finished, but the teacher only wanted to see the outline today. The topic I had chosen, motifs in Shakespearean tragedies, was so open-ended that I could have outlined forever. I shouldn't have any problems hitting the twenty-page mark.

The lemon scent caught me by surprise as I was about to enter the classroom. I froze in the doorway, eyes on my outline, afraid even to look up. What if I made eye contact with whoever it was?

But I knew who it was. English was not one of the classes I had to worry about. Which meant somebody new was here.

My stomach muscles tightened, and I debated what to do. The scent grew stronger, and someone bumped my shoulder. "Oh, sorry."

There was no mistaking that accent. I closed my eyes, my shoulder tingling where he'd bumped me.

"Hey, don't I know you?" His footsteps paused and then came closer, the lemon getting stronger.

I drew in a hasty breath, turning my back to him before I opened my eyes. "Not feeling well. Sorry!" I fled down the hallway, my heart beating in my eardrums.

Great. Not only was he in my English class, but he wasn't going to avoid me. Which meant I had to avoid him.

But first I had to go to the nurse's office and pretend to be sick. Otherwise, I'd get marked truant.

I hung out with the nurse through fourth period, claiming to have horrible cramps. She gave me some medication and let me sit for half an hour until it kicked in. Then she sent me back to class.

I didn't go, though. I slipped into the bathroom and waited it out. Dana was right. I was nothing but a coward.

At lunch I waited for Dana by the vending machine, our usual meeting place. I tossed an apple in one hand and fingered a bag of Doritos in the other. My usual mix. I definitely ate healthier on the weekends. Or at least, I ate more.

The line in front of the machines began to die down, and still no Dana. Where was she? I distinctly remembered her saying she'd talk to me at lunch.

"Jayne?"

I'd know that voice in my sleep. I could picture Stephen's Adam's apple bobbing up with the word, his deep voice pushing the sounds out as if it required effort. But I turned around anyway, willing myself to breathe easy. "Stephen. Hey. How are you?"

His light green eyes flickered over my lunch, then up to my face. I knew he must be busy with team workouts; his lean torso and chiseled arms said as much. "You haven't eaten yet. Come outside?" He inclined his head to the picnic tables just outside the door.

Dana and I usually ate outside, but not there. We chose the grass in front of the school, where we could watch most of the student population and feel the warm sunshine beating down on us.

I ran a hand through my wavy hair, letting my fingers free fall. "I'm waiting for Dana, Stephen. Have you seen her?"

"Oh, yeah." Both eyebrows went up. "I saw her at her locker. She told me where to find you."

And then decided not to show up. There would be time to kill her later. "Well." I looked down at my sleeveless lavender dress, suddenly self-conscious. What did my face look like? Was I blushing? "Sure. That would be fine."

Stephen escorted me outside. A slow breeze blew, and a tree above us dappled the picnic table with the shadow of its leaves. He sat on one side and patted the spot next to him.

"I met your dad." I felt like an idiot right after I blurted out the words. Certainly there was more for Stephen and me to talk about than his parents.

"Really?" Stephen pulled a bottle of soda and three peanut butter and jelly sandwiches from his lacrosse bag. I eyed them, feeling a lump in my throat. His mom probably made those. "Where?"

Oh, great. The only answer to that would be to explain my failed interview. "Just saw him, really. We didn't talk." *But I know how he's going to die.* In my head, I saw Mr. Harris step off the edge of the balcony.

Maybe getting to Mr. Harris wasn't the answer. Maybe I should tell Stephen that his mom was sick.

And Stephen. What happened to him in all this? My head shot up, my eyes studying him, memorizing the scattering of freckles across his nose.

He squirmed a bit, looking uncomfortable under my scrutiny. "I tried to call you the other day."

"Uh-huh." I turned back to my food, suddenly not hungry. "The day Jessica broke up with you, you mean."

"Hopefully you didn't find out about it before I did."

I recognized his attempt to lighten the conversation. I gave him a crooked grin. "I doubt it."

"I totally know what you're thinking. That I'm a jerk for dumping you. An idiot for liking her. You and I were totally friends before all that, and now we don't even talk."

I stayed silent, twiddling with the stem on my apple. What was I supposed to say? He was right, of course. That's what I thought.

"Jayne, you're such a nice girl."

I winced. Nice. Not really what I wanted. "But Jessica was fun," I said. "And outgoing. And popular."

"No, Jessica was a ditz. It could never last. She wasn't the type to be serious with."

I glanced at him through narrowed eyes, wondering which had attracted him more, her boobs or the freedom. "Yeah, I bet she wasn't. You could've waited to break up with me before you made out with her."

"Jayne, quit it. I made some mistakes, okay? I'm sorry." He took a bite of his sandwich, but his eyes never left mine. "I want to be friends again. I want to try again."

My heart gave a little pitter-patter, grasping at strands of hope in spite of myself. "You want to try being friends again?"

"Are you trying to be dumb?" Stephen put his sandwich down and grabbed my shoulders, pressing his mouth to mine. He tasted like grape jelly. But it only took a moment before his lips pushed mine open and I stopped noticing the essence of pb and j.

I leaned into him, hungering for the warmth of his mouth. I'd missed kissing him. I wanted this back. I closed my eyes, getting lost in the memories for a moment. Hanging out in Stephen's car, singing to 80s music while Stephen howled. Homecoming—leaning into his embrace, feeling like we would be together forever. We were meant to be together.

Except I knew better now.

"There." Stephen pulled back and stroked my face. "Give me a second chance." His thumb rubbed my lip. "Go to prom with me."

I held the moment close to my heart, feeling the tears behind my eyes. What would happen if I said yes? How far would the preparations and charade go before Miss Blond showed up, offering Stephen something better than what he could get with me? I would be a fool to pretend like it would work. "I can't." I blinked and the tears overflowed. I pushed away from the table and grabbed my apple and chips, holding back a sob.

"Sure you can." Stephen stood, taking my elbow. "I know I hurt you. I know it. I'm not just asking you 'cause I got dumped. I want to be with you."

He brought up a good point, though. I looked at him through blurry eyes. "Now you want to be with me. What about a month ago? Two months ago? How about in a month? Will you still want to be with me?" I shook my head. "No. I can't." I pushed past him, cursing Dana for making me go through that.

CHAPTER FIVE

I CLOCKED IN to my second day of work already tense from school. I'd avoided Dana for the rest of the day, turning the other direction when I saw her by my locker and barely talking to her in calculus. I wanted to make it very clear that I was angry with her.

I knew she got the message. She hadn't bothered trying to call me, though she'd sent me several texts. I ignored them. We both knew I'd check them later, when I wasn't so mad.

"Hey, what's up?" Friendly coworker Matt came over and held up a hand. His blond hair curled up a bit around the edges of his baseball cap, courtesy of the humidity. I stared at his hand, wondering what he wanted me to do.

"Don't leave me hanging." Matt grinned at me around a toothpick. "If giving five's not your thing, we can do a knuckle bump." He made a fist with his hand.

"Oh." Feeling like an idiot, I made a fist also and bumped his knuckles. "Sorry. Been a rough day."

"Nothing like working in the kitchen to make you forget your troubles. Come on, let's show you the food prep."

I groaned inwardly. Somehow I had managed to forget that this would also be part of my duties. I much preferred ringing people up.

Of course, I had to admit to myself, making bagel appetizers and bagel sandwiches wasn't nearly as bad as flipping burgers or folding tortillas. At least, the reputation was better. The afternoon went by quickly in the back. A fan whirred, blowing the air around but not really cooling it. Before I knew it, Matt stood beside me.

"You're doing great, new kid. Break time."

"Really?" I wiped my brow with a paper towel. The hair around my head was frizzing under the hairnet, more from sweat than anything else. "Great, thanks."

I used my employee discount to purchase a large chocolate chip muffin. I needed it. I sat at a corner table facing the window and unwrapped the calorie-laden indulgence. The fresh chocolaty smell wafted up to me and a smile caressed my lips.

I lifted the muffin to my mouth and took a bite, feeling the chocolate bits melt against my tongue. My eyes closed and I relished the taste. I was all set to take a second bite when my nostrils picked up a hint of citrus.

My eyes flew open. We baked the muffins fresh every morning, and I knew there was no orange or lemon in the chocolate ones. I spun my chair around and inhaled sharply.

There he was, standing at the register. I knew just from the back of his head. Aaron. What was he doing here? He'd been here yesterday! Surely he didn't come from England with an addiction to JT's.

I watched him place an order, then I swiveled back around, staring at my muffin. He didn't know I was here. He'd get his food, eat, and leave. Tomorrow I'd figure out what to do about English class.

Several sets of footsteps danced in different rhythms around me as customers went to their tables with trays of food. Quick, hesitant, light, heavy. My ears perked up as one set drew steadily closer. With them came that oppressive lemon smell.

"Jayne?"

My heartbeat hammered in my neck. I didn't turn, certainly didn't stand up. "Yes?" I hoped he wasn't expecting an invitation to sit, because I was fresh out.

Apparently he didn't care. The table wobbled as he stepped around the corner. I stared at my muffin while wrapping a strand of hair around and around my finger.

"I hope you don't mind," he said, his accented voice lyrical, "but I asked the girl at the register if you were working today. She sent me back here."

Gabby. Another person to add to my hit list.

"I'm Aaron, by the way. I met you yesterday, but I don't think you met me." He sounded amused and held his hand out to me.

Mine trembled as I took his. "Nice to meet you." I wrapped up the uneaten pieces of my muffin. "Well, I think my break is about over. I better get back."

"Oh." I got a good look at his brown leather tennis shoes as he pushed off the linoleum floor and leaned back in his seat. "That's too bad. I hoped to talk to you. We have English together, you know."

"Right." I nodded.

"Are you feeling okay?" Concern tinged his voice. "You left before class started."

"I feel a little better. Thanks for asking." I stood up and walked away, clutching my muffin. It was rude, but I didn't know how else to get out of the conversation.

"Jayne."

I hadn't counted on him following me. His hand closed on my forearm, practically begging me to turn around. I stopped walking and squeezed my eyes shut.

"I'm new here, Jayne, and I was wondering if you wouldn't mind showing me around town. Maybe Friday night we could go out for a bit."

He was asking me out. Superman was asking me out. "Sorry, Aaron. I can't. There's a game Friday night." Did I seriously just turn him down? "I have to get the stats right for the school paper. I'm sorry."

"Hey, that's no problem." His hand dropped from my arm. "I'll come to the game. I'm not a writer, but I know a lot about basketball."

Why, oh why, had I told him what I was doing? Yet I couldn't deny the twinge of excitement I felt. "Right," I said. "See ya."

"See you," he echoed.

I waited until I heard the footsteps walking away, then turned around and watched Aaron shoulder his way out of JT's. I couldn't figure out why he was interested in me, hairnet and all. I wouldn't even look at him, for goodness sake. That couldn't be a turn on.

I went back behind the counter, finishing my muffin quickly before entering the kitchen. He was super hot, after all. Maybe I could pull this off? As long as I didn't see his death, we could have a normal, carefree experience, like most teenagers. I hummed to myself, elevated by the thought of spending Friday evening with Aaron.

Gabby and I helped Matt close up the restaurant. Not fun. It was my first time to do that. By the time I clocked out and changed into my regular clothes, it was ten-thirty. I threw my stinky uniform in my backpack, grateful I had a second set I could use tomorrow. I wouldn't have a chance to wash this one before then.

Thinking about tomorrow made me remember Friday. Aaron. I got butterflies in my stomach at the mere memory. Tom, my manager, had agreed to let me off early on Friday if I worked all day Saturday. Open to close. Good thing basketball season was almost over.

In the back of my mind, I knew I should also be concerned with catching the lacrosse games. But that just made me think of Stephen and his kiss. Was that really just earlier today? I felt so confused now. Stephen and Aaron.

On one hand, Stephen was entirely out of the question. I didn't want to be at his side when he met Beautiful Mysterious Blondie, not to mention that he'd totally cheated on me and dumped me. On the other hand, how could I even consider Aaron? It's not like I could make him wear sunglasses to prevent me seeing his eyes whenever we spent time together.

The very thought made me giggle.

Gabby stepped out of the bathroom, sporting a black tank top and fishnet stockings under her shorts.

"Aren't you two out of here yet?" Matt poked his head into the back. "You and Gabby take off. I'll lock up."

"We're almost gone," Gabby said. Now that her hairnet was off, I saw a streak of electric blue in her short brown bob. "Don't ask twice, Jayne. Just get out as fast as you can."

I followed her. "Where are you parked?"

She jerked her head behind the restaurant. "Out back. Aren't you?"

"Oh." I inclined my head in a similar manner. "In the front."

"Employees aren't allowed to park there. See ya later." She walked out before I could say another word.

"Thanks," I muttered to myself, stepping into the parking lot. "Would've been nice to know earlier."

I clutched my car keys in one hand and my bag in the other. Mine was the only car in the lot. Large overhead lights flooded the parking lot, which helped to ease some of my disquiet. I hated being in dark shadows.

I bent over the door handle of my old white Honda and turned the key in the lock. A car pulled up behind me, and I whirled around, feeling my eyes widen in surprise. The girl in the driver's seat met my eyes a second before she rolled down the window.

"Excuse me," she began, but I was already gone, swept away in the vision that came before her citrusy perfume ever reached me.

Hannah doesn't move from where she lays in the alley. The cold air pricks at her skin, but she is numb. Flashing neon lights from a dance club paint the gray walls blue and then red, over and over again, like the lights from a police cruiser. She stopped fighting against the gag in her mouth ages ago, and now she just stares at the man hovering above her. His brown eyes sink into the pock-marked face, and a pink tongue wiggles inside his mouth as he concentrates. A long scar gouges the right side of his jaw and neck.

He's going to kill me. Hannah closes her eyes for a moment, heavy regret nearly crushing her. Not from death itself, which is hardly as frightening at this moment as it was an hour ago. Regret for the pain her mother will feel when she finds out how Hannah died.

His hands move away from her body, and Hannah opens her eyes. He grips a knife in his gloved hand, and it moves like lightning against her neck. Hannah doesn't even have a chance to gasp against her gag before the world fades into blackness.

The vision left me and I sank to the ground, burying my face in my hands and trembling.

"Hey, are you okay?" Hannah climbed out of her car and bent over me, her hands on my shoulders.

"No. No." I reached up and gripped her hands, seeing the concerned expression on this young girl's face, only a few years older than me. "Hannah! Don't go near the night club! Don't be alone at night, don't trust anyone! Promise me!"

She stepped away from me, suspicion replacing her concern. "Do I know you?"

"No." I sobbed into my hands, unable to face her again. I didn't know what else to tell her. She wouldn't believe me. I shook with the trauma of what I'd Seen.

I heard her footsteps on the pavement, and then the car door shut and it revved away. Whatever she'd wanted, she decided it wasn't worth asking the crazy lady. Crazy Jayne.

I forced myself to my feet and climbed into my car. I banged my hand down on the lock and sat there for a moment, scared out of my wits. I had never Seen a murder before. Accidents, even suicides. But never a homicide. I knew I'd have nightmares tonight.

Halfway through my left-hand turn out of JT's, I saw *her*, standing in front of a closed beauty salon as if waiting for a bus. On sudden impulse, I yanked my car over to the side of the road. I got out, slamming the door behind me.

She turned her head, tracking my movement. The white dress clung to her lithe body, the blond hair loose around her shoulders.

I was not about to let her unnerve me. "Who are you?" I shouted. My hands curled into fists and I stopped ten feet from her. "Why is this happening? I know you have something to do with it!"

She lifted her eyes to mine, a deep dark blue, and stared at me. I stared back, waiting for answers, a revelation, something. Nothing came.

I screeched in frustration and pulled at my hair. "I can't deal with this anymore!" A sob wracked my body, and I pressed my hands into my face.

"De-claw."

The word whispered into my ears, driven by the soft breeze blowing the night air. It wasn't quite "de-claw," but that was the closest word I could come up with. I dropped my hands and looked at her. She was gone, of course.

De-claw? How was that ambiguous hint supposed to help me?

My hands shook with pent up anger and fear, and it took me three tries to get the car door open. De-claw? What on earth...?

I pulled my car into the drive at home, surprised at how quickly I'd arrived. My hands still trembled around the steering wheel and the silence invaded the car. I hadn't even thought to turn the radio on. I pulled my phone out and scanned through Dana's messages, no longer mad at my best friend.

> 6:03 p.m.: sry I ditched you. R u mad at me?
>
> 6:14 p.m.: r you there? Call me, plz
>
> 6:16 p.m.: W8, ur at work, huh? Call me when you can! K?
>
> 7:19 p.m.: Just thinking about u. R u mad @ me? At least txt back.
>
> 9:40 p.m.: Was just watching celebrity apprentice. Reminded me of that science project we did. LOL call me! XD
>
> 10:03 p.m.: Call, I don't care how l8 it is. U got me worried. :/

I scrolled through the six messages, then shouldered my bag and hurried up the porch steps. The bushes swayed in the breeze and I jumped. My nervous fingers dropped the keys twice before I got the door open. I slipped inside, locked the door, and leaned against it, finally breathing a sigh of relief.

I was about to open my bedroom door when I noticed the light creeping out from under it. I frowned, glancing at my wristwatch even though I knew the time. Almost eleven. I doubted my mom would be hanging out in my room at this hour. Which meant it had to be my sister.

I pushed open the door and Beth whirled around, turquoise taffeta up to her chin.

"What are you doing here, Beth?" The sight of her brought such a strong feeling of irrational fear that it overshadowed the darkness in my heart. I cast my eyes about, searching for some place to look besides at my little sister. If Seeing Hannah unnerved me, Seeing my sister would be so much worse. I walked to my vanity and fluffed my hair in the reflection, feigning nonchalance.

"Oh, Jayne!" Her breathy voice came out sounding a bit guilty. "I just wanted to try on your prom dress. Since, you know, you're not going now. Right?"

Prom. The word brought a bit of normalcy to my reality. I allowed the feelings of hurt and embarrassment to push out my fear and unease. This was to be my first year at prom, and I had splurged three-hundred dollars on the heavily layered turquoise dress. And yes, I wasn't going. I had made that very clear to Stephen this afternoon.

"Nice, Beth. Thanks for rubbing it in." It was a shame I hadn't been able to keep the break-up from my family. "You've tried it on. Now take it off."

The dress rustled and shook as Beth heaved it up over her head. "I'm stuck, Jayne. Help?"

I risked a cautious glance at her. Beth's head was completely swallowed up in lace, only her two arms poking above the fabric. Suppressing a smile, I stepped to her and tugged on the dress, averting my eyes before her head emerged. "There. Now go to bed." Whew. Yet another day that I'd averted disaster.

"Jayne?" Beth's voice came out soft and meek. "Can I talk to you?"

I groaned inwardly. I yanked open my candle drawer on the vanity and pulled out the Sweet Pea scented one. It wouldn't be very effective with Beth in the room, leaving her lemon musk everywhere. But I had to try. My fingers shook as I lit the wick. The longer she stayed in here, the more likely that I would accidentally make eye contact. "What?"

She bounded over and lay down on my bed. She kept her long brown hair straight, and it fell around my pillow, which she grabbed up and hugged in front of her. "I like a guy at school."

"Beth, it's late. Do we have to talk now?" I glanced at my watch, hoping she'd get the hint.

She stuck out her lower lip. "We never talk, Jayne. You used to tell me everything."

I didn't need a guilt trip. Not now. I flipped off the light and climbed into bed next to her. My head pounded and I wanted to smother myself with the pillow. "Then talk, Beth. But I'm tired. Don't expect me to stay awake."

Beth broke into a happy babble, which I listened to in a half-daze. Memories of my vision with Hannah floated in and out of my head. Tomorrow I would write it down in my file, where I kept of list of all the people I'd Seen and what happened to them.

My eyes burned and I shut them. Beth's voice droned on, but my mind was elsewhere.

Declare.

My eyes snapped open and I stared at the darkened ceiling above me. Was that what she meant? Declare? Declare what? I already tried to tell people how they were going to die, and it never accomplished anything.

My brain felt thick and mushy, and I gave up. Tomorrow I'd think on this.

CHAPTER SIX

"J AYNE!"

Someone shook my arm. I recognized Beth's voice in time to squeeze my eyes tighter. My breathing quickened, and I fought off an anxiety attack. *Don't look, don't look.* "What, Beth?"

"You'll be late for school, Jayne!"

I could smell her so clearly, lying in bed next to me. It was like fate mocked me, tempted me to open my eyes.

I flailed out with my hands and stumbled off the bed. Only when I knew she was behind me did I blink, exhaling and picking through the clothes on my floor. "Then go get ready, Beth. You take longer than me."

She flounced out of my room. Her hair had regained its natural wave during the night, and it bounced around her shoulders.

Just like mine.

A knot formed in my chest. I couldn't avoid her eyes forever, and one of these days I would See her death. How could I prepare myself?

I got Beth to school on time, but not myself. The tardy bell rang as I jerked open my locker. I muttered self-deprecating insults and ran through the empty halls.

Luckily, Mr. Livingston was my first period teacher. He glanced from the board at me when I walked in, then turned around, saying only, "*Cierra la puerta,* Jayne."

I closed the door quietly, feeling a great sense of relief. He wouldn't count me tardy. I put my head on my desk and rested my eyes. They burned with desire to sleep. I had relived Hannah's murder over and over again in my dreams.

I didn't see Dana until second hour in calculus. I sank into my chair at the desk we shared and gave her a meek smile, just to let her know I wasn't mad, and then I threw myself into my assignment. Horrible images of Hannah's murder haunted me. I pressed my hand to my forehead.

My phone vibrated in my backpack pocket. I glanced down, pulling it out just enough to scan it. Dana's text read, "u OK?"

I looked at her and gave her a bleak smile. "Yeah," I mouthed.

She texted again. "What happened w SH?"

Stephen Harris. I forgot that I hadn't even told her. I leaned over, pretending like I was fishing for a pencil, and texted back, "Talk @ lunch."

Dana gave me a quick hug as soon as class was done. "Gotta go. If I'm late for gym one more time, I'll have detention for a week. I'll tell you at lunch all about that new kid in my stats class!"

Aaron. "Sure." I pasted a smile on my face while Aaron's face threw itself into the jumbled crockpot of my mind. Yesterday after he asked me out, I'd planned how I'd pump Dana all about him: how did he act, was he flirtatious or quiet, did he seem sincere or like a player, smart or silly?

But after last night, I just couldn't rouse the excitement to feel anything. My emotions were drained. I didn't feel like spending the next hour trying to avoid seeing Aaron's death.

There was no way I could skip English class again. I waited in the classroom like a wallflower, not sure where to sit so I could avoid Aaron. I watched the girls huddle around each other and giggle while the boys stood around flexing their muscles. I'm sure they thought the girls were watching them, but I saw the surreptitious glances the female posse shot toward the open door.

Seconds before the tardy bell rang, Aaron walked in. He held his head high with a poise and confidence that belonged to royalty. His eyes darted around the room. I lowered my head, trying to make myself invisible.

"Hey, Aaron!" Poppy Miles flashed a smile and snapped her gum with a crack. "I saved a seat for you!" She scooted off the desk and patted a chair next to her.

If Poppy's shirt were any tighter, her boobs would pop right out of it. Hmm. Maybe it wasn't a coincidence that her name was Poppy. I rolled my eyes and wedged myself into a safe seat two rows back.

Ms. Seigfried's words about Shakespeare's deliberate mixing of comedy and tragedy floated around my ears. For once I couldn't seem to concentrate. I watched Poppy scribble something in big, loopy letters and then pass the paper to Aaron. What did it say? Was she asking him out? He took the paper and wrote back with small, crooked writing. Poppy passed the paper over to her brunette cohort, Shannon, and the two girls exchanged a giggle. Then Poppy wrote something else and sent the paper back over to Aaron.

I bristled, wondering why I would feel the insane emotion of jealousy. From here I could see the curve of Aaron's jaw, the way the dark brown hair fell over his forehead. His lemon odor drifted my direction, reminding me of why he was off limits. *Stop drooling,* I told myself. *You can't have him.*

Aaron's shoulders tensed as if he were going to turn around, and I quickly looked down at my paper, going through the motions of taking copious notes. Oh, well. With girls like Poppy and Shannon chasing him, what would Aaron need with quiet old me? About as much as Stephen had, probably.

The bell rang, and I paused. Should I fly out as fast as I could, or should I wait until everyone had left and then file out?

I took too long to decide. I knew from the cloyingly sweet lemon smell mixed with musky aftershave that Aaron approached my desk. I worked hard to keep my eyes riveted on my books, which I carefully organized into my bag.

"Hey, Jayne."

"Hey."

Aaron crouched next to me, and for a moment the scent of his cologne overpowered the lemons. He smelled like evergreens and leather. I inhaled, relishing the scent.

"Do you have lunch next?"

"Yes." I pulled out my pens and pencils and began rearranging them. "But I'm meeting my best friend, Dana. We like to have a private lunch everyday. You know, girl time."

"Oh?" I heard a smile in his voice. Again I fought the urge to look at him. Did he have dimples? "And what are you going to talk about today?"

"We have some important things to discuss."

"Any boys on the list?"

I felt my face flush. *As a matter of fact, yes. Two, to be exact.* "Wouldn't you like to know?" I stood up, shouldering my bag and keeping my eyes trained in front of me.

Aaron reached out and moved my hand further down my backpack strap. "You'll balance the weight better if you hold it down here." His fingers lingered on mine, the thumb touching the back of my knuckles.

I tugged my hand free and walked out of the classroom, struggling to maintain a neutral expression. "Thanks."

Poppy and Shannon waited outside the room. Poppy raised an eyebrow at the sight of me and whispered something to Shannon, who nodded.

Aaron leaned closer to me. I lowered my eyes, keeping them on his brown oxford shoes.

"Are you working tonight, Jayne?" he asked, his minty breath washing over my face. The English accent made the casual sentence feel formal and important.

Yes or no? For a moment I couldn't remember. "Yes. Closing again."

"Then I'll see you tonight."

I stood where I was, staring at the ground until his Oxfords disappeared around the corner. Poppy's voice made me jump.

"Well, you don't wait long, do you? Though I will admit, Aaron is a step up from Stephen."

I looked at her and felt a flash of anger. Boobs and money, and she thought she ruled. I gave her a cool smile. "Don't worry, sweets. Stephen's up for grabs, if you were looking for leftovers." A flicker of guilt pricked me for speaking so callously about Stephen, but it was for the greater good.

Poppy's face turned red and she sputtered. I left before she could get her wits together and slam me with a rebuttal.

One thing was for sure. Aaron's mere presence got my mind off last night's vision.

☙

"Let me get this straight." Dana stared at me over her Reuben sandwich, her blue eyes wide. "Stephen asked you out—and you turned him down?"

"Yes, I've already said that. Then he—"

"You turned him down?"

She wasn't ever going to let me finish. I brushed it off, anxious to tell her about Aaron. "Dana, I couldn't go out with him. He would've dumped me again for someone else."

"You don't *know* that!" she shrieked.

I didn't bother arguing with that. "He didn't stick by me the first time. Why would he for another round?"

Dana groaned and put her head in her hands. "Jayne! Maybe he really was sorry! You should've given him a chance!"

"How's your prom date coming along?" I asked, trying to steer the topic off of Stephen.

"No, no, we're not done." She held a hand up, palm out. "How did Stephen react?"

I tried to remember the exact order of events. "He seemed to think I was being melodramatic. He was trying to make a point, so he kissed me."

"He *what*?"

The shriek again. I put a finger to my lips and shushed her. "Dana, hush. No need for everyone to know."

"But Jayne! A kiss means something! He likes you!"

My finger pulled down on my lip and I couldn't help remembering the taste of his mouth on mine. "Now he does. Wait and see. He won't try again. We'll see him at prom with a beautiful blond on his arm."

"Jayne, I could cry." Indeed, Dana's mouth trembled. "Aren't you just sick inside?"

"I would be, but..." I took a deep breath. The excited flutter bubbled up in my stomach again. Having a new crush could be quite intoxicating. "I think I might like someone else."

This time, at least, she covered her mouth to muffle the squeal. "No wonder you turned him down! Why didn't you say something? Jayne, you better tell me who it is, now!"

I felt a smile toying with the corners of my mouth. "Well, he's new in school."

"Aaron!"

Guessing games were no fun with Dana. I wrinkled my nose at her. "You could at least pretend not to know so I could draw out the suspense longer."

"Jayne!" Dana grabbed my hand. "I can't believe you have a crush on him! Where did you meet?"

I considered explaining how I'd met him at work and all, but opted for the easiest explanation. "He's in my English class."

"Wait. Do you have a crush on him just because he's 'safe'?" She made quotation marks with her fingers. "Because every other girl in school is crushing on him too?"

"No. That's just my bad luck."

A smile danced around Dana's mouth. "Jaynie, this is great. This will really help you get over Stephen."

"Uh-huh." I played with my apple, picking at the peel. "I thought you kind of liked Aaron?"

"No way. He's definitely hot, but you know I like my men older."

"Any developments in that direction?"

"No." She sighed and leaned back, one hand digging in her backpack. "Come on, I know I have another Dum-Dum in here... ah, here it is." She dropped the wrapper on the green grass and stuck the candy in her mouth. "There is this guy I met at the university library. He was so nice, helping me find my book. I gave him my number, but... he hasn't called." She shrugged. "I guess the smart ones have better things to do than hang out with high school girls."

She sounded really bummed about it. "Sorry, Dana. Next year, you won't be in high school. Then they won't act that way."

She gave me a wan smile. "Maybe I'm just not exciting enough."

I couldn't imagine anyone thinking Dana wasn't exciting. I mean, she wasn't crazy or anything like that, but she was lively and spontaneous and fun. "Don't ever change yourself, Danes. You're the best."

The bell rang, and she stood up. "I hope you're always around to boost my confidence, Jayne."

"I will be." I meant it, too. We didn't have to be in the same state to be close. "See ya after school."

"See ya."

The rest of my classes went by in a blur, and finally the last bell rang. Most of my peers made a bee-line for the parking lot, but I lingered by my locker. Spanish club didn't start for another fifteen minutes.

"Think about what I said, okay?" Dana popped up next to me, sucker in her mouth, and I jumped, startled. She pulled a new bag of Dum-Dums out of her backpack and ripped it open.

"Ah, you scared me. Think about...?" It took me a moment to realize she was referring back to lunch and my supposed conquest of Aaron. "Sure, Danes. I'll think on it."

"Right, you will." She handed me a Dum-Dum. "Call me when you get done with work."

Work. Hannah. My stomach twisted up. "I'm closing. It'll be late."

"No prob." She waved at me over her shoulder and started down the hall.

"Coming, Jayne?" Meredith Singer, a short girl with brown hair and glasses, stopped next to my locker. Meredith was probably my closest friend after Dana. We had journalism together and had been doing Spanish club for three years. Spanish club met every Monday, Wednesday, and Thursday after school, but I usually only went on Wednesdays and Thursdays. Mondays and Fridays were game days.

"Yes. On my way."

Mr. Livingston, my Spanish teacher and Spanish club adviser, was handing out newspapers to students as we came in. "*Hola, amigos,*" he said in what sounded to me like a perfect accent. He had lived in Argentina for a few years as an English teacher, and he still spoke with ease.

Spanish club had a mostly female population, a fact that I attributed to Mr. Livingston's dark lashes and blue eyes, not to mention the dimple in his cheek when he smiled. He handed me a newspaper as I came in. "Come on in, Jayne. Assignment's on the board."

In Spanish club we went beyond grammar and memorization and tried to dive into life as a Spanish-speaker. So today, according to the white board, we were choosing articles in the paper and translating them into Spanish.

Meredith sat down next to me. "Partners?"

"Of course."

She flipped through the pages we'd been given. "Shall we do something involving *comida*?"

"Always easy," I agreed, still flipping through. An article continuing from page 2a stopped me short.

> ...third body found in as many weeks.
>
> "This is a sign of a serial killer," Prof. Daniels warns. "This killer is following the same pattern: finding a young girl late at night, killing her in the same manner, and dumping the body behind a dumpster. These crimes won't stop until he's caught."
>
> Police are cautioning all women to travel in pairs, to carry pepper spray...

The rest of the article blurred before my eyes, and I dropped the paper. It couldn't have been Hannah. I'd just Seen her last night. She couldn't be dead already. The visions didn't come true that fast.

I jumped up so quickly I slammed my hip into my desk. Wincing, I hobbled over to another table and fished through the various paper segments. 2a. I scanned the page until I found the beginning of the article.

> The name of the most recent victim, discovered Tuesday night at ten p.m., has not been released at this time.

I breathed a little easier. It wasn't Hannah. I met her yesterday, Tuesday night. I put my head in my hands, trying to clear my thoughts. But this was how Hannah would die.

"Jayne?" Meredith touched my shoulder, and I pulled my head up. "Hey, I found a great article on the food festival. Did you find anything else?"

"No." I shook my head quickly. "No, let's get started."

"Everything going okay here?" Mr. Livingston paused by our table.

"Great." I gave him my brightest smile, hoping it didn't tremble. I fumbled with the paper, pressing my thumb over the headline.

Mr. Livingston's eyes followed my movement. He picked up the paper and scanned the article on the latest victim, a shadow darkening his eyes. "You shouldn't let these things bother you. Keep good company and you'll be safe."

So my teachers knew about the serial killer too. "Of course. We're just about to dive into *la seccion de comida*."

He smiled and nodded. "Very good. Much more appropriate. You should write an article on the club for the school paper, Jayne. You're such a great writer."

Mr. Livingston asked me to include the club in the newspaper at least once a month. Since I knew everyone in there, I usually did, giving the Spanish club coverage in a quarter of our school papers. Technically, I was a sports writer, but I could be versatile for Mr. Livingston. The paper came out every Friday, and sometimes the other members of the staff had a hard time coming up with new topics. "That's a great idea. Maybe I'll write an article for *Cinco de Mayo*. It's coming up."

He brightened. "Yes, it is! And we're going to have a *fiesta*. Let's get the word out!"

He walked away, and Meredith giggled. "He's kind of dorky."

"But so nice," I defended.

"Oh, no argument from me!" she agreed. "I love Mr. Livingston…'s class." She smiled, and I laughed, relieved by the light-hearted banter.

CHAPTER SEVEN

JT's Bagel Shop was growing on me; either that, or I was desperate for a distraction. As I parked my car in the back, I realized I looked forward to my shift.

"Jayne!" Matt crowed when I came in. He tossed an apron and a hairnet at me. "You've got kitchen today."

It wasn't hot outside, but the kitchen felt warmer than a tanning bed. "Thanks," I said, my enthusiasm dimming a bit.

Gabby's voice echoed from the drive-thru window as she spoke to Melissa, a girl I had only worked with once. "No, I was so not at that party."

"You were!" Melissa exclaimed. Her long hair hung from a single braid down her back. "I saw you! You were wearing—"

Gabby lifted a finger and switched her mic back on. "Welcome to JT's, would you like to try our cheddar bagel combo meal today?"

I shuddered and sprinkled more cheese on the bagel dough. Drive-thru was even worse than the check-out line. I had only worked it once, and nobody had come through smelling of lemons, but the panic I had felt at each new car nearly gave me a heart attack. I spilled seven drinks—a new record, I was told—dropped three debit cards, lost lots of change, and gave four orders to the wrong people.

The good news was, Matt said I'd never do drive-thru again.

As if hearing my thoughts, Matt loped into the kitchen, one hand hitching up his pants. He held a clipboard in the other hand and a pencil stuck out under his trademark baseball cap. "Here's your checklist."

I wiped my hands on my apron and took the clipboard with a deep sigh. How soon before the serial killer struck again? Would it be Hannah this time?

Matt peered at me under the bill of his cap. "You okay?"

His genuine concern brought a lump to my throat. "I'm fine." I swallowed back a sudden urge to cry. "Just going through a stressful phase."

"Wanna talk?"

I gave a cynical laugh. "No." Crazy Jayne. Another good way to get fired.

"I need help at the registers!" Melissa hollered. She yelled a lot when she needed something.

"Look that over and let me know if you have questions," Matt said, all business again. He lumbered out of the kitchen.

I glanced at the closing checklist. My break had been assigned to me at seven-fifteen. Two more hours.

Melissa came into the back room. "Jayne. There's someone here to see you."

I ran a mental list of who might be here as I followed her back to the front. My family hardly ever headed to this side of town. Could be Dana, if she had nothing else to do. I was afraid to hope it was Aaron.

A knot made of equal parts dread and expectation tightened my stomach as soon as I smelled the clean lemon scent. I focused on the brown leather shoes. Yep. Aaron.

"Hey," I said, giving my fingernails a close inspection as I leaned against the wall.

"Jayne," Aaron replied, his crisp British accent making me feel more like Jane Austen than Jayne Lockwood. "What time are you off?"

"I'm closing today," I replied, feeling the familiar mixture of relief and disappointment. I wanted so badly to look at him, to study that chiseled jaw and touch the lock of hair that kept falling in his face.

"Yes, you mentioned that. When's your break?"

"In two hours." I pressed a hand on the wall when I realized I was leaning toward him. There was no denying the pull of attraction I felt.

"And are you planning on eating bagels for dinner?" There was a hint of teasing in his voice.

"Doesn't sound very appetizing." I dropped my hand and smiled at the counter, tracing my fuzzy reflection on the hard surface.

"Then I'll be back with dinner."

He just assumed I wanted to eat his food. Which I did, of course. "Don't you have homework or a job or something?"

"My schedule's flexible. Is that all right?"

I shrugged, trying not to appear too eager. "Sure. I'll be here."

"Great." He leaned over and mussed the top of my hair. "Thank you, Jayne."

I stared at the back of his khaki pants as he walked away and touched my fingers to my hair, lightheaded with giddiness. He liked me. I was quite sure of it.

༄

"You only get a half hour break," Matt warned me as I punched out. "Don't go too far with your boyfriend."

"He's not my boyfriend," I growled, thoroughly embarrassed and annoyed that everyone at JT's had witness Aaron's entrance and departure. "And I don't think we're going anywhere."

"Maybe Matt meant the other 'too far,'" Gabby teased. She slipped something into my pocket and snapped her gum in my ear. "Just in case."

I closed my eyes, mortified. "That won't be necessary, Gabby."

"Ope, here he is." Gabby moved away just as the heady scent of lemons spread through the fast food joint. My eyes dropped to the register.

"Ready?" Aaron asked, his elbows resting on the countertop.

"Yeah." I shouldered my backpack. "I only have half an hour, though."

"That's fine." Aaron pushed away from the counter. I almost expected him to take my hand, but he stayed two steps in front of me.

I followed him out of JT's. The sun was setting, and I squinted against the rosy light. "Where are we going?"

"I don't know. I just moved here."

I risked a quick glance at his profile and saw a smile teasing his lips. His eyes stared straight ahead as he walked up to a dark green BMW. Though in general cars didn't interest me, I couldn't help noticing how nice this one was. I arched an eyebrow. "What, no convertible?"

"It would be a great finishing touch, wouldn't it?" Aaron unlocked the car. "Couldn't afford it. But I have a really sweet sunroof."

I turned my gaze to the roof of the car as I slid into the passenger seat. "What do you mean, you couldn't afford it?"

"Ah." He slid a pair of sunglasses on and then swiveled around in his seat, looking behind us as he backed up. It was mostly dark outside, but some sunlight hovered on the horizon, right at eye-height. "You think all English kids get handed exotic European sports cars by their rich mummies and daddies."

"Something like that," I said, feeling my face warm. "I'm guessing I'm wrong?" The good thing about him wearing sunglasses was I could look at him. I couldn't see his eyes at all, only my own reflection looking back at me. I instantly felt more at ease.

"You're wrong in my case." Aaron flashed me a smile, exposing a dimple on his right cheek. "My parents paid for half."

I still wouldn't have been able to pay for half of a car like this. "And where did you get your half?"

We stopped at a light and Aaron pulled up the GPS on the dash. "All right, I admit it, I took some out of my savings account. But I had a job in England. I earned my own money."

"I'm impressed," I said. I couldn't imagine Dana working. She had no need to, not when everything was handed to her. "What did you do?"

He cleared his throat. "I, er, worked in a hospital."

I squinted at him. "Like a nurse? A medical assistant? They let kids do that in England?"

He fidgeted in his chair, running one hand over the steering wheel. "Not exactly. Here we are."

I turned my attention to the view outside as we parked. We were at a playground. It was empty except for the ducks on the pond this time of day, with the light-posts already turned on and crickets starting their evening chorus. "What are we doing here?"

"I thought we'd have a picnic." Aaron got out of the car and went to the trunk. I climbed out also.

"A picnic?" I echoed, rubbing my arms as a cool breeze tickled the hairs. A large white swan settled on the pond, and I watched the majestic creature fold its wings in as it floated on the water. Swans always gave me a peaceful feeling.

Aaron retrieved a picnic basket and a thick blanket. "It would be better with moonlight, but this will work. Maybe we'll see a star or two." He spread the cloth out on the grass and sat down. "I hope you like salads."

I settled next to him. "Are you telling me I need to be on a diet?"

"Not that kind of salad." He pulled out several containers. "Potato salad, macaroni salad, chicken salad. And just for fun, a can of sardines."

"No way." I laughed. "You don't actually eat those."

He held the can to his nose and sniffed it. "Mmm. You have no idea what you're missing."

"I'd like to keep it that way, thanks. Did you make all this food?"

"No. A cook I am not. But the deli by your work seems to be quite adept at such tasks."

"Well, you're in luck. I happen to love anything slathered in mayo." I spooned some of all three salads onto a paper plate. "Why the picnic?"

I could feel his eyes on me as I ate. "It sounded like fun." He shrugged, a motion I saw from my peripheral vision. "So you want to be a journalist?"

I sputtered on some chicken salad. Aaron popped open a can of juice and handed it to me. I took several gulps before trusting myself to speak again. "Who told you that?"

"I saw the school newspaper from last week. You have a byline."

Of course. I relaxed. "Well, kind of. I want to be a sportscaster. But I'd prefer not to be seen. So the written medium works well for me."

"You would be a natural on television."

I smiled and tucked a strand of hair behind my ear. "Thanks." The wavy hair popped free again.

"So why journalism? Are you a curious person? Do you like to solve mysteries?"

At the mention of mysteries, I felt a stirring in my heart. Sometimes I did find myself wanting to go out and play detective when I heard about crimes or missing persons on T.V. But I knew that would bring me face to face with too many unwanteds. So I contented myself with letting someone else make the front-page news.

But thanks to Hannah, I was in the middle of a mystery right now.

I shrugged and lay back on the blanket, staring up at the darkening sky. "Nah. I'd rather not know about things, really. What about you?"

He moved his sunglasses to the top of his head, a dangerous move that instantly increased my heart rate. "I'm generally pretty curious. Like, about prom. I can't figure out why it's such a big deal. It's just a high school dance."

I propped myself up on my elbows, being careful to direct my line of vision just to the right of his face. "You are so not American. Prom is way more than that. It's a chance for a girl to star in her own fairy tale. To get dressed up, pampered, and ride off into the night with her prince charming." I sighed, my romantic aspirations for that magical night returning for a moment.

"I see you take it very seriously."

I glared in his general direction, wishing he'd left his sunglasses on. "Very."

"So who are you going with?"

I dropped my eyes, deflated. "Haven't figured that out yet."

He straightened one leg and rested his elbow on his knee. "You don't like to meet my eyes. Is that a self-confidence issue?"

Irritation surged in my chest. Dang it, he'd noticed. "No."

He waited, but I didn't bother explaining. Instead, I took the easy way out: I changed the subject. "How are you liking Forked River?"

"Fork-ed," he repeated, the stress on the second syllable sounding awkward and unsure. "Several times people have laughed at me for saying 'forked.'"

"Yeah? At least it's an easy way for us to spot an outsider. Messing up the name."

"Why the strange pronunciation?"

"You're one to speak," I returned. "Everything you say is pronounced strangely."

He laughed and stood up, brushing his hands on his khakis. The light color was the only thing I could see clearly, now that the sun had dipped below the horizon. "Funny, I think everything you say is cute." He extended a hand. "You're going to be late for your shift."

Dang it. I accepted his hand. He effortlessly pulled me up, his hand drifting up to my shoulder before letting go. It only took a minute to gather up the picnic items.

"Thanks for coming," he said as he dropped me off at JT's. "Sorry for making you late."

"Thanks for inviting me," I replied, ducking my head and climbing out. I hesitated, wanting to say something more but finding it impossible to say something sincere while my eyes were on the pavement. So I just shrugged. "I'll see you tomorrow."

CHAPTER EIGHT

"Y͟O͟U͟ ͟D͟I͟D͟ *what* last night?" Dana's question rang out over the heads of the student body as everyone scurried to first hour.

"Shh!" I hissed, waving a hand at her. "I'll tell you all about it in calculus. He came to my work and took me out on my break."

I'd waylaid Dana in the hallway with my good news, too excited to keep it to myself. I felt a stirring of guilt for being so happy when the serial killer was still out there, about to strike Hannah down. But what could I do about it? I couldn't prevent it. I couldn't even find her. The most I could do was learn from it and not go out alone. I shoved the negative emotions aside, telling myself I was powerless in the situation.

Dana's blue eyes gleamed. "To where?" she asked, bringing me back to the Aaron situation. "What can you possibly do in half an hour?" She arched an eyebrow. "Well, Miss Jayne?"

I was ready for her question. "He took me on a picnic. He had it all prepared." I couldn't keep the pride from my voice.

"Jayne, he likes you!" She squeezed my forearm. "A picnic! Such an English thing to do! Do you like him?"

The tardy bell rang, saving me from having to answer. I waved to Dana. "See you in an hour!"

By the time I got to English for fourth hour, I was exhausted. Dana had peppered me with questions all through second hour, and then she'd stuck silly fantasies in my head about kissing and prom and my senior year.

After all the hype, I kind of dreaded facing Aaron. What if I'd made a big deal out of nothing?

How was I supposed to act, anyway? Like we were a couple or like we barely knew each other? Did I wait for Aaron by the classroom door? Save a seat for him? Sit next to where he usually sat? Or pretend like there was nothing going on between us?

I debated the issue in the hall for about ten seconds, and then I went inside the classroom. I would just play it cool. I put my books down on a table in the middle row, leaving a space beside me.

The lemon scent entered the room first, giving me a two-second warning, during which I dropped my head and pulled out my notebook. I pretended to study my outline, all the while holding my breath.

"Hi," Aaron said, moving my books out of the way and sinking into the empty spot next to me.

I smiled and tucked my rogue piece of hair behind my ear. "Hi," I replied, not turning my neck to face him.

He scooted his chair in to the desk and leaned forward, resting his elbows on the desk. I watched his fingers swirl a pencil between them, agile even in their larger size. I glanced down at my own hand. His had to be twice as big.

Ms. Siegfried called the class to order and we started to discuss the sexual tension in Othello. Aaron shuffled in his seat, his jean-clad thigh bumping mine.

My pulse fluttered. Talk about sexual tension.

He turned toward me and whispered, "Did you get in trouble last night?"

I shook my head. "No. The restaurant was pretty quiet. I was only a few minutes late." I couldn't resist asking, "Why do you come to JT's all the time? Do you live close or just have a hankering for bagels?"

"I like talking to this cute girl that works there."

I doodled a vine on my paper. I added blossoming flowers with five points, spreading out along the margin. "What color are your eyes?"

I could feel his gaze burning into the side of my head. "Why don't you check for yourself?"

Tempting. But the thought of finding out how Aaron was going to die made my throat constrict. I couldn't bear to find out that he was going to suffer a horrible and ignominious death, whether it be in a few months or a few years. "I can't. I've got laser vision and I'll burn your retinas."

He laughed softly, a deep sound that warmed my chest like a cup of hot chocolate. "Fine. Have it your way. They're blue."

Of course they were. He was Superman, after all.

We drifted into silence and I tried to add some class notes to my doodles. Mostly I was thinking about Aaron and his blue eyes and how much I wanted to stare into them.

The bell rang and I stood, focusing on my backpack while I shoved pencils and books into it.

"Do you work tonight?" Aaron asked.

I nodded. "Yeah. Just till nine, though. Easy night."

"I'll come by before you get off. Maybe we can do something afterward."

"Sure. That would be fun."

He tapped his fingertip on my knuckle. "See ya."

"Bye," I answered. I studied the back of his head as he walked away. Dana was not going to believe this.

෧ඌ

Ms. Montgomery handed us a stack of newspapers in journalism. "I noticed with the last school paper that some of you didn't have your columns and bylines formatted correctly. That could have been my fault, as perhaps I didn't teach you correctly. More likely, though, the culprit is hasty editing. Your assignment is to find five bylines that are formatted incorrectly and fix them."

I didn't ask if I was one of the guilty parties. I very well could have been; I got lazy sometimes. I sifted through a newspaper from two weeks ago when an opinion article on the fourth page caught my attention.

Is Lacey Township becoming too large? After the second murder in three weeks, citizens are beginning to wonder if they are not as safe from the big city crime as they once thought.

This paper was from a few weeks ago. How many murders had there been now? Three? Maybe even four, if Hannah was already dead. My fingers twitched and I fought back nausea, again pricked by guilt. *Stop it!* I chided myself. *It's not like you could help her!*

Then why did I feel like I should be doing something? I began scanning all the articles and headlines for any information about the murders. There had to be clues as to how this guy operated.

There were no more references to the murders in that paper, so I put it aside and picked up another. Nothing in this one either. I exhaled, feeling my shoulders slump. This could take awhile. An online search would probably prove more helpful.

I swiveled around to a computer, pulling up a web browser. I had gotten as far as typing "Lacey Township serial killer" in the search bar when a hand landed on my shoulder. I shrieked.

"Jayne," Ms. Montgomery said, peering at me over her glasses, "what are you doing?"

I swiveled in my chair and smiled my best innocent smile. "Research."

"Save it for home."

"Yes, ma'am" My face burned at being called out in class. I waved a hand to cool it off, watching her move on to supervise other students. Fine. This could wait until tonight.

☙

"Hey, Jayne."

I didn't look up from the cash register. I had smelled Aaron the moment he walked into JT's, and I felt too emotionally drained to get excited about it now. I'd spent the rest of the school day thinking about that newspaper article. The anxiety to get home and start my own research sat like a rock in my stomach. I'd almost skipped Spanish club with the intent to do my own private research. Then I thought better of it. I didn't need my teachers thinking I was obsessed with this topic.

Even though it was in a vision, I'd seen the murderer's face. What if there was a way I could help identify him? The woman had told me to declare. Could I still prevent Hannah's death? Should I declare what I knew to someone?

I focused on the keys on my register. "Hey, welcome to JT's. What can I get you?"

He stood just far enough away from the counter that I could see his feet shift over the linoleum. Brown leather shoes again. "Do you have a moment? I need to talk to you."

The grinning confidence was missing from his voice. He sounded uncomfortable, nervous, even. His tone distracted me from my state of mind, and I found myself wanting so badly to look at him. *Get a grip, girl.* I checked my watch. 7:05 p.m. "I'm going on break in ten minutes. Can you wait?"

"Sure." He shoved his hands in his pockets. "Corner table."

He shuffled away and my heart beat out a staccato note. His attitude was making *me* nervous. He wasn't my boyfriend, so he couldn't break up with me. I had nothing to worry about.

At least it gave me something else to brood about. The next ten minutes couldn't pass fast enough. Finally I slipped out from the counter and wandered over to the table, my fingers trailing the chairs that I passed.

"What's up?" I sat down in front of Aaron and focused my eyes on his mouth. He licked his lips, and I wondered what it would be like to kiss them.

Bad idea. I dropped my eyes to my hands.

"I came by at four and you weren't here. What time did you come in to work?"

"Are you stalking me?" I tried to tease, but then I remembered the serial killer, and it fell flat. A shiver ran down my spine. "I had a club meeting after school. So I didn't come in until five."

"Oh? What club?" He sounded interested. Or was he just avoiding whatever it was he wanted to talk to me about?

"Spanish." I tapped my fingers on the table. "I only have a fifteen-minute break."

"Right." He cleared his throat. His fingers crept across the table like they were going to touch mine, but didn't. "I'm not going to make it to the game tomorrow. I didn't want you to think I was ditching you."

"Oh." I exhaled. So much for our kind-of date. "That's fine. Thanks for letting me know."

"Jayne?"

I almost lifted my eyes out of habit before I caught myself. "Yes?"

"I have a friend coming into town tomorrow from England. That's why I won't be there."

I cocked an eyebrow. "A family friend?"

"Er, no. Kind of a personal friend."

"Like, a girlfriend?" I blurted, jerking my head up. I knew even as I did so what would happen, but I couldn't seem to stop myself. Did he really mean a girlfriend? How could he be flirting with me, leading me on, if there was another girl on the scene? His light blue eyes took my breath away seconds before my vision blurred.

Aaron lies on a bed next to Libby, his beautiful redhead girlfriend. She has his phone open and scrolls through his contacts with one hand while the other runs along his chest, covered except where she has undone the buttons.

"What about this one?" She pauses on a snapshot of Jayne. "Who is this?"

Aaron rolls on his side and takes the phone, an emotion like regret filling him. "No one. Just someone I met in the States." He hits the delete button, erasing Jayne and her memory from his life.

Libby leans over, her straight hair falling in front of her face, and kisses his neck. "Oh good. The picture kind of made it look like she was more than no one."

The scene changes again. "No, this is not a fair arrangement," Aaron argues. A wedding ring glints on his finger as he pushes his hand through his thick dark hair, streaked with gray. Wrinkles line his eyes and mouth. He glances out the wall-to-wall window, looking over a green golf course. "You leave me for a dead-beat, has-been rock star and think you're getting the house? Don't call me again. Have your lawyer talk to mine."

He slams the phone down and glares at a picture of Libby on the end table. Aaron snatches it and throws it across the room, where the glass shatters. He grabs his wedding band and starts to twist it off, and then stops in mid-motion at a crash downstairs.

"Hello?" he calls, leaning over the spiral staircase, still clutching his ring finger. "Is someone there?"

A man appears at the bottom of the stairs. "Sorry to bother you. Just doing your wife a favor." The man lifts a gun in his gloved hand and shoots Aaron three times. Aaron gasps and falls over the banister.

I screamed and jumped to my feet, pressing my hands to my heart.

"Jayne?" Aaron was at my side in an instant, one hand on my elbow and the other on my shoulder. "Are you okay?"

I gasped and shook my head, tears streaming down my face. I lowered my eyes, aware of people in the restaurant staring at me.

Aaron's hand reached for mine, and I jerked away. "Jayne, I'm sorry. Listen, I'll make it up to you."

"No." I pushed him away, my legs trembling. "You should've told me you had a girlfriend. Just go away." I turned and fled out of JT's.

My mood progressively worsened on my drive home. How could I even warn Aaron about this one? "Don't marry her! She'll kill you!" He'd think I was just jealous.

I let out a sob and pounded the steering wheel. Why? Why Aaron? How could I convince him to be with me instead? I yearned to be able to change what I'd seen. I threw myself from the car, stumbling toward the house. Tears fell down my cheeks, and I swiped at them with one hand while opening the front door with the other.

I almost didn't see the woman watching me from under the streetlight. My lip twisted and I glared at her. Then I slammed the front door shut and ran up the stairs, plowing straight into my room and onto the bed. Leaning across it, I fumbled for my sweet pea candle and the matches. The fragrant aroma reached my senses, flooding out the earlier feelings of despair.

I closed my eyes and lay back on my bed, letting my mind give in to the nothingness.

My eyes snapped open when my phone began to ring loudly on the dresser. How long had I been lying here? It felt like only a few minutes, but outside it was dark. I glanced at my watch, confirming that it had been nearly half an hour.

The phone stopped for a moment and then started again, the display flashing. I grabbed it up and groaned. JT's Bagels. I gritted my teeth and answered. "Hello?"

"Jayne? This is Tom."

My manager. I pinched my nose. This was it. I was about to get fired. "Hi, Tom."

"Jayne, what happened? You just took off without saying a word. Where are you?"

"I'm at home. I, uh..." I let out a shaky sigh. "I all of the sudden got really sick. I couldn't think straight, I just had to go."

Silence on the other end. I wondered what Tom was thinking. Would he give me a second chance? Did I even want a second chance?

"Jayne, you can't leave without telling anyone. Take the evening off, be here tomorrow for your shift. People get sick, but if you ever take off like that again

" Tom paused and then sighed. "I'll have to let you go."

I could hardly believe it. JT's must be more desperate for workers than I'd realized. "Um, okay. Thanks, Tom. I won't let it happen again."

I collapsed on my back, trying to decide if I was better or worse off than before. I pounded my pillow in frustration.

The murders. I sat up, suddenly glad for something to focus on besides Aaron. I took the steps two at a time to the downstairs den, where the family computer sat at a desk. My parents told me I could have my own laptop—when I went to college. If I wanted one before then, I had to buy it. Fat chance of that happening, considering I never kept a job.

Beth sat at the card table, headphones on while she worked on her homework. I took a deep breath and looked away. I couldn't stand to See someone else today. *Don't think about her. Think about the serial killer.*

Even I thought it was a weird thing to comfort myself with.

I pulled up a search engine and typed in, "Lacey Township serial killer." Several different hits popped up, some from several years ago, others taking place in other parts of New Jersey or even New York. I ignored those and clicked on the one connected to the local paper. A message popped up.

"Please enter your name and phone number to confirm your subscription to the Lacey-Barnegat Times."

We didn't have a subscription. Heaving a sigh, I ran upstairs to get my check card. I didn't have a lot of money in my checking account, but it would cover a newspaper subscription. I filled out the required information, lied about my age, and started my subscription. It wasn't too bad, since I only wanted the e-version.

Then I read each article slowly, absorbing the information.

The first murder came as a shock to the community. Twenty-three year old college student Claire Eastman was found in an alley behind a dance club. She had been sexually assaulted before he slit her throat and threw her in the dumpster, where the body was discovered the next morning. Her black leather purse, which hadn't been touched, quickly identified her. The article included a smiling photograph of a brunette in a tank top.

I thought I was going to puke. I put my head in my hands. Just like Hannah, Claire had been at the prime of her life. So much in front of her. And then to have it taken from her in such an ugly, cruel way...I could only hope that she had also been numb to those last moments, as Hannah had.

Shaking it off, I flipped open my notebook and started a new list.

Name: Claire Eastmon

Age: 23

Occupation: student

Hair color: brown

Eyes: brown

I studied my list. I needed more. Like where Claire lived, where she worked. Did something about her make her a target? Or was he choosing girls on a whim?

Finding her address was easy. She lived over by Tom's River, about ten miles from my own house. She worked as a waitress at the Lobster Shanty, a rather expensive seafood restaurant with the best crispy spinach I'd ever eaten.

I tapped my pencil on the desk. There had to be more. More about Claire's life. I wasn't likely to find it here, though. If I were a real journalist, I'd get in my car and drive out there, interview her family and friends. But I wasn't, and I quickly dismissed the idea. I'd have to find the information another way.

Next one.

Name: Emily Gardner

Age: 17

Occupation: student/cheerleader

Hair color: brown

Eyes: brown

Neighborhood: Crestwood Village

Place of death: Pine Barrens

So far all the girls had brown hair and brown eyes.

I searched my memory. Did Hannah? I was pretty sure she did. Maybe that was the link. I stuck my thumb in my mouth and nibbled on the nail, scanning the next few articles until I found the headliner about the third murder.

Name: Melanie Swift

Age: 19

Occupation: hair stylist

Hair color: blond

Eyes: blue

Neighborhood: Waretown

So much for that theory.

Number three was the last one. There were no more murders. I exhaled. Hannah was still alive, then, somewhere.

I put my pencil down and studied my notes. I was familiar with all of these towns; they were close by. I knew the police were doing the exact same thing, and probably with more information. But I knew something they didn't: I knew who one of the future victims was. I needed to at least find Hannah's last name. How? I winced when I bit off too much nail and shoved my hand under the chair.

"I'm going to bed," Beth said, standing and stretching. "Night, Jayne."

"Night," I murmured. I had the sudden urge to warn Beth, to tell her to be careful. The desire to meet her eyes and know for a certainty how she would die almost overwhelmed me. But I couldn't. What if it *was* the serial killer? To know, to warn her, and then still have her die, would absolutely destroy me. "You know there's a serial killer out there, right?"

"Oh?" She glanced toward me, but I stared at the computer screen. "I think I heard something about it."

"Be careful," I murmured. "Stay in groups when you're out."

"Sure. Of course." She waited a moment, and, when I said nothing more, stepped out of the den. I heard her footsteps ascending the staircase.

I shut the computer down and gathered my papers. I'd sleep on this. Maybe something would be clearer tomorrow.

CHAPTER NINE

"APRIL SHOWERS bring May flowers," I murmured as I parked my car at school. I preferred the sunshine, personally. I flipped down the visor and narrowed my eyes at the frizzy strands of hair framing my heart-shaped face. I had tried to get my hair into a ponytail, but the rain made a rebel of it.

I jumped out of the car and hurried into the front entrance. Kids stood in groups inside, water dripping into small puddles at their feet. I shivered in the manufactured air of the A/C and headed for my locker.

The black Doc Marten's standing next to my locker caught my attention as soon as I got to the top of the staircase. I lifted my eyes and caught sight of the back of Aaron's head as he talked to Dana. I took a deep breath, inhaling the lemon-free air. I knew all there was to know.

Dana met my eyes over his shoulder. I marched up and took her by the elbow, pulling her down the hall to her own locker.

"What's going on?" she murmured, swinging the metal door open and grabbing a book. She glanced behind us. "You avoiding him?"

"Yeah." I patted the strands of hair around my face, trying to coax them down. "We kind of had a disagreement."

Her eyes raked over me, begging for details. "Bad?"

"Yes." My mouth twitched. I concentrated on keeping my features placid. "Let's just say, he's no longer an option."

Dana's eyes went over my shoulder again. "Does he know it?"

I was so tempted to turn around. I knew Aaron was there at my locker, watching us. "I told him. He has to accept it."

We started down the stairs. I made a plan to come back to my locker before the tardy bell and get my books.

Dana hooked her arm through mine. "You have to tell me everything."

I shrugged. "There's not much to tell. He's not over his ex-girlfriend, actually. She's coming into town this weekend and he canceled our date to be with her." *And he's going to marry her,* I added to myself.

Dana gave a low whistle. "Yikes. That is low. Good for you for sticking to your guns." She squeezed my arm. "Are you okay?"

I nodded, feeling my eyes tear up a bit at the question. Sensitivity was my middle name lately. "I feel like a stupid idiot, that's all. At least I found out before I got too involved."

"Yeah. Come over to my house tomorrow. We'll go out. I'll find you a dream guy."

I let out a weak laugh. "Thanks, but I'm working. All day." Dana and I had different dreams. I didn't want one of her guys.

"Your loss, babe." She kissed me loudly on the cheek and pushed off of my arm. "See ya in math!"

The warning bell rang and the halls filled with students, all in a mad rush to get to their first class. I fought the crowds back up to my locker. The halls emptied quickly, and Aaron was nowhere to be seen. I felt a twinge of disappointment.

You don't like him anymore, I chastised myself. I grabbed my books for the next two classes and trotted to Spanish.

I couldn't help but remember last night's research while I listened to Mr. Livingston talk about the past perfect progressive conjugation, or something like that. I glanced at my classmate, Troy Mason, who was texting away on his iPhone, like he did in every class.

"Troy," I whispered, learning over.

He looked up at me, surprise flickering in his gray eyes. "What's up, Jayne?"

I kept my grimace to myself. Troy was friends with Stephen, and though he was cordial, I hadn't spoken to him since Stephen and I broke up. I suspected Troy had something to do with the Jessica element. "Can you look up news on that thing?"

"Sure." He moved his hand over it as quickly as if he were waving a wand. The exact dynamics of the movement were lost to me. "What do you want to look up?"

Out of my peripheral vision I saw Mr. Livingston glance my direction. But he didn't say anything, and I knew he wouldn't. There was a fine line between students and teachers as far as friendship went, and I felt pretty secure knowing he'd let me get away with almost anything. I couldn't push it, though. "Look up that serial killer. See if there are any new murders."

"Serial killer, huh?" Troy arched a bleached blond eyebrow. "I hadn't heard of one." A few more touches, and he handed me the phone. "Yep, you're right. Here's an article."

I read the date and my heart started to pound. This morning. Something must've happened for them to be writing about him again.

> A 21-year old woman was found last night in Barnegat Bay. Police suspect she is another victim to the Lacey Township Serial Killer. Forensics determined the death to be approximately 24 hours before the body was discovered by Deputy Sheriff Clyde Williams.

Twenty-four hours. My mind did the math. It could've been Hannah. But wasn't I supposed to save her? I handed the phone back, my hands shaking. I had to find out who the victim was.

"You good?" Troy whispered, and I snapped back to the present.

"Yeah." I steadied myself with a deep breath. "I'm good." I reached into my backpack and pulled out my lists. Goosebumps popped up on my arms. The article hadn't disclosed the name of the victim. What if it was Hannah? What did that mean for my mission to declare? My fingers trembled as I added her information to the list, searching for a common denominator.

Name: Hannah

Age: 21

Occupation: ?

Hair color: brown

Eyes: brown

Neighborhood: Barnegat Bay

Another town too close for comfort. In fact, the hit towns seemed to circle Forked River.

I had to put my concern for Hannah aside in math. Dana bugged me about Aaron. I staved off most of her questions by asking my own about calculus. This class was too hard for me, but Dana had convinced me to take it with her. She was a math whiz, taking both calculus and statistics in one school year.

"Come on, Jayne," she said, pursing her lips and erasing my figures. "You can do this."

"You talked me into this," I reminded her, glad that I'd distracted her from Aaron. "You promised to help."

"Yes, but you're not even trying." She launched into a simplified version of how to solve the equation, and I smiled to myself. She was too annoyed with me to care about my love life at the moment.

The bell rang, and I got up, stuffing the books into my bag. "I have to go to my locker. I'm going to skip lunch today and study for our physics test sixth hour. See you there?"

"Yes." She blinked her light blue eyes up at me. "Meet at my locker after school."

"Thanks." I smiled and hurried away.

I managed to avoid Aaron during English class by squishing in between Derek Mills and Kyle Larson, two guys who were too smart to still be in high school. They always sat in the back, spewing out cosmic ideas that were way beyond my mental capacity. They looked at me funny but otherwise ignored me.

Aaron sat in front of me to the left, his body twisted slightly to see the whiteboard. I spent the entire class staring at the board or my notebook, doing a great job of not studying his profile or admiring that square jaw. Mostly. Pity that now that I could look at him without Seeing any crazy visions, there was no reason to. I shot out of the room as soon as class was over, not giving him the chance to catch up to me.

My half an hour cram session at lunch didn't help my physics test any. I was in a foul mood by the time class let out. My forehead felt permanently creased in a scowl. Dana shot me a questioning glance and I shook my head.

She waited by my desk after class, watching as I put my stuff in my backpack. "Didn't go so well, huh?"

"Not so great." What a crummy day. My head throbbed with exhaustion, the effort of avoiding Aaron, too much school, and the serial killer. We paused at my locker. I stuffed my books inside and slammed it shut. "I'll see you at the game tonight."

She followed me out the double doors to the front of the building. "Is it just the physics test? You seem a little off."

"Yeah, I am." I rubbed my eyebrow. "I have to go to work."

"Bye, then." Dana turned around and walked back into the school, and I knew I'd snubbed her. I felt a twinge of guilt. Keeping such a big secret from her weighed on me. But I couldn't tell her about the serial killer.

I could tell the police, however. I made up my mind to do so as soon as I could.

☯

I looked forward to the mindlessness that accompanied working in a fast-food joint. I parked at JT's and hauled myself out of the car.

Memories of Aaron assaulted me as I walked through the glass doors: our first meeting, his subsequent return visit, our "break-up." Panic seized me. Why did I think I would be safe here? This was where we always bumped into each other!

For a brief moment, I froze. The impulse to turn and run enticed me.

"Oh, good, you're here." Matt came around the counter, his jeans clinging to his hips as if by magic. If I wore pants like that, they'd fall down to my ankles with the first step. He slapped a wet towel at me.

"You're so very lucky we saved a spot for you. Clock in and take register one."

"Right." *Get it together, Jayne.* Aaron wouldn't come in today. Everything would be fine. I dumped my stuff in the back and started behind the register. I tried not to focus on the entrance, but I jumped every time the door opened.

"You okay?" Matt's deep voice came from behind my ear, and again, I jumped.

"Huh? Oh, yeah. Fine."

"Tom said you left sick yesterday. And today, you seem—jumpy." His lip curled up like he'd said something incredibly witty, a toothpick dangling from the other side of his mouth.

"Ah, well…" I couldn't really deny being sick. That wouldn't be good for my career. "I'm a tad under the weather, if you know what I mean. But I'm not contagious. And I washed my hands." I pointed to the plastic bottle of hand sanitizer on the counter.

"Maybe you need a break from all the people. Wanna work in the kitchen today?"

"The kitchen?" I echoed, thinking of how I hated messing with the food. Then my mind flashed back to Aaron. "Yeah. That sounds great."

The kitchen was hot. Beads of sweat gathered on my forehead while I kneaded the bagel dough into elastic strands. I used a paper towel to wipe at my face, but that didn't keep bits of cream cheese and bagel from sticking to me.

"Hey." Gabby came in and tossed a peppermint at me, which I made a half-hearted attempt to catch in my dough-covered gloves. "Matt sent me to relieve you. Said you're taking off?"

"Oh!" I pulled my hands out of the onion bagel dough, yanking off the plastic gloves. "I forgot I'm off early today!" I'd made it through my shift! If Aaron came in, I hadn't even noticed. "Thanks, Gabby!"

Gabby tucked her blue-striped hair into a hair net. "No prob. Later, Chickadee."

"See ya." I threw my apron in my bag to wash at home and grabbed my purse. I barely had enough time to change. I hoped perfume could cover the smell of my bagel experiences.

I arrived at the game fifteen minutes before it started. A quick search of my car revealed that I'd forgotten my tape recorder, so I grabbed a notepad and pencil.

Even before the game started, the gym already smelled of sweat and dirty socks. I didn't spot any friends on the bleachers, so I settled behind the score keepers, propping the pencil behind my ear and placing my camera in my lap.

This was where things got fun. I studied the players as they came out and warmed up, jotting quick notes about who did what and when. I made a guessing game of who seemed in top form tonight. I fancied myself pretty good at predicting the way the coach would play his team.

The bleacher wobbled, and I looked up to see Dana straddle the bench next to me, the usual Dum-Dum in her mouth. She popped it out. "So. What's the news?"

I exhaled, a flood of warmth filling my chest. "You're a gem, you know?" I reached forward and hugged her. "I know I was ornery today. Thanks for not being mad."

"I *am* mad." She popped the candy back in. "But I'll get over it if you spill. What's the news?" she repeated.

I had no clue what she was talking about. I twirled a curl around my finger and played dumb. "What news?"

"You know." She inclined her head and widened her eyes, pointing without using her fingers. "With homeboy."

My blood congealed in my veins. Surely Aaron wasn't here. "Is he here?" I hissed. "He said he wasn't coming!" I inched my head forward and peered around Dana.

He was here. Hanging on his arm was a tall, thin girl whose red hair cascaded down her back like a shiny sheet. The black stilettos she wore made her seem taller and older than she was.

Aaron's head turned in my direction and I jerked back. "Let's move." I began to gather up my notebook and camera, shoving papers back into my backpack.

"Move where?" Dana crinkled her nose at me. "We've got the best spots for the game."

The whistle blew and I groaned. I couldn't leave now. The beginning and ending of the game were especially critical to capture. "Keep guard, will you?"

Dana chuckled. "What, you think he's going to try and kidnap you?"

He wasn't even supposed to be here. For the first ten minutes, I kept one eye out for Aaron. But by the second quarter, I was intent on the game, nodding along to Dana's rambling while jotting down scores and plays.

"And anyway, here comes Aaron."

I pulled my eyes away from the basketball court. "What?"

Dana laughed. "Just kidding. Just wanted to see if you were paying attention."

I scowled at her. "Not funny."

Dana lowered her voice. I had to lean closer to hear her. "Have you guys talked? Since, you know, he told you about his GF."

I shook my head. "No. He hasn't even tried to call me." Which kind of annoyed me. What part of me wasn't living up to his expectations? I shook my head and laughed to myself. I didn't want him in love with me, after all.

I didn't.

Dana took a sharp breath only a second before stilettos and tennis shoes appeared in my right peripheral vision. I pressed my lips together and focused on the game.

"Hi, Aaron," Dana said. I could picture her looking up at him. "Who's your friend?"

"Oh, hi." The sound of his melodic accent turned my spine to jelly, and my shoulders relaxed out of tense-mode. I found myself being persuaded to let go of my determination not to look at him. "You're Jayne's friend, right?"

"Dana," she purred, amusement in her voice. "And this is...?"

I suppressed a smile. Dana would not, of course, be put off.

"This is Libby, from England. She's my—"

"Girlfriend," Libby interrupted before Aaron could finish, one foot tapping against the hardwood floor. Her deep, flawless voice matched Aaron's accent, but on her it wasn't so cute. I shot her a glance as she leaned closer to him, giving him an adoring smile. Her white, straight teeth could not be a product of nature. "At least, that's what we call them in England."

"Oh?" Dana widened her eyes and leaned back on the palms of her hands, looking up at Aaron. "For some reason I thought you were single. You just seemed rather available." She smirked.

Libby swiveled her head toward Aaron, and he cleared his throat, one thumb rubbing his eyebrow. "Urm. I mentioned her to Jayne, and I wanted to introduce them."

His eyes tracked toward me, and I saw a flash of blue before quickly averting my gaze. What on earth made him think I wanted to meet his girlfriend? So he could rub her in my face? I preferred to look at the enemy, so I met Libby's large brown eyes instead. "Nice to meet you, Libby. I'm so glad Aaron mentioned you when he did. Thank goodness Aaron has someone like you to keep him happy." I kept my voice thick with sugar, hoping she would interpret my words very differently than Aaron did. "I hope you'll come to visit often. Don't let Aaron forget he has a girlfriend."

Aaron's shoes shifted in the corner of my gaze, and I knew he was uncomfortable. Well, served him right. I didn't ask him to come over and introduce her. I turned my head, fixing him with a cold stare. I bit my lip to keep from smiling at how he fidgeted.

"The pleasure is mine, Jayne." Libby sidestepped closer to Aaron, her shoulder brushing his. She took several steps toward some other seats, though he didn't budge. "Aaron?"

"I'll talk to you in class on Monday, Jayne." Aaron's tone made it sound like a command.

I lifted a shoulder and snapped a few pictures of the game. "Sure. Have a fun weekend, you two."

They walked away, and Dana burst out laughing. "Jayne! You were positively vicious!"

I looked at her and gave a sheepish grin. "Was I? Well, what's he thinking? He played me! And he thinks I want to meet his girlfriend?"

"But you did hear, right? He didn't call her his girlfriend. That's the title she gave herself."

Oh, I'd definitely caught that. I shrugged. "He didn't correct her."

Dana grabbed my arm. "Jayne, it's because he hasn't told her yet that's she's not. Trust me, I'm reading this guy right. He's going to break up with her. He likes you."

I stared at Dana. Over the drumming of my heart, I was vaguely aware of the coach yelling at the referee. I should be writing his words down, but my thoughts were all twisted up in Aaron. Why did I feel so mixed up about this? I wanted Dana to be right. Yet I couldn't let that happen. I shook my head. "Forget it. I don't even like him anymore."

Dana's blue eyes flickered over my face, trying to read me. "Yes, you do. You just don't want to."

I turned away from her. "Oh man, what did I miss? Something's going on in the game!" I leaned forward, jotting down everything I could hear from where I was.

One of the players on the other team got a foul, and I lifted my camera to snap a picture of the coach's face. Right before I could, though, a man walked in front of me and stopped, staring at the court. I lowered my camera. "Excuse me!" I yelled. I didn't sit on the front row for nothing. "Trying to take a picture!" I waved the camera, and he turned around. I gasped, dropping my camera as terror and shock chilled my body.

"Sorry." The man I'd seen murder Hannah bent over and picked up my camera. "You dropped this."

He extended his hand and I recoiled. I wanted to puke, yet I couldn't take my eyes off his face, the light eyes and sandy brown hair, the scar that sliced down his jaw and neck. His features were as familiar as if it were me he'd murdered.

His eyes narrowed and his jaw hardened. "Do I know you?"

"No, no." I took the camera and dropped my gaze, trying hard to get myself under control.

Dana put a hand on my back. "Jayne?"

"I think your friend is having an anxiety attack." His voice was smooth and nonchalant with a hint of a professional diagnosis. "I'll take her to get a drink of water."

"I'm fine." I grabbed Dana's hand and squeezed it. "I was startled by the play. I'm fine."

"She's fine." Dana nodded at him. "Thanks for the offer, though."

"Anytime, Jayne."

I jerked my head up when he said my name. He nodded at me before continuing on his way.

"What was that about?" Dana scowled. "Creep."

I grabbed her purse and dug through it until I found her phone. "Get me on the internet," I demanded, handing it to her.

"Okay, okay. Calm down." She touched her phone and handed it back to me.

I put in a search on the Lacey Township serial killer. Right away, it brought up a newer article than the one I'd seen in class.

The latest victim in a string of killings has been identified as Hannah Morgan, a twenty-year-old junior at...

The words blurred in front of me and I handed the phone bag, taking small, shallow breaths. Hannah was dead. I'd failed her, and the killer was still out there. Out here, attending my high school basketball game and probably looking for his next victim.

That did it. I couldn't put off visiting the police one more day.

CHAPTER TEN

WORK WENT by in a blur on Saturday. I stuffed my hair up under a baseball cap and kept my head down, not wanting to talk to anyone. All I could think about was my plan to visit the police during my thirty-minute lunch break. I had to act fast. The Lacey Township Police Department was less than a mile from JT's. The problem would be parking. Hopefully, at one o'clock on a Saturday, that wouldn't be an issue. I only had half an hour.

A pair of purple pumps stopped several feet in front of my register, one jean clad leg swiveling back and forth impatiently. I was in no mood for customer service. "Yes?" I glanced at my wrist. Twelve fifty-two. I would take lunch in eight minutes.

The woman still stood there, so I lifted my head, hoping my annoyance showed in my eyes. "Oh. Hey Gabby. What are you doing?"

My coworker smirked at me and popped a big pink bubble. "Where's your mind today? Definitely not at work. Guy problems?"

Aaron's tanned face with dark brown hair and dimples popped into my mind. *Not today.* "No. I have an appointment during lunch and it's kind of stressing me out. I don't have a lot of time."

"Oh." She leaned forward, the one blue streak in her shoulder-length black hair brushing the counter top. "Well, I'm not supposed to come in until two, but I'm here. I can stick around and cover for you if you don't make it back in time."

I looked at her, at this girl who always seemed so cold and uninterested, and felt a rush of gratitude. "You'd do that for me?"

She shrugged and leaned back. "Who wouldn't?"

"Oh, Gabby," I gushed. "I'll cover for you anytime. I'll do whatever you want. This is really important, and I hate the thought of having to rush it—"

She waved me off. "Forget it. I've got ya covered."

"Thank you! Thank you!" I had a few minutes left, but I ran into the back and grabbed my stuff anyway. I punched out on the register. "Matt! I'm off!"

"See ya!" he shouted from the kitchen.

My hands started to tremble as I drove, and I tried not to think too much. I had no idea how the police were going to react. I jammed my Sarah Brightman CD into the player and lost myself in her high soprano voice.

Parking was a beast at the police station. Even Sarah's lilting Italian couldn't distract me from the fact that I had already wasted ten minutes driving around. Giving up, I parallel-parked on the street one block over from the station. I cursed myself for not just walking. I could see JT's from here.

I ran inside the red brick building, ignoring the elevator and taking the stairs to the second floor. The digital clock in the hallway blinked one twenty-three. A woman greeted me as I pushed through the glass doors.

"Can I help you?"

"Yes." I stepped up to her desk, trying to appear confident. "I need to speak to someone who's working the serial killer case. I have a tip."

"Just a moment. Your name?"

"Can I be anonymous?"

"Okay. If you'll take a seat?" She gestured to three plastic chairs against the wall. Judging from her expression, I'd just gotten myself priority seating. I settled myself on the edge, checking my watch. My foot started to tap and I stilled it.

"Ma'am?" A trim man wearing a dark suit and tie stepped over to my chair. "If you'll come with me?"

I stood, clutching my bag in both hands. I followed him over to a cubicle office. He sat and motioned to the other chair. "Please, sit. I'm Lieutenant Bailey. You said you have a tip?"

I took a deep breath and said in a rush, "I know who the killer is. Well, not his name, but I can describe him to you."

Whatever Bailey had been expecting, this obviously wasn't it. He leaned forward, smoothing his brown mustache with one thumb. "How do you know?"

Now I wished I'd role-played a bit before I got here. Of course he would ask that. Time to lie. "One of the victims was my friend. She—she told me that someone was—following her."

His pen was out now, and he was scribbling as quickly as I spoke. I relaxed a bit. He was taking me seriously, at least. "Which victim?"

My throat tightened, and I whispered, "Hannah." I looked away, feeling the tears burn my eyes.

He grabbed a box of tissues and handed it to me. "So she told you what this guy looked like?"

I nodded. "In great detail. She was scared."

"When did you see her last?"

I bit my lip, realizing that I was treading in deep water. If he checked Hannah's routine and discovered that she wasn't with me when I said she was, this whole thing would be over. "Thursday night. She stopped by my work before I went home."

"And what did she say?"

"That she was scared." The vision flashed before my eyes, and I pressed my palms over them. "I told her to be careful." I began to cry in earnest now. It wasn't fair that I hadn't been able to help her.

"Can I get your name?"

"No." I shook my head. "Here." My hands shook as I pulled my rough sketch out of my bag. "It's not very good, but I tried to draw him. Based off what Hannah said, anyway."

He took it from me and spread it out on his desk. "This is very good for second-hand."

My face flushed. "She wanted me to watch out for him."

"Have you seen him?"

"I-I-" I stammered. Taking a deep breath, I tried again. "I saw him at the Township High basketball game."

He sat up straighter, grabbing his notepad and pen. "You're sure?"

"Yes." I gestured the length of my neck. "The scar."

He glanced at the paper again. "Uh-huh." He squinted at me. "Did he talk to you?"

"Yes," I whispered, squeezing the table. "He called me by name."

The man studied me, and I shifted under his scrutiny. Did he believe me? Did he think I was crazy? "How does he know you?"

I shook my head. "He doesn't. He overheard my friend."

"Have you seen him at the games before?"

"No."

He stood and handed me a card. "I have an appointment in five minutes, but I want to meet with you again. Call me." He waved the paper at me. "Thanks for this."

I watched him walk away and exhaled in relief. I did it. Now he had the drawing and could find the guy. Maybe the police would send a patrol to all the games. I glanced at my watch and jumped up. One fifty-eight! Where had the past twenty minutes gone? There was no way I could make it back to work in two minutes.

I hurried down the sidewalk toward my car, keeping my head down so the wind didn't blow into my eyes. Shiny black shoes stepped into view only seconds before I collided with the owner. I threw an arm out to keep myself from falling and managed to smack the man in the face, knocking him off the sidewalk. And I still fell on my rear.

"I'm so sorry!" I cried, my eyes darting toward my car, wondering how quickly I could apologize and escape the scene.

"Jayne?"

I blinked and turned my attention to him. My Spanish teacher took my hand and helped me to my feet.

"Mr. Livingston! I didn't see you there."

He chuckled, though the lines around his light brown eyes made them seem tense. The dimple that so often made an appearance when he laughed stayed hidden. "No, you weren't looking." He glanced over his shoulder and pressed his lips together.

"Yeah." I gestured behind me. "Just leaving the police station. They make me nervous. And I'm late for work!"

Mr. Livingston frowned. "Traffic ticket?" He clutched his fingers, popping each knuckle.

"No, no." I shook my head. I couldn't have him thinking I was a bad driver. "I just had some information for them about that case."

"Case?" He dropped his key ring and bent to retrieve it. His eyes flicked upward as he stood, searching my face. "Are you in trouble, Jayne?"

I knew he was just concerned for me, but my face reddened. Did he think I was a delinquent in hiding? "No, no, not me. The serial killer one."

"Oh." One eyebrow lifted and his frown deepened. He went back to work on his fingers, pulling on the joints. "Sounds dangerous." *Crack. Crack.*

"Yeah, well." I fished my keys out of my purse. "What about you? Traffic ticket?"

"Hm? Oh, yes. Teachers aren't immune, you know."

"Right." Time was up. "I've gotta run, Mr. Livingston. See you Monday!" I waved and hurried off. Late late late. "I'm so gonna get fired," I murmured to myself, starting my car up.

Must be a bad ticket. I'd never seen Mr. Livingston so agitated. I glanced toward the police station as I backed out of my parking spot. He still hadn't gotten up the nerve to enter; just stood in front of it, studying it.

CHAPTER ELEVEN

"I'M SORRY, Ms. Lockwood, but we only have a month left in the school year. I can't transfer you into a different English class at this time."

I stared back at the receptionist, feeling desperation creep through my chest. This Monday couldn't get any worse. After Saturday's police fiasco, I'd gotten the tongue-lashing of a lifetime from Tom, who just happened to check in at the restaurant while I was late getting back. To make matters worse, he'd gotten Matt in trouble. I'd spent the whole weekend feeling guilty.

But JT's drama faded into oblivion when I stepped into the Lacey Township High and spotted Aaron at his locker, surrounded by the dance team posse. It was too much. I knew right away that I couldn't deal with seeing him every day in class.

"I can't stay in there!" My poor English teacher would see my transfer as a direct betrayal, but it couldn't be helped. "I can't focus. I can't get anything done in there!"

The receptionist looked over her computer. "Hmm. I'm showing you have an A in the class. What seems to be the problem?" She peered at me, silver chains dangling from her wire-rimmed glasses.

"It's a recent development." I glowered at her, daring her to ask any more questions.

"Ah." She folded her arms across the desk, her eyes taking on a placid expression. "Does this involve a boy?"

I *know* my face flushed. I felt the heat rise from my cheeks to my forehead. "Never mind." I gathered my books up and headed for the door.

"Has he threatened you?" she called after me. "Harassed you? I can transfer you if he has."

I turned around. "No. I just don't want to see him anymore."

"Is he stalking you?"

I considered that one. Depending on the definition, maybe. But I couldn't get Aaron in trouble. He hadn't done anything wrong, really. "No."

She reached up and patted her hair-sprayed white hair, looking sympathetic. "Then I'm afraid we can't do a transfer."

"I know," I sighed. "I heard you the first time." I walked out, letting the door swing shut behind me. I should have expected as much. Of course they weren't going to just let me switch classes. And I couldn't skip, either.

When fourth hour came, I tried waiting in the classroom across the hall until Aaron went into English. But when he arrived, he stayed in the doorway, chatting with each classmate before they entered, but not entering himself. I felt my heart sink. "Go on, Aaron!" I hissed. "Get in there!"

Someone tapped me on the shoulder, and I spun around. Mr. Joenks, the chemistry teacher, hovered above me.

"Yes?" I squeaked, pulling my books against my chest.

"The tardy bell will ring in a moment." His bushy brows met in a ridge above his eyes. "Don't you have somewhere you need to be?"

"Yeah." I backed out of the room. "Just getting there." I turned around and faced my destiny.

"Jayne." Aaron stepped toward me. It took every ounce of determination that I had to keep walking and not stop to talk to him. "I —"

I brushed past him, my shoulder momentarily touching his before I crossed the doorway and dropped into an empty chair between the wall and another student. Then I busied myself with getting out my English assignment, knowing my face was flushed with shame at having treated Aaron that way. But what was I supposed to do? If I was rude enough, maybe he would lose interest.

I put my hands in my hair and pulled on my scalp. Oh why, oh why, did I have to return his interest? It made everything twice as hard!

As soon as class finished, I shot out of the room, practically climbing over my desk to get ahead of the other students. *Next time*, I thought to myself, *sit close to the door*. I felt more confident already. I'd get this avoiding thing down.

Luckily, I didn't have to work tonight, and I doubted he would be at the lacrosse game. One less avenue for Aaron to hunt me in.

I stayed late after school, working on my sports column. I had journalism seventh hour, but I was a bit behind on my deadlines. The journalism room was more like a closet with a window surrounded by computers. Cozy.

I got to work, pausing for a break only after I'd finished my write-up of last Friday's basketball game. I glanced at my watch. It was a quarter to four, and the sun warmed my shoulders through the window behind me.

My stomach churned a little at the thought of the lacrosse game. Stephen would be there, and much as I tried not to, I couldn't help remembering the kiss between us. We hadn't spoken since that incident, though I'd ignored countless phone calls. Was ignoring boys my new lifestyle?

Don't think about it. Another girl was about to walk into his life. And I, apparently, was to be the second choice for every guy I met. I hated that feeling.

I turned back to the computer and started on the March game highlights. Sports were the only thing I wrote about. I never interviewed the players, and therefore never got close enough to them to See anyone. One time I'd tried to write about the homecoming court when our activities columnist was down with mono. I only Saw one person in the court, but it was enough. Every time I typed her name for the article, her numbered days passed before me, leaving me trembling and crying. I ended up giving my notes to someone else so they could write it.

Never again. Now I stuck to sports.

Dana caught me by surprise when she opened the door and dumped a bag full of Taco Bell in front of me.

I lifted my head, the smell of cheese and spicy ground beef bringing me back to the present. Suddenly famished, I tore open a sauce packet and layered a burrito.

"Who says that's for you?" Dana laughed, plunking down in the seat across from me. She picked up a chalupa and took a bite. "Saw your car out front," she said around a mouth full of taco. "Thought you might be hungry."

"Thought right. Thanks so much." Though I hadn't noticed the hunger until she came in. I glanced over my finished column. "I'm done with this anyway. I'll just do some homework before the game. What are you doing?"

Dana cleared her throat. I lifted my eyes to her face, recognizing the sound. Something was on her mind. "What?"

Dana shrugged one shoulder. "Well, listen, I don't know what's going on in your pretty little head over Aaron—" I dropped my eyes. "And it's really none of my business. But..." She pulled out a slip of paper and waved it at me. "Homeboy wanted me to give you this."

I stared at it, dancing seductively in front of my face. There was no way I was touching that paper.

"Don't want it?" She arched her brows. "That's fine." She pulled her hand back.

I reached out and snatched it from her before she could put it away. "Give it here," I grumbled.

She settled back in her chair, sipping her soda with a satisfied smile on her face.

I opened the paper, my heart pounding, not sure what to expect. Staring back at me were seven digits. "His phone number?"

"Yep." Dana leaned forward again. "Listen, I don't know what went down between you two after the game Friday. But I don't think he's ready to be written off yet. He asked for your number."

I gaped at my best friend, a shiver of expectation racing down my spine. "But you didn't give it to him, did you?"

"Oh, Jaynie." Dana gave me her most pathetic expression. "He looked so forlorn and cast off. I had to ease his pain."

I groaned. "Dana! How am I supposed to avoid him if he can call me?"

She shrugged, not looking at all remorseful. "You've been managing just fine with Stephen, haven't you?" Before I could retort or even ask how she knew that, she continued. "Don't answer his calls if you don't want to talk to him. He'll get the hint. Besides, he seems like such a nice guy. Do you know where he was going?" She didn't give me a chance to tell her that I didn't care. "To the hospital. He works there. In the children's ward." She leaned back in her chair and sucked on her straw, eyes on me.

I glared at her. She knew me too well. She knew I would cave every time I saw his number on my phone, and I would answer it. "Some best friend you are."

She picked up a gordita and handed it to me. "No need to thank me. I know you're grateful." She flashed me a grin. "Looks like one of us might have a date to prom after all."

"Dana." I took the gordita and bit into it viciously. "Did you miss the whole other *girl* at the game? He is *not* going to ask me to prom. He's just going to torment me."

"Hmm." Dana winked her blue eyes at me. "We'll see."

We finished up our Taco Bell and headed outside to the field. The game didn't start until four-thirty, but it was such a beautiful day that I couldn't help wanting to get outside and soak up some sunshine. I squinted up at the sky above me, thoughts of serial killers seeming much less tangible in the radiant sunlight. Aaron, on the other hand, felt very real.

"Maybe spring is finally here." Dana sat sideways on the metal bleachers, spreading her white eyelet dress around her.

"Wouldn't that be nice," I agreed. Sometimes the weather had a hard time making up its mind in New Jersey. We wouldn't have consistent warmth until May or even June.

A whistle blew, and we turned our attention to the field as the lacrosse team trotted out. My eyes were drawn to number eleven. I watched Stephen go through his warm-up drill, the movements of his shoulders and legs so familiar to me. I felt a longing in my chest and shook it off.

As if sensing my eyes, Stephen looked up. He waved.

"Did Stephen just wave at you?" Dana hissed.

Fairly obvious. I ducked my head, busying myself with my recorder.

The whistle blew a few minutes later. I didn't have to look to know they were taking a break from the pre-game workout.

"Jayne? Stephen's coming."

I lifted my eyes to see him jogging over. Stephen Harris. Sweat dripped down his chin and his face was flushed, but there was no denying how attractive he was.

He paused in front of us and leaned over, putting a foot up on the bleachers and resting an elbow on his knee. "Hey ladies," he said, his green eyes lighting on me. He panted, still catching his breath. "Nice of you to come watch."

Did he actually look hopeful? I exhaled and stuck the tip of my ring finger in my mouth, nibbling away at the nail. "I'm just here for class. The paper. You know." I waved my recorder at him in case he had any doubt.

"Of course. Thanks for coming." He pulled a towel from his shoulders and rubbed his face. "Want to hang out after the game?"

I did, but not because of Stephen. Aaron's face flashed through my mind, and I realized with a rush of guilt that I wanted to hang out more to make Aaron jealous than to be with Stephen. I couldn't do that to him. We had a long history together, and I couldn't hurt him just because he'd hurt me.

Aaron was a different story. I wanted desperately to get back at him. How petty of me.

The whistle blew again, and Coach Matthews yelled, "Harris! Get over here!"

Stephen jumped up. "Call me," he said as he mimed holding a phone to his ear.

I nodded, and he smiled. Then he hurried off.

He was barely out of earshot when Dana jumped all over me—well, not literally. "What gives, Jayne? You look at him like you want to be with him, but then you blow him off. Are you playing hard to get?"

"I miss him," I admitted, trying to understand my feelings myself. "I know Stephen. It feels natural to be with him. But I can't stop thinking of…" My voice trailed off as I remembered how useless it was to pursue the boy I was thinking of.

"Aaron," Dana finished for me. She gave me a soulful look. "I'm so sorry."

"It's okay." I turned my recorder on and began video-taping, making a conscious effort to focus on more than just Stephen.

"You have too many admirers. Who's that guy up there?" Dana cocked her head up to the bleachers behind us.

I turned to see a guy with a baseball cap watching us. His face was hidden by the bill, but his gaze seemed to focus right on us. I studied his physique. Didn't look like Aaron. "Maybe he's one of your admirers. I don't know him."

Dana laughed. "My admirers would never come to a high school lacrosse game."

"Well, you're just way cooler than me," I replied, annoyed. I turned back to the game, my good mood completely dampened.

It was almost six by the time I got home. I didn't stay for the post-game activities lest Stephen should try and talk to me. In spite of trying not to look for Aaron, I couldn't deny the disappointment sitting heavily in my chest when he didn't show up.

Mom must have had a rough day showing houses, because the first thing that greeted me when I walked in the door was the smell of banana bread. I inhaled deeply. My mom made the best banana bread, complete with a lavender glaze on top. I knew why she did it, too; the lavender had a soothing, calming effect. Just the scent of that bread washed away my anxiety over Stephen, Aaron, and my crappy weekend.

"Mom?" I paused in the kitchen.

"Hi, honey." She gave me a quick hug, then wiped some flour from my face. "Oh, sorry. How was the game?"

I saw the way her eyes appraised me, and I knew she saw in me almost a carbon copy of herself. Her brown hair, the same color as mine, was done up in a loose, stylish bun on top of her head, a few stubborn curls escaping around her petite face. The only thing that gave away her age were the tiny wrinkles starting to show around her blue-green eyes.

"Fine," I said. "What about you? Bad day?"

She rolled her eyes and turned back to her baking. "I didn't sell the big house. But Susan sold the one I showed last week. Looks like someone else gets the giant commission."

We weren't lacking for money, but I knew it hurt my mom's ego not to get the commission. "Hang in there. Maybe you'll make up for it somewhere."

"Maybe." She shrugged, her back still to me.

I settled in at the kitchen table, helping myself to some warm bread and spreading out my math homework. It wasn't too late to get going on Monday's assignments. I checked to make sure my phone wasn't on silent. "Dad home?"

"No, honey, his flight won't get in until late tonight, remember?"

"Right." I nodded, though I never could keep track of my dad's schedule. His job as a computer consultant often took him away from home for days at a time. I was closer to my dad than my mom...though sometimes I still felt the sting of betrayal when I remembered his reaction when I told him about my Sight. "What time's dinner? And where's Beth?"

"Cheerleading practice. Leftover night, help yourself if you're hungry."

Oh yeah, Beth was trying out for cheerleading. I hoped she made it. She might as well have some fun in her life before she died. My eyes teared up and I coughed.

"Need help with your math?"

I shook my head, grateful for my mom's reminder to live in the now. I opened my math book and stared at the equations in front of me. "I'll do what I can. Maybe Dad can help me later."

Mom grunted in response, already distracted by her bread dough.

I managed to get the first two equations done without too much trouble, but when it came to the third one, I was stuck. Something about understanding one-sided limits and considering the function of (x)... I cursed Dana for convincing me to sign up for calculus.

The doorbell rang, pulling me out of my diagnostics.

"Oh, Jayne, can you get the door?" my mother asked, wiping the back of her hand across her forehead and leaving flour in her eyebrow.

I stiffened. I hated answering the door. The person on the other side was a complete unknown factor. "Um, yeah, sure." Trying to ignore the sudden dryness in my throat, I pushed my chair from the table.

I opened the door and came face to face with a box of lollipops. But it wasn't the lemon lollipop creating the aroma around me.

"Hi, I'm Herold," a high-pitched child's voice said. "I'm selling candy to earn money for a trip to Coney Island for my class. Would you like to buy a lollipop?"

"Nothing—Nota—No thank you." I stumbled over my words in my haste to get the door closed.

"Please!" Herold reached out to grab my arm and in the process lost his box. Lollipops flew everywhere. "Sorry! I'll pick those up!"

Heaving a sigh, I knelt to help him. "That's alright. It was an accident." I reached a hand out, feeling for the box.

"Are you blind?" the boy asked, ducking his head to look up at me.

"No!" I cried.

"Mommy!" Coughing, sputtering, Herold weaves through a smoke-filled room. The ear-splitting sound of a fire alarm rings through his head. He stops at his parents' bedroom and presses his hand to the door. Not hot.

"Herold!"

Herold whirls around at the sound of his little sister. He can't see the end of the hallway, but he knows she is in her room. "April! Remember how they told us in school? Crawl to me!"

Her whimper is barely audible over the fire alarm.

"Mommy!" Herold screams again. Why doesn't she come out of her room?

April's hysterical sobbing reaches him now. "Herold, I can't get Kojo! He's stuck!"

Oh. Her stuffed crocodile. Of course she won't leave him.

Herold looks toward the stairs leading to the main level, feeling them taunt him. So close to the exit. "Let him go, April!" But he knows she won't. Herold drops to the ground, trying to find cleaner air. Quickly he moves to April's bedroom.

Her tiny arms wrap around him when he enters, her little body shaking.

"I'm here, April." Mommy. He has to get Mommy.

Another sound fights to be heard over the alarm, a roaring and snapping. Sweat drips from Herold's brow and his heart races. Instinctively, he knows time is running out.

"Come on." Herold lifts April up, ignoring her cries for the crocodile, and runs for the doorway. He sees it—he's almost there—and then the floor gives way, dropping the two of them into the fiery abyss below.

The connection broke the moment Herold died, and I jerked away. I pressed my hands to my cheeks, feeling the tears that streamed down my face. It wasn't too far into the future, either, because I hadn't seen any other events in Herold's life. Just his death.

"I'm so sorry," Herold said. I knew now that he couldn't be older than nine or ten. "Did I do something?"

"No." I shook my head. Pulling out my wallet, I handed him several twenties. "Ill take all your lollipops." *Just go. Go and enjoy Coney Island.*

"Really?" I could hear the awe in his voice. "Thank you, lady! I mean, ma'am!"

"Herold?" I paused, my throat aching. How could I warn him? "If you're ever in a fire, you need to get out of the house. You know that, right?"

He looked at me oddly. "Right."

I closed my eyes. *But the little sister.* What could I tell him, to leave her behind? No way would he do that. "That's all," I whispered. I waved him off and resumed picking up the spilled lollipops. At least the kid would see Coney Island before he died.

He hurried away with his empty box of candies, and I couldn't help it; I looked for her.

This time she stood in the middle of the street. I wondered if she ever got tired of wearing the same white dress. I crossed my arms over my chest. "It doesn't mean anything to me, you know!" I shouted. "Declare. Declare what?"

I turned around and went into the house and straight to my room, ignoring my math homework still laid out on the kitchen table. My hands trembled as I grabbed the matches, fumbling to light my Sweet Pea candle. In a moment, the essence filled the room and I threw myself on my bed, inhaling deeply. Tears leaked out the sides of my eyes and I fought back a sob, images of the last minutes of that little boy's life invading my mind.

I groaned and pulled a pillow over my head. What could I do? How could I get these visions to stop? I didn't want them anymore, I didn't want to See anymore.

My pocket vibrated, followed quickly by the perky jingle of my cell phone. I took several deep breaths before answering. "Hello?" The smoke and the candle were calming me. I exhaled lightly.

"Hello, Jayne?"

Aaron. I'd know that British accent anywhere. My eyes flashed open. Sitting up, I ran a hand through my hair. "Yes?"

"Jayne, it's Aaron. Don't hang up, please." He paused, as if checking to make sure I was still there.

"Okay..." I let the word draw out doubtfully.

"I need to talk to you. Can I come to your house?"

Aaron, at my house. I closed my eyes again and quickly opened them when Herold's face popped into my head. I needed a distraction. Suddenly I longed for Aaron to be here, to hold me and comfort me. I wanted to lay on my bed with him, my head on his chest, his arms wrapped around me.

"Jayne?"

"Yes." My face grew hot and I fanned myself. "Do you know where I live?"

"No." The relief was evident in his voice. "What's your address?"

I rattled the numbers off distractedly while running my fingers around the edge of my candle. The hot, soft wax molded under my fingertip.

"All right. I'll be there within the hour."

"Kay." I tossed the phone on my bed and stared into the flickering flame. What on earth was I getting myself into?

Once I felt good enough to leave my room, I headed downstairs and gathered my homework into a neat pile on the kitchen table. I wasn't done with it, but my head wasn't in the right place for mathematical calculations. Mom had left the kitchen and the oven was off, the last loaf of bread cooling on the stove. She was probably sleeping.

I hovered between the kitchen and the living room, anxious for Aaron's arrival. I couldn't get my heart to stop racing.

My phone rang at the same time that the doorbell did. I pulled it out. My sister. No, not now. I hit ignore and quickly opened the door.

"Jayne? Are you alright?" Aaron drew his brows together, a frown etching lines into his face.

I realized I was staring at him. At that brown curl on his forehead that would look ridiculous on anyone else, the way his light blue jeans clung tightly to his form. His deep blue eyes, which I could gaze into as long as I wanted now. Now that I already knew how he died. I took a deep breath and shook myself. "Yes, I'm fine. Sorry. Was just... thinking about something important." *Like how extremely sexy you are.*

The brows lifted. "Have you been crying?"

Oh, drat. I'd almost forgotten. "Come on in, Aaron." I ducked my head, avoiding his eyes out of habit.

I continued toward the kitchen and stopped when I realized he wasn't following. I turned around. Aaron still stood in the entry way. "Well? You coming in or not?"

"I want to make sure you know why I'm here."

I didn't want to speculate about what brought him to my side of town. Suddenly weary, I waved a hand and rested my head against the kitchen doorway. "Go on."

He cleared his throat and shoved his hands into his jeans pockets. "Well, about that girl you saw me with—"

"That girl?" I echoed. The painful, embarrassing moments at the game on Friday came flashing back to me as clearly as if they had just happened. I jerked my head up. "You mean, Libby? Your girlfriend from England? The one you never bothered mentioning when you canceled our date?" I worked hard not to sound spiteful. But really, I didn't know why I bothered. I knew what he was going to say. I'd already seen them married.

For a moment he looked more like Clark Kent than Superman, a pathetic and forlorn expression on his face, his dark eyebrows raised over those blue eyes.

I sighed, the fight going out of me. He didn't have any more say in the matter than I did. Fate would have its way with us. "Just tell your story."

"Okay." Aaron nodded. "Libby was my girlfriend in England. I didn't know she would expect the relationship to continue once I moved."

I kept my expression impassive. Did he ever break up with her? What else was she to expect? Men. At least I knew better. When Aaron left the States, he also left me.

"It was quite unexpected when she showed up this week. It wasn't very comfortable. I had to let her know that she isn't my girlfriend anymore." He met my eyes on the last sentence, as if this were some big reveal and he wanted me to put the pieces together.

But it wasn't a big reveal. All of this I'd already known. I'd known everything he was going to say. I didn't feel the least bit of excitement—just apprehension. This was the beginning of the end.

No. I wouldn't let it go that way. I could end this here. If I never became his girlfriend, he couldn't break up with me just to go back to Libby, marry her and…die. Wow. Happily ever after for both of us. I would not let him shatter my life that way.

"As long as you're happy, Aaron. I'm glad you two worked something out." I gestured to the door behind him. "You've made yourself clear. Now, if you don't mind, I've got things to do."

Aaron crossed the foyer to where I stood in the kitchen, his chest touching my shoulder. I caught my breath. I felt his gaze on me but didn't dare look up. Then he moved past me to the dining room table. "You're upset, Jayne. I can't leave you like this. What's wrong?"

Everything. My thoughts ran from Aaron, Libby, and my heartbreak, to the last moments of Herold's life, to the lemon scent enshrouding my sister, to Hannah and the serial killer. Goosebumps popped up on my arms. I rubbed my eyes. "It's nothing."

"Are you having a row with your parents?"

I let out a laugh and shook my head.

"Trouble at work?"

"Would you stop?" I stalked into the kitchen and poured a glass of water. "I'm fine. Now if you'll please—"

"Is this your homework?"

I turned around. Aaron stood over the table, looking at my math assignment.

"Looks like you got stuck on number three." He glanced up and flashed me a grin, his eyes crinkling in the corners.

I slammed my glass down on the counter, unable to tear my eyes away from his disturbingly blue eyes. And that strong jawline. "I'll get it. Math is my best subject."

He snorted, causing my face to flush. "You're having a laugh."

Did we even speak the same language? "What?"

"It means you're joking. Because I can see from the scribbles in the first two problems, math is not your best subject."

I licked my lips and rubbed my fingers together. He wasn't going to leave. I couldn't get this incredibly handsome and persistent guy out of my house. Should I even bother? I threw up my arms.

"Fine, boy genius. Help me with my math."

Aaron cocked a brow and sat at the table. I scooted my chair up beside him, careful to maintain an arm's length between us.

"Let me show you what you're doing wrong."

I closed my eyes, letting his British accent caress my ears. Some European cologne clung to his ribbed sweater, and I inhaled. Nothing he said made any more sense than it had in class, but at least it sounded more pleasant.

"Are you listening, Jayne?" Aaron's voice held a note of amusement.

"Of course." I shrugged. "You understand it all so well. So what's the answer?"

Aaron wrote the final result on my paper. "Math isn't your thing, huh."

"I'm more of a words person."

"That's why you write for the school paper?" He put the pencil in my hand.

"Yes. That's more my element." I held the pencil up, waiting for him to tell me what to do.

"That's well neat." He pointed to two numbers in the equation and I wrote them down. "Are you going to study journalism in college?"

"Hopefully." I worked out the rest of the problem, beginning to feel more optimistic. It wasn't exactly easy, but it was starting to make sense.

"What paper do you want to write for?"

I shrugged. "Anything I can do from home. I don't want to be in an office. I want to get my assignment, have my column, and head home. Or maybe even do freelancing. But not around people."

"You're not a people-person?"

I clucked my tongue and stared at the book. "You could say that."

"Where do you want to go to school?"

"Oh, just the local community college."

We drifted into silence. I copied the next equation onto my paper, shooting glances at Aaron out of the corner of my eye.

He caught me and smiled. "Well. Let's get started!"

I became as passive as possible, letting Aaron do the work without letting him realize it. He helped me find the right numbers and prompted me if I started to work them incorrectly.

"You're not as bad at math as you think. You just don't like to try. Well, my parents want me to go to Oxford."

Aaron's comment caught me off-guard, and then I realized he must think it weird that I hadn't asked any questions about him. I probably appeared very uninterested. He had no way of knowing that I already knew everything about him. I knew he was going back to England for college. I knew he would meet back up with Libby and marry her. Okay, so I didn't know he went to Oxford, but that was a minor detail in the big scheme of things.

"Oh?" I feigned intrigue. "I could've guessed that. You being from there and all, and it's such a prestigious school. Aren't you excited?"

"My parents have no doubt I'll get in."

"No doubt," I agreed, noting that he didn't give his own emotional reaction to the idea. "What do you want to study?" I gnawed at the nail of my index finger. Polish chipped off onto my tongue, reminding me of Dana's effort after Friday's game to get me to stop biting my nails.

He favored me with a grin. "Classics and English."

"So you must like English, too."

"I'm in your advanced English class, aren't I?" He nudged me with his elbow. "Did you think I was just a dumb English bloke?"

I shook my head, flustered by his touch. "No, I just—well, you're good at math. I didn't expect you to be good at both."

"Oh, yes. Guys with more than one talent are a rarity." His arm bumped me again, and I dropped my pencil on the floor. It rolled under the table.

"Let me get that." Aaron pushed his chair back.

"No, that's okay." I jumped up, not wanting him on my kitchen floor, searching for my pencil. Dropping to my knees, I scurried under the table, wishing I weren't in a skirt. Bad, bad idea. Backing out, I found Aaron standing behind me, lips curved upward, hands on his hips.

"I would have done that for you."

I put the pencil down and fanned my face. "Um, did you want a drink or anything?" I put my thumbnail in my mouth and bit down.

"No. I should go now."

"Oh. Already?" I felt a pang of disappointment and berated myself for caving into my human longings.

"My parents will worry." Aaron walked through the foyer to the front door. I followed him, wondering if he would try to kiss me before he left.

He paused with his hand on the doorknob and turned around, facing me where I stood in more or less expectant anticipation. "Jayne, I'll call you." He closed the door behind him.

I sighed and leaned against it, feeling wholly unsatisfied. I had expected to be the one refusing his advances. As they had been entirely non-existent, I found myself yearning for them. He hadn't even tried to hug me or touch me or anything. Knocking my pencil out of my hand didn't count.

Sticking my lower lip out in a pout, I pushed myself up the stairs. It was time for bed. It was only eight o'clock, but it was time.

CHAPTER TWELVE

I CHANGED INTO my Mickey Mouse flannel pajamas and wrote Herold's stats in my file folder. I put it away, closing his chapter. That gave me sufficient closure for the moment.

Beth! I'd forgotten to call her back! I panicked at the thought of her out there alone. Quickly I dialed her number.

"Hello?" Her voice carried from across the hall, and I exhaled in relief.

"Oh, good. You're home."

"No thanks to you," she responded, her tone too light to be angry. "Anyway, I've got homework to do, Jayne, so if you really want to chat, feel free to come to my room."

"Um, sure." I felt so bad for not taking her up on her offer. "Maybe I will."

"'Kay. Bye."

I sighed and put my phone down. Lifting my eyes to the mirror of the vanity in front of me, I gasped, goosebumps popping out on my flesh. There was a man in my closet.

I whirled around, heart thumping so hard I expected it to burst. There was no one there. Not even the shape of a man, just my gray towel hanging from a hook on the closet door.

I rubbed my arms and shivered, creeped out.

A light breeze blew in from my open window. I crossed to it and closed it, making sure the lock latched in place. I chewed on my lower lip and tried to talk myself out of it, but I still checked under my bed and behind the door. No one was in my room.

I climbed under the blankets and squeezed my eyes shut, trying to slow my racing heart. There was a serial killer out there, and I'd seen him face to face. Did he have a girl with him now? Was he, at this moment, murdering someone?

I rolled over onto my stomach and buried my head in the sheets. *Think of something else. Something good.* Christmas, sugar cookies, the taste of brine in the air, Aaron—

My mind seized on Aaron, grasping at the memory like a lifeline. Clenching his jaw, studying my math book, touching my hand.

This is counterproductive. I needed to stop thinking about him. But it felt so nice. I let the image of his deep blue eyes and smug smile dance in front of my eyes. My body relaxed, and I slowly drifted to sleep.

By morning, nothing I did could get my mind off Aaron, or the way my stomach exploded with butterflies every time I remembered him bumping my elbow. I could picture quite clearly the way those eyes looked when narrowed in concentration, his lips pursed over that square jaw.

I paused by my car in front of my house, squinting in the bright sunshine. How would I be able to face him in class today?

"Jayne!" Beth flounced down the driveway, shiny brown hair bouncing off her shoulders. "I don't need a ride today. Theresa's picking me up!"

"Great. I'll see you later." I jumped in the car and drove around the corner. But when I reached the intersection to go to school, I made a quick decision and headed east instead. I felt like going sand walking.

The beach had a tendency to be crowded with tourists no matter what day of the week it was. But I knew a spot overlooking the ocean that was usually deserted, and I headed there now. Losing myself in the frigid water with a surfboard had a certain appeal to it, but I didn't have my wetsuit. And it wasn't safe to do such activities alone.

Instead, I parked my car and myself on the rocky sand, pulled out several books, and settled back to lose myself in the world of literature. At least if I did homework, I wouldn't feel so bad about skipping.

I let the scenery distract me for a bit. Seagulls dove at the grass around me, daring me to throw food at them. Below the bluff, a few ducks and a swan waddled over the sand. I studied them a moment before turning back to the books.

At nine a.m., my phone started ringing. I glanced at it and saw that it was Dana. Of course she'd be wondering where I was. How could I begin to explain to her everything that was going on? She was so out of the loop. I heaved a sigh and buried the phone under my backpack, ignoring the twinge of guilt. I just didn't feel like getting into it now.

Dana called again at ten. At eleven she left me a message. "Where are you, little miss Jayne? I know you're not *sick* because you would have called me! Or should I call your mommy and ask her where you are? I will if you don't call me back!"

The threat in her voicemail was all too real. I groaned and gave in. I pressed Dana's number on the speed dial.

"Where are you?" Dana demanded as soon as she answered.

"Hello to you too," I said dryly. "I'm great, thanks for asking."

"Cut it out. You lost the right to cordiality when you ditched your BFF with no word. Why are you skipping school and where are you?"

"I'm at the beach. You know the place. And I'm fine. Just dealing with things."

I could practically see the wheels turning in Dana's mind. I'd haunted this beach a few months ago—back when Stephen and I broke up. "What things?" she asked.

"Things."

"Jayne, I'm warning you," she growled. "Don't make me come get you."

And she could. She knew where this spot was. I grasped onto the item that required the least explanation. "I'm trying to figure things out about Aaron, okay?"

There was silence while she digested that. "Aaron? You mean the guy who dropped you like a rock when his Wales princess came waltzing in?"

"Yes, that would be the one." This was getting redundant.

When she spoke again, her voice was nothing more than a hiss. "Did something happen? Something you're not telling me?"

"No," I sighed, and even I could hear the regret in my tone. "Nothing happened." Not even a good bye hug as he left my house.

Dana laughed out loud. "You like him still! Fabulous! Hey girl, we'll get it worked out. We'll have him running circles around you again!"

"Dana!" I cast my eyes about, even though I knew I was alone. "I'm not desperate!" My face warmed as I imagined what ridiculous charades Dana might come up with to get his attention. "I can handle this on my own."

"Sure you can," she purred. "Well, at least let me take your mind off it. There's a bonfire at Mike's beach house tonight. Lots of hot college guys will be there. Come?"

"On a Tuesday night?"

"Parties have no boundaries, sister."

I could see Dana in my head now, tossing her springy blond curls over her shoulder and flirting in the flickering firelight, while I stood close by, can of soda in hand, a painfully awkward smile on my face. "I don't think that will help."

"Don't make me go alone!" Dana gasped. "You're my conscience! You'll keep me from doing something irresponsible!"

Whatever. I rolled my eyes. "Dana, you're a big girl. And you're smart. I'm not worried about you. And anyway, I have to work." *Thank goodness.*

"Fine. Ditch your best friend. I don't care."

This conversation was exhausting me. "See ya later," I sighed, clicking the end button.

The phone jangled in my hand as soon as I hung up, making me jump. I looked down with a scowl, expecting to see Dana's number. *Aaron.* My heart fluttered and I popped the phone to my ear. "Hello?"

"Jayne, it's Aaron." His lilting voice washed over me and I smiled. The sun suddenly felt warmer, the ocean brighter. No! I wasn't supposed to fall for him!

"Yes, I know. It's a cell phone."

"Oh, of course. Are you well?"

"Am I well?" I repeated.

"You're not in school. I thought you might be ill. You seemed rather down yesterday."

"Oh." I cleared my throat, not about to tell him the reason for today's melancholy. "I've been a bit under, but I'm okay. How are you?" Oh, that sounded stupid. I winced at myself.

He chuckled, and this time I heard the familiar self-assuredness. "I'm fine. In that case, there's apparently a big get-together tonight on the beach. Would you like to ride with me?"

"At Mike's house?" I asked, suddenly suspicious that Dana was behind this.

"Oh, you already know." His surprise sounded genuine, and I pushed my suspicions aside. "I can pick you up. Do you work tonight?"

"I do. It's so sweet of you to offer, though."

"It's not a problem. What time are you off work?"

"I'm off at nine," I said, and then it dawned on me what he was saying. "But it's a school night, Aaron. I can't be up all hours."

"Just a few hours, then." I could hear the smile in his voice. "I'll pick you up."

"Aaron."

No response.

The lack of static on the other side was the only indication that he'd hung up. I pulled the phone away from my ear and glared at it in frustration. Such confidence. He had no doubt that I would agree. I hit the send button and redialed. Straight to voice mail. I tried two more times before giving up. Looked like I had a date tonight.

A flicker of excitement stirred in my belly, and I stood up, shaking off the sand. I needed to get home and find something nice to change into after work.

I chuckled, imaging the look on Dana's face when I arrived at the bonfire on Aaron's arm.

CHAPTER THIRTEEN

AT FIFTEEN after nine, Aaron still hadn't arrived. At first I was relieved by the opportunity to change my clothes, pull my hair down, and put on some lipstick. But after another five minutes of anxiously waiting outside, the chilly spring air blowing on my bare shoulders, I began to feel apprehensive.

Tom, our manager, was closing tonight, so Matt had the rare opportunity to leave the restaurant before ten. He waited with me for a few minutes, then pulled his keys out. "I hate to leave you, Jayne, but I gotta get. You should go. It's not safe lately, you know?"

Believe me, I did. I put on my best fake smile. "You're right, Matt. It wouldn't be the first time I've been stood up."

He dipped his head, probably not sure how to respond to that. "Right. See you tomorrow, Jayne." He loped away, hitching up his falling pants in mid stride.

I checked my phone for any missed calls. None.

How long should I wait? I headed for my car, feeling like an idiot. Anger battled with humiliation at having been stood up this way. Opening the door, I tossed in my work bag.

"Ready, Jayne?"

I turned around, pressing my hands to my chest. A dark sports car purred up beside me, silent and invisible in the night. Aaron stepped out, his tight jeans and blue polo setting off the blue in his eyes. In an instant, my fright dissipated.

"Oh, right." My eyes trailed over his legs and I slammed my car door. Inhaling, I noticed the musky sent of his aftershave and the citrus scent of his deodorant. But no lemon.

"Are you sure you won't be cold?" His fingers ran over the tops of my shoulders and down my arms. I shivered.

"That's why we're going to a bonfire." I tried to play it cool, but his face mere inches from mine did me in.

"Of course." He grinned, the corners of his eyes crinkling. "But we won't get there if you don't get in the car." He gestured to his green speed demon, so dark it looked black in the night.

I grabbed my bag from my car and slid in, wondering how many times in ten minutes he could make me feel like an idiot. Aaron settled in to the driver's seat. The seat leaned back to provide room for his legs.

"Did I miss anything special in school today?"

"Nothing." Aaron kept his eyes on the road, merging with the traffic. "In fact, next time you skip, take me along."

"Will do." I pictured Aaron up on the sandy cliff with me. He'd love lobbing rocks into the white-crested water. "So who invited you to Mike's party?"

He shrugged. "A few people mentioned it to me."

Translation: All the cheerleaders at Lacey Township High followed Aaron around today, making sure he knew about the party. "Are you a partier?"

"I like to hang out with my friends." He shot me a glance. "You?"

I nodded. "Yeah." Mostly, anyway. Dana and I usually went, though we were definitely the milder girls. Neither of us drank or snuck out with guys, preferring to keep sober heads. Though lately I'd sensed a reluctance in Dana to linger with me. I didn't let it bother me. She'd get her chance to branch out in a few months when she left me for her big city college.

"Good thing I'm driving, then."

It took me a moment to realize what Aaron meant. "Oh! Well, I don't drink. I just go to socialize." Actually I hadn't really been to a party since Stephen and I broke up. And Stephen was always the life of the party, expecting me to drag his drunk butt home when it was over. "So, yeah, I can drive us home."

Aaron cocked an eyebrow. "Well, I don't drink either."

"Really?" I looked at him and felt a flood of admiration that bordered on worship. Drinking, besides making people do stupid things like make out with the hostess of the party and jump off balconies, was illegal. I always wished I had a guy who was man enough to do the right thing, even if no one else was. I felt myself slipping further down the road to delirium. *Careful, girl.* I smiled. "What, Superman doesn't drink?"

"Superman?" He blinked at me.

I pursed my lips, a blush creeping over my cheeks. No point in stopping now. "Yeah, you know, the superhero identity of Clark Kent? Wears tights and a cape?"

"I know Superman." Aaron sounded puzzled.

"Well, you sort of remind me of him."

He glanced over his shoulder at the backseat. "Oh, right. My cape's in the back. Don't let me forget it."

I laughed. "It's not so much the cape as the blue eyes and hair and stuff. Anyway." I fought to change the subject before he realized I was as obsessed with him as every other girl. "So you don't drink?"

"Nah. It messes with my super powers."

I laughed and hit his forearm, then jerked my arm back. I was *not* supposed to be the one making the moves. "Huh. I wonder if it would mess with mine. Oh, turn here."

Aaron curved left sharply, almost missing the driveway. "What are your super powers?"

"Oh. I'm kind of an... enigma. I see dead people." *Before they die.*

He parked his car in the grass behind several other cars. "Unoriginal. That super power's been taken." He got out of the car and pulled me from my seat.

"Oh," I said. "Guess I'll have to think of another one."

The air was colder than it had been when we left town. I shivered and rubbed my bare arms.

Aaron grabbed a windbreaker and wrapped it around my shoulders. "This will have to do for my cape," he teased. He gripped my hand and led me toward the flickering light and laughing voices closer to the shoreline.

I resisted the urge to pull away from him. *Relax. It's okay to have a romantic fling, even if it doesn't last.* My stomach clenched at the thought of falling in love with Aaron, only to lose him. And to lose him forever.

But that was high school, right? Most relationships didn't last.

"Are you going to prom?"

Aaron's question came out of nowhere and caught me off guard. This was the second time he'd brought it up. I laughed. "Surely you're not as worried about it as every other girl at school."

He shrugged. "It's my only chance to participate in this very important American tradition. I want to make the most of it."

"I'm not planning on going." *Yet.*

"And why aren't you as concerned about it as every other girl?"

A single curl dropped in front of my eyes, and I tucked it back behind my ear. "No one's convinced me that I should be." I met his eyes and quickly turned away. Too bold.

Our arrival went unnoticed by the dozens of teenagers milling around the fire. I spotted Dana sitting on a log roasting a marshmallow, looking so good in her mini-skirt that I regretted wearing jeans. Then I remembered the mosquitoes. No, jeans were better for bonfires.

"She's your friend, isn't she?" Aaron nodded toward Dana, who was tossing back her head and laughing wildly for the benefit of the boys around her. I felt a little embarrassed.

"Yeah, that's Dana." I paused, not sure if I should go over. I hadn't even told her I was coming.

"Let's say hi." Aaron put an arm around my waist as if he wanted people to see us together.

The thought warmed me, making me feel confident and exhilarated. "Okay."

Dana glanced up as we approached, her eyes widening. "Jaynie! You're here!" Her mouth fell open in a small 'o' when she saw Aaron. "Hey, guys!" She jumped up and headed our way.

I stopped moving. A lemony balm smell mixed with bonfire smoke drifted over to me. My heart pitter-pattered in my chest. Which one? Which of the boys around her carried the scent?

"What's wrong?" Aaron asked, his eyes trained on me.

"Hey!" Dana had reached us, and she threw her arms around me. "Wow! I can't believe you're here!" She looked up at Aaron. "Good for you, getting her out in public. This girl never leaves the house."

Nice. Before I could come up with a retort, one of the boys slipped over and put his hands around Dana's tiny waist. "Come back over, little bird. We're just getting started."

She giggled like a maniac and batted her eyes at him. This kid wasn't from our school. In fact, he looked like he was in college. He handed Dana a can of beer. I felt a jolt of alarm.

"Oh, thanks." She winked at me and set it down on a log. "I'll just get to that later."

"Let's go back by the fire." The boy nuzzled her neck. "We were just getting cozy."

"You two enjoy yourselves!" She waved at us and started back.

"Dana!" I reached out a hand to grab her arm, but she had already danced away.

"She's a party-animal, huh?"

"I-I don't know." I hated to admit that Dana and I hadn't gone to a party together in months. If this was how she acted away from me, I wasn't the only one keeping secrets.

My cell phone vibrated in my pocket, and I pulled it out. Text message from a number I didn't recognize. I opened it.

> Jayne?

Getting my thumbs into texting mode, I replied.

> Yes. Who is this?

The response was almost immediate.

> Ive got ur number Jayne.

Okay, definitely alarming. I stared at my phone, all of my fears about a crazy psycho stalking me coming back in full-force. I had the police officer's card in my wallet. Should I call him right now and tell him about this?

It was just a text message, after all.

"You okay?" Aaron asked.

I shook myself and forwarded the message to the police officer, hoping he had texting.

Unknown number. Possible stalker?

I put the phone in my pocket and the incident out of my mind. There was nothing I could do about it now. "Huh?"

"Are you okay?"

"Oh. Yes." Great. I was acting weird again.

Aaron shifted his weight. "You want to stand by the fire? It's a bit warmer."

"Great idea. Come on." I hurried toward the music and the fire. I had to lift my arms above my head and thread my way through the jibing, shaking crowd which thickened the closer I got to the fire. "Dana!" This time I succeeded in reaching her. "Dana, have you been drinking?"

"No." She glanced at the beer that had somehow opened itself and placed itself in her hand. "Oh, Jaynie." She looked back at me, large eyes pleading. "Just a little. It's a party, okay? Don't spazz on me."

Don't spazz? My best friend was drinking!

She had already forgotten about me standing there. She wrapped her arms around another dude, not even the same one that had given her the beer. I felt a hard pit in my stomach. What else did she do that I didn't know about?

"Aaron! Hey!"

A couple of kids I recognized but didn't know came over to Aaron. It looked like they were trying to do the whole boy-swagger-handshake thing, but Aaron didn't quite know how. Which made me bite my lip to keep from laughing. These guys were on the football team, and they walked as if each step weighed their shoulders to the ground. Most shouldered their letter jackets next to hair that was either too long and in their eyes, or too short and spiky.

And then there was Aaron, standing straight like a concert pianist, his hair nicely parted and combed to the side. His form-fitting jeans were similar to theirs, but his sweater and white shirt with the top two buttons undone gave him the look of a law student at a frat party.

Fingers closed around my forearm, and I jumped, startled out of my deep study of Aaron. I came face to face with Stephen, a chunk of golden-brown hair falling across his tanned forehead. I resisted the urge to reach up and brush it back.

"Jayne." He smiled at me, and the faint hint of alcohol that emitted from his breath killed all tender urges I might have for him.

"Stephen." I sighed and pulled my arm away. Stephen had his father's tendency when it came to alcohol, and he was always inebriated within ten minutes of arriving at a party. "I should have known you'd be here."

"The surprising thing is that you are," he countered. "I never see you anywhere these days."

I peered over his shoulder. "Where's your girlfriend?"

He gave a grunt that I recognized as annoyance. "I told you. We broke up."

I crossed my arms and settled back to stare at him. "So you came alone?"

He wrapped an arm around me and nuzzled my neck, his stubble tickling me. "I'm not alone now."

"I hope I'm not interrupting." Aaron's voice caused me to jerk back. He had a bemused expression on his face while he regarded us.

Stephen peered at him, blinking a few times. "Do we know you?"

"Jayne does." Aaron looked at me, though he made no motion to approach me.

I swallowed and took a step back from Stephen. "Aaron, this is Stephen. He's on the lacrosse team. We're—" I choked and forced the word out, "friends. Stephen, this is Aaron. He's new, from England."

"We're together." Now Aaron hooked a finger through one of my belt loops and pulled me closer to him. I leaned into him, relief warming my body. He claimed me. We were together. At least for the moment.

Stephen rubbed a fist into his eye and looked at me again. "Wait, I don't get it. You're seeing someone, Jayne?"

I stuck the tip of a finger in my mouth, anxiously seeking a fingernail. Finding it already chewed off, I gnawed on the side of my finger instead. What should I say? What did Aaron expect me to say?

"Looks like it," Aaron replied, and for the first time I heard a note of a challenge in his voice. "Is that a problem?"

"Hell it is!" Stephen's green eyes flashed and he glared at me. "Did you start seeing him before or after you kissed me?"

I was glad it was dark, because I knew my face was burning crimson. "You kissed me!" Oh heck, why did he bring that up? What would Aaron think of me now? "Stephen, don't make a scene. We can discuss this later."

"Right." Stephen glared at me, his jaw clenching and unclenching. My gut twisted when I saw that he was genuinely distressed. "Whenever you decide it's worth your time to call me, that is."

I pushed my guilt aside. He hadn't been too concerned about my feelings when he cheated on me with Jessica, after all. "I'll call." I hoped he would read my eyes. I was begging him to go.

Stephen met my gaze. He knew I hated confrontations. "Whatever, Jayne." He paused a moment, then shrugged and walked away. Probably to get another beer.

I felt bad for thinking it, but it was true. That's what he did when he was upset.

The pressure on my jeans relented, and Aaron pulled back. "Is that over?"

"I'm sorry." I pressed a hand to my head. "Maybe we should just go."

"If you want. So." He smiled, the corners of his eyes crinkling. "You should have told me you have a boyfriend."

"Ex. Ex-boyfriend." Such a shallow way to describe the extent of mine and Stephen's relationship. I was wrecking this, I could feel it. No wonder Aaron preferred Libby over me. What a mess this night was turning out to be. I gnawed anxiously on my thumb nail, looking anywhere but at Aaron.

He pried my hand from my mouth. "Let's start over and pretend like we just got here. Look, there's Dana. Shall we say hello?"

"Yes." I took a deep breath.

"Come on, then." Aaron slipped his fingers around mine and pulled me forward. My stomach fluttered at the contact and some of my nerves relaxed. I'd offered Aaron an out, and he hadn't taken it. For now, at least, he was only interested in me. The question was, should I run while I still could? Or should I take what I could get?

CHAPTER FOURTEEN

WE NEARED the group of kids next to Dana. She no longer danced, but lay sideways on the rotting leaves next to the fire, singing to herself. Twigs and dirt clung to her face and hair.

Aaron glanced at me, and I knew what he thought.

"I've never seen her like this," I tried to explain. But it was useless. Dana was making a fool of herself.

"I'm sure it's not her," Aaron said. "It's those blokes she's with."

Right. We could blame the stupid college kids. I pulled away from him and marched into the group of boys, ready to tell them off. Just because they were of legal drinking age (and I had my doubts) didn't mean they could be so irresponsible. I grabbed one by the arm.

"Hey, pretty sister," he said, hooking me by my jeans. "Wanna play?"

"Let me go!" I yanked backwards, angry words on the tip of my tongue.

"What's the matter?" He slinked closer, fingers clutching at my pants again. "You grabbed me, remember?"

"Let her go." Aaron was suddenly there behind me, his jaw tight.

"Hey! She grabbed on to me."

"Is there a problem here?" A third guy, this one with greasy hair and a gold hoop in his left ear, stepped between us. He was so covered in bonfire smoke that I didn't realize he was the bearer of the lemon smell until our eyes met.

In an instant, the world around me faded.

The car is careening down an empty street. Laughing, Hank takes another swig from his beer. "Who's up for dancing? Let's go Samba!" He shakes the steering wheel to mimic the gesture of hips moving, the car swerving from lane to lane.

"I'm up for it!" Chad, in the backseat, has his arm around Dana, whose face is flushed, eyelids heavy. "I bet you can shake it, huh?"

Dana offers a limp smile, eyes drooping closed for a moment.

Hank checks them out in the rearview mirror. "She's plastered, man. You gonna get some."

Sirens start up close by, and he jerks the wheel, nearly taking out a fire hydrant. He swears violently. "Cops! On my tail!"

"Lose 'em!" Chad looks visibly alarmed, excitement and stupor gone. "Faster!"

Hank speeds up, jumping through the empty street. The police car gains on them, coming close enough to ram the vehicle. He pumps his foot on the gas, willing the stupid car to move.

Around the corner another police car, lights already flashing, enters the intersection and stops in front of Hank's car. Gasping, he yanks the steering wheel to the side and tries to avoid the roadblock. His reflexes are too slow, though, and his car jumps onto the sidewalk.

For a moment Hank sees everything in slow motion: the police lights, the bumping sidewalk, the approaching light pole. And then his side of the car smashes into the pole. The window shatters on impact and Hank cracks his head on the pole before everything goes black.

I took a step back, sputtering and shaking. Where was I? Nausea curled around my stomach and I swallowed several times. Breathing deeply, my head aching, I bent over, resting my hands on my knees.

Hank laughed, an ugly, nasal sound. "I think it's time for her to go home. She's already had too much."

Strong hands gripped my shoulders and pulled me up. "Jayne?" Aaron said. "Are you all right?"

"Yes." I straightened, coming back to my senses. "I'm fine." Lifting my eyes, I saw her, standing on the other side of the bonfire. The flames struck strange shadows across her hollowed cheekbones, the evanescent white gown blowing in a non-existent breeze. I yanked on Aaron's arm. "Aaron. Look there, through the bonfire."

He squinted and followed my finger. "Okay?"

"Do you see a woman?"

He glanced at me and turned back to the fire, his brow furrowing. "You mean, like in the flames?"

"No, no. On the other side."

"No." He squinted at me. "Did you see someone?"

She still stood there, only now I thought I saw a smile on her lips. I let his arm go, feeling triumphant. I had just proved it. Only I could see her. "No, I didn't. Just wondering."

Forget the woman. I had to talk to Dana. My heart raced with anxiety. What happened to her? I hadn't Seen her future. Did she die in the car accident, like Hank? No matter what happened, I had to keep her out of that car. I spun toward where she lay on the ground, only she wasn't there anymore. I panicked. Had they left already? "Where's Dana?"

Aaron pointed a few yards across the sand. Dana leaned into Chad, the dude who had been in the backseat with her, and swayed to music. "Give me a minute."

Aaron's eyes were creased with concern. "Can I help?"

With a sinking feeling I realized I wasn't helping our date much. I kept getting weirder and weirder. Well, it wasn't in our destiny to be together. Dana, I still had a chance to save. "Not right now." I steeled myself and walked away from him, approaching my best friend. "Dana." I touched her arm, annoyed at the uncertainty I felt. "Can I talk to you?"

She turned and regarded me. "Hey, was that you that caused the commotion back there?"

I flushed. "I need to talk to you."

Dana glanced around and lowered her voice. "Jayne, you're acting strange. People are noticing. Lighten up, okay? It's a party."

Tell me about it. I took a deep breath. "Dana, let's go. Let's leave this place."

"'Scuse us a sec." Dana flashed a smile at Chad and moved a few steps away. As soon as we were alone, the smile dropped off her face. "What's your problem?"

"My problem?" I echoed. "Since when do you drink?"

She had the grace to blush. "I don't usually drink, okay? But these are older kids. They'll take care of us."

"We're leaving." I took her hand and started to pull.

"Whoa, Nelly!" Dana backed up. "Who *are* you? I don't think so, girl. I'm having fun. You don't like it, you go." She shooed her hands at me.

This was not going the way I wanted it to at all. Why had I thought she would just come with me? She needed more evidence. With a sinking heart, I knew she wouldn't believe me. I should've told her years ago.

But I had to try. "Okay, I'm going to tell you something." I took a deep breath and blurted, "I can see the future. I know I've never told you about it, and I'm sorry. But I saw you getting in the car with that guy," I inclined my head toward Hank, "and getting in a car wreck. I don't know if you were hurt or not, but the thing is, Dana, you can't get in that car with him. You need to leave with me."

She stared at me, mouth agape, for a full five seconds, and then burst out laughing. "Oh, girl. Fabulous story! And I was feeling bad for drinking. How many have you had?"

"What?" I blinked. "Dana! I haven't been drinking! Are you insane? I'm telling you the truth!"

She shook her head, her lips compressing into a tight line. "Forget it, Jayne. I don't know what you're playing at, but I'm officially annoyed. See ya." She flounced back to Chad, ostentatiously avoiding my eyes.

I curled my hands into fists. Well, what had I really expected? That she'd just believe me?

I'd hoped, anyway.

Fighting tears, I turned around to see Aaron standing a few yards away. In the flickering firelight, leaning against a thick tree trunk with his hands in his pockets, he looked like Clark Kent, reincarnated. Just needed a pair of round glasses.

I took a deep breath and stumbled toward him, twisting my ankle on a dead branch. I bent to massage my leg, hoping he couldn't see the moisture in my eyes.

"What's going on?" he asked softly.

What was I supposed to say? If Dana didn't believe me about my Sight, Aaron certainly wouldn't. I decided to go with gut feelings. Nobody could argue with those. "Something doesn't feel right. About those boys Dana's hanging out with. But I couldn't convince her to leave them."

Aaron touched my forearm, a brief gesture that left a bubbly feeling in my chest. "What don't you like about them?"

I hugged my torso. "The way they touch her, the alcohol, their ages—they don't care about Dana. She's going to get hurt."

"Dana seems like a smart girl, Jayne. She'll be careful."

"She's drunk." I spat the words out, anger washing over me again. "She's not being careful. She's not acting like herself at all." Dana, a flirt, sure. That's who she was. Dana, getting slammed at parties and going home with strange men—that was not her.

"Tell you what." I could tell Aaron didn't think my doubts were warranted. But I knew he was searching for a way to appease me, as well. "Let's go to a coffee shop, get something to drink. We can invite Dana."

I put my head in my hands. He'd never want to see me again after tonight. I must look like such a psycho to him: coming along to a party, getting in an argument with my ex over who kissed who, spazzing out on my best friend, insisting that the guys with her were nutty... yeah, I'd probably never want to see me again, either. "Sure. Whatever. It's worth a try."

I watched through my fingers as Aaron walked over to Dana and talked to her.

She shook her head, gestured to the people around her, then waved. Aaron trudged back, his brown shoes kicking up small clouds of sand.

"Well, she doesn't want to come. Shall we go?"

I nodded, the taste of defeat bitter on my tongue. I followed Aaron through the sand, my heart heavy. What was going to happen tonight? Was that the last time I would see Dana?

I stopped walking. What was wrong with me? I couldn't give up like that. This was her *life* we were talking about! "We have to make her come with us, Aaron." I turned around and ran back.

Before I got to Dana, though, Hank stepped into view. He had his own ditzy chick on his arm. I switched directions and converged on him. "Hey, you! What's the matter with you? How can you be here giving beer to high schoolers? And then you think you can drive after this? You're freaking drunk!" I shook with anger. At least he didn't smell like lemons anymore.

He glanced at his friends and then started laughing. "I like 'em feisty, but you take the cake, baby. Cool yourself in the water and then come back."

I shook my finger in his face. "You listen to me. You're not driving anywhere tonight, and you are certainly not taking her"—I shoved a thumb toward Dana, who turned to watch the conversation—"with you!"

His eyes roved to Dana. "She don't have to go anywhere she don't want to. She's a free woman."

"Jayne!" Dana's face turned bright red. "What are you doing?"

I turned on her. "You're drunk. And being stupid. Let's go now, before I call your parents and tell them where you are."

I thought the parents card would be a trump, but I was wrong. Dana sputtered a moment before marching toward me. "You dare, Jayne Elizabeth Lockwood, and I will never speak to you again. Never! I'm not leaving with you, so go!"

I was ready to drag her away forcibly, but Hank intercepted me. "Now, one thing's pretty clear, spaz girl. She don't want you here. So go ahead and exit the scene. Nice and pretty. Good girl." He patted my rump and gave me a shove.

"Don't you touch her!" I don't know where Aaron came from, but suddenly he was there, fists clenched, ready to fight for my honor. As touching at that was, now wasn't the place.

"Let's just go." I grabbed his wrist and tugged him backwards. My hands shook with frustrated anger. I wasn't going to lose this one. Somehow, I had to find a way to change it.

CHAPTER FIFTEEN

AARON STARTED the car in silence. I didn't want to talk about what had just happened, either, so instead I pulled out my cell phone. My fingers trembled as I dialed Dana's house phone. Sure, she might never speak to me again, but at least she'd be alive.

"Hello?" The deep, groggy voice of Dana's father answered on the second ring. I glanced at Aaron's car clock and my heart skipped a beat. Twelve eleven. Almost a quarter after midnight.

"Mr. Sparks, it's Jayne."

He cleared his throat, and I knew I'd waken him. "What's the matter, Jayne?"

"It's Dana." I gripped the phone tighter, trying to control my tremors. In my peripheral vision, I saw Aaron looking at me. "She's at a party, and she's with a bad crowd. I couldn't get her to leave."

"Is she in trouble?"

I almost said no but changed my mind. "Yes." I closed my eyes. I'd doomed her. Her father would either call the police or personally retrieve her, and Dana would be caught. She'd hate me.

"What's the address?"

I fed it to him before hanging up my phone, letting my hand drop into my lap. Tears leaked from my eyes, and I stared out the window. I brushed the tears away as they rolled down my cheeks.

"What's going on, Jayne?"

Aaron's soft voice broke through my reverie, and I looked at him. "I can't really explain it. But I know something bad is going to happen. Dana's got to leave there, and not with those guys."

I saw the way he studied me, intense blue eyes flicking over my face. "She's going to be well angry with you."

"Yeah." I nodded. "I had to, though."

The car gave a sudden lurch, sped up, and stopped. I stared at the road in front of us, not comprehending why we weren't moving.

Aaron sat for a moment before hitting the steering wheel and throwing the door open. "I just bought this two bob car! What a mug! What's wrong with it now?"

I climbed out as well, the air a lot nippier without the bonfire. My face felt stiff where the salty tears had dried. "Now? Does this keep happening?" I looked over the dark green BMW, wondering how something so expensive could be faulty.

Aaron popped the hood. "Last time it was the battery. Replaced it. Then it was an oil leak. In England you'd get nicked for selling a bad car!"

"Here we have someone inspect it before we pay," I tried to joke. Aaron pressed his lips together, obviously not amused.

"Yes, well, let's see where the problem lies this time."

I fished around in my purse. "We can just call a tow truck. I'm covered for emergencies on my parents' insurance."

"Give me a minute," Aaron grunted.

I waited while Aaron messed with the car. Every time he started it, the engine turned over, but that was it. It didn't respond to any attempts to go forward or backward.

I didn't know anything about cars, but I felt like a useless log sitting inside, so I got out and hovered by Aaron, pulling his jacket close around my shoulders. It smelled like him.

"I give up." Aaron closed the hood. "Guess we'll use your emergency card." He climbed back into the car and sat there, drumming his fingers on the steering wheel and gazing out the window.

I made the necessary call and joined him. "All right." Out of habit, I ran my hands in front of the vents, which, of course, weren't on. "They should be here in about twenty minutes."

He nodded, still not looking at me.

Well, that was that. I'd managed to freak him out. The night was black outside the windows, the trees flanking the road noisy with crickets and frogs and whatever else was out there.

I leaned against the seat and heaved a sigh, my chest feeling like someone had put a leaden ball in it.

"Hey, sorry."

I moved my head, looking at Aaron when he spoke. "Why are you sorry? I'm the one who ruined everything."

He blinked. "Did you put cooking oil in my engine? If so, then yes, you owe me an apology. And plenty of money."

I tried to smile. "I ruined our evening. I ruined—" I thought of Dana and squeezed back tears.

The phone in my hand rattled, and I looked down. Dana's father. "Hello?" I answered nervously. Certainly Dana wouldn't call right now to tell me off.

"Jayne," his deep voice boomed in my ear, "we went to the location of the bonfire, but Dana was already gone. She left her car there. Do you know where she went?"

Already gone. The words echoed around my mind. I pictured the street I'd seen them driving on. It wasn't familiar to me. "I don't. But I think they said something about maybe going dancing."

He exhaled into the phone. "All right. Will you call me if you hear from her?"

I swallowed past a lump in my throat. "Yes. Of course." I dropped the phone and put my head in my hands. Failure. Again.

"Do you want to talk about it?" Aaron asked softly.

"I...I..." Dang it all, now I was crying. "Something bad is going to happen to Dana."

"What is it?"

"Those guys she was with. They're really drunk. They shouldn't be driving."

"Maybe they have a designated driver."

I knew what he was trying to do, but I was in no mood to be comforted. "They don't."

"How do you know?"

Somewhere in this car was my bag. I turned around and fished through it, trying to find something to clean my face. All I came up with was a napkin from the bagel shop. I dragged it under my eyes. "I just know, okay? Sometimes when something bad is going to happen, I know it ahead of time. But no matter what I try to do, I can't change it. I'm such an idiot."

"What do you mean, you just know? Are you psychic?"

I didn't answer.

Crazy Jayne, Crazy Jayne. The middle school taunts whispered in my ears. When I was ten, my father took me to a psycho-therapist because I told some people about my visions. He diagnosed me with schizophrenia and put me on tons of medications. The only way I'd escaped the nickname was switching schools and not telling a soul about my curse.

"Okay," Aaron said with the attitude of a parent who is playing along with a child. "So what do you think is going to happen to Dana?"

The way he phrased that question irked me. "Nothing. Just forget it."

"Just tell me."

"There's going to an accident." I flinched, seeing the car wrap itself around the light pole in my head. "Somebody dies."

"Who?"

"The driver. I don't know who else." I couldn't meet Aaron's eyes. Why had I told him, anyway?

Lights flashed behind us, and we both turned around to see a tow truck. Aaron got out and conversed with the driver, gesturing emphatically at the car.

The tow truck driver nodded, threw down a cigarette, and came over to investigate. He walked around the car, then called Aaron over to look at something.

Aaron listened to him, nodding his head, and then got back in the car, looking chagrined. His cheeks were rosy. Flushed from the chill outside?

"Well?" I asked.

"I'm out of gas. Either the light indicator on my console is burnt out, or the gauge in the tank is broken. Bloke's going to fill us up and we'll be on our way."

I wanted to laugh. Gas? That was it? But I could tell from Aaron's face that he was embarrassed. "At least it's an easy fix. And it wasn't because of the cooking oil I put in your engine."

Aaron's eyes shot to my face, and then he laughed. "Yeah. You'll have to try better next time."

The driver finished filling up the tank and brought over a paper for me to sign.

"All right." Aaron sighed and turned the key. The car roared to life, luke-warm air blowing out of the vents. "Let's get you to your car, Jayne."

An awkward silence descended over us. I knew Aaron was trying to figure out how to tell me goodbye. What could he possibly say after my eerie confession?

We pulled up to the restaurant and Aaron put the car in park. Well, at least he wasn't just dumping me at the curb. He leaned over the seat and grabbed my backpack. I was suddenly aware of his musky scent, the way his arm moved when he pulled my bag up to the front.

He looked at me and exhaled, the scent of spearmint gum lingering in the air between us. "Are you going to be okay, Jayne?"

Way to go, Jayne. You ruined everything. My heart thumped in my chest, and I realized how much I wanted to stay in the car with him. I managed a weak smile. "Yeah. Yeah, I'm good." I shouldered my bag just as my cell phone buzzed. My heart skipped a beat when I saw Dana's number. Immediately I answered. "Dana?"

"Jayne." She sounded funny, like her nose was stuffed up. I gripped the dashboard in front of me, feeling dizzy.

"Dana, are you hurt? Where are you?"

"I'm at the police station. Can you come get me?"

"Of course." I turned to Aaron and mouthed, "Bye," and then pushed the door open.

Aaron grabbed my backpack strap. "Wait."

"I'll be right there, Dana." I hung up and pushed a hand through my hair. Lucky for her, I'd just been to the police station and knew it was a block away from JT's.

"Who was that?"

I swung my head toward Aaron. I'd almost forgotten he was there. "Dana's at the police station. She needs me to go get her."

Aaron pulled me back in and put the car into drive. "Do you know where it is?"

"Yes." I closed the door and put my seatbelt back on while trying not to think about the fact that he wasn't ditching me by my car.

Five minutes later we pulled up to the squat, red-brick building. "I'll wait here," Aaron said, turning the car off.

"Sure." I clattered up the five steps leading inside. An officer directed me to a waiting room. I could see Dana through the blinds on the glass windows, her arms clutched around her shoulders, staring at the linoleum flooring. I walked around the corner. "Dana?"

She looked up at me, her mouth working for a moment before she burst into tears. I ran to her and wrapped my arms around her. "Are you okay? Were you hurt?"

She shook her head. "They said I might have some whiplash tomorrow. But I didn't want to go to the hospital, and since I'm not a minor, they didn't make me." She paused and drew her head back, looking at me with bloodshot eyes. "How did you know about the accident?"

I helped her wobble out the door. "It was a guess. They were pretty drunk. Did the police book you?"

She choked back a sob. "No, just gave me a warning. Since it was my first offense." Dana lifted her eyes and scanned the parking lot. "Where's your car?"

"I came with Aaron."

She let out a groan. "Oh, please! I don't want anyone to see me this way!"

I tried to calm her down. "It's alright. Let's just get you home, sweetie. Do your parents know?"

Aaron opened the passenger side door and helped me arrange Dana in the front seat.

"Oh!" Dana tossed her head back, tears leaking out the sides of her eyes. "The worst part! My dad had the police looking for me! As soon as I came in they called him." Her words were totally slurring together, but they did that anyway when she was excited, so I got the gist. "And he refused to come get me! Said I needed to learn to take responsibility for my own actions!"

I had to admit his reaction was a bit harsh, but it probably worked. "Do you want to come to my house?"

"I better not." She wiped her tears on her arm. "He'll be in a much better mood if I'm there when he wakes up tomorrow."

I patted her shoulder and climbed into the back. "Do you know how to get us out of here, Aaron?"

"Yeah, I think I got it," he responded, revving the car engine. Dana whimpered and put her head in her hands. "Are you all right, Dana?"

"I'm okay," she whispered, dropping her hands. "Hank was driving. He ran off the road." She pressed her face into her elbow, blond ringlets falling forward. "He died on impact." Her sobs filled the space in the tiny car.

Dana quieted down as we drove. I murmured directions to her house over Aaron's shoulder, leaning as far forward as my seatbealt would allow me. When we got there, I realized she was asleep. I half dragged her up the walkway and used her key to let us in. The house was quiet, with only one light on in the hall. Getting her up the stairs was a bit of an issue, but Dana barely stirred. I laid her in bed and took her shoes off.

"Jayne?" she whispered.

"I'm here, Dana." I hovered close to her, feeling such relief that she was alive that I hardly noticed how bad she smelled.

"I'm sorry for what I said."

"It's okay. Go to sleep. I'll see you tomorrow."

Aaron had his head down on the steering wheel when I opened the door. He jerked up, blinking several times.

I didn't really know what to say, so I just climbed in and closed the door. "Thanks for taking me to get her."

Still he didn't start the car. "You really did know, didn't you?"

My eyes darted to his face and then I looked away quickly. "Yes."

"Do you know things about everyone?"

I inhaled slowly. Uh-oh. Here it came. "No. Just—some people."

"Do you know things about me?"

I squeezed my eyes shut and shook my head quickly. I couldn't tell him about Libby and his death. Not yet.

Aaron backed the car out of the driveway and got back on the freeway. "It's really late, you know."

The clock on the dash blinked, moving to two fourteen. "I know." My parents hadn't called. Having a clean slate gave me loads of freedom and trust.

We reached the bagel shop, and once again I grabbed up my backpack. The adrenaline rush had worn off now, and I felt the tiredness pulling at my eyes. "Maybe I'll see you in school tomorrow."

"Maybe?" He gave a ghost of a smile. "Planning on skipping again?" His smile faded. "Listen, why don't I follow you home? You look about ready to pass out."

I gave my head a shake, more to wake myself up than anything else. "No, I'm good. Get this car home before it dies on you again."

"Right." His eyes flicked over my face. Did I imagine it, or did they linger a moment on my mouth? "Call me when you get home. So I know you made it."

I saluted. "Yes, sir." I closed the door and spun to my car, hoping I could convince my body to stay awake a little bit longer.

CHAPTER SIXTEEN

THE SUN streamed across my bed, forming a stripe over my eyes. I squeezed them tighter, desperate to block the light out and get back to dreamland. A heavy ache in my chest warned me that I didn't want to face reality.

My bedroom door bounced open, bringing with it the lemon perfume. I wrinkled my nose, rolled over, and shoved my head under the pillow. "Beth! You're not supposed to be in my room!"

"And you're not supposed to be in bed." I heard her at my vanity, picking up candles, smelling them, and putting them back. "Are you sick? How am I getting to school?"

I took a deep breath, trying to remain calm. "I don't know. Ask Dad."

She harrumphed and trotted out of the room. "Mom! I need a ride to school!"

I groaned and sat up, listening to my mom and Beth yell back and forth from the kitchen to the stairs. A quick glance at the alarm clock confirmed my fears: seven twenty. It was time to leave for school, not wake up for school.

My room stank. I lit one of my cucumber melon candles and opened a window, shooing out the musty air. I didn't like sleeping with the windows closed, but I couldn't shake the creepy feeling I had that someone was watching me. Which reminded me, I needed to call the police station today.

A knock on my door gave me a two-second warning before my dad walked in, straightening his tie.

"What's wrong, Sis? I'm almost out the door and your sister tells me she needs a ride. Feeling sick, honey?"

My dad. Always so kind and gentle. I'd seen it as a betrayal all those years ago when he took me to the shrink. Now I knew it was out of concern for me.

The events of last night came rushing back to me, and I longed to throw myself into his embrace and let him make it all better. "No, not sick. I just didn't sleep well. I'll go to school late."

Mom appeared behind him, her expression not nearly so sympathetic. "What time did you get in last night, Jayne?"

"Well…" I made a big show of yawning and thinking. "It was pretty late."

"How late?" Mom pursued, not about to be put off.

"Mom," I said, putting some bite into my tone. "I'm not a kid. I was out with some friends and time got away from us. But I'm up and I'm getting ready for school now, okay? So how about some privacy?"

Dad scooted out the door, eager to give me that privacy. But Mom just folded her arms across her chest. "Take your sister to school. Your dad and I have to work and we won't be late because you were out having fun on a school night. We'll talk about this later." She turned and walked out.

"Fine," I grumbled, kicking at my dresser. "After work and after Spanish club, we'll talk." The thought of all those after school activities made my head hurt. I just wanted to go back to bed.

I left my phone charging in the bathroom while I took Beth to school. Then I came home and threw myself back in bed. Sure, I'd said I was going to school. But I was really tired…and no one was around to stop me.

I finally woke up around noon. My bedroom was warm even with the breeze blowing in through the window. The candle had burnt itself out.

Stretching, I made my way into the bathroom and examined my reflection. Yeah, definitely not going to school today. I felt the first inkling of panic. Two days of in a row of skipping. My parents would probably get a call today. Even worse, I was officially behind in my homework.

I shrugged it off. *This is my junior year!* I told myself. *Not like my school of choice cares about my grades.* Yeah, all those straight As, except for calculus—for nothing.

I picked up my phone, feeling my heart start to pound as I contemplated calling the police. Finding the number in my contact list, I hit send.

"Lieutenant Bailey speaking."

"Hi, Lieutenant." I swallowed down my nerves. "I met with you a few days ago about the serial killer. Gave you a drawing?"

"Yes! I was hoping to speak with you some more. Can you come back in this afternoon?"

"No." I gripped the phone, noticing that my hand shook. "But someone texted me last night. I think it might have been him." Saying that aloud freaked me out. My knees buckled, and I put one hand on the sink to steady myself. " I tried to forward it to your number. Did you get it?"

"I did, I just wasn't sure who it was from or what it meant. Now it makes sense. So you think he's targeting you?"

"Yes," I whispered.

"It's Jayne, right? What's your last name, hon?"

Oh, crud. I'd forgotten that the text included my name. I hesitated. If I gave him my full name, he might figure out that Hannah and I hadn't been friends. But I couldn't really stay anonymous if I wanted protection. "Lockwood."

"Jayne, what you are telling me is very serious. I don't want you to get hurt. When can you come to the station?"

A door slammed downstairs, and I froze, the skin on the back of my neck crawling. "I think there's someone in here," I whispered. The room darkened on the edges of my vision, and I reached for something to hold me up.

"Give me your address. I'll send a patrol by."

The calm authoritativeness in his voice gave me an anchor. I turned the light off in the bathroom and crouched next to the toilet. "Thirty-five Wentworth Ave."

Radio crackled on the other side, though I couldn't make out the words. "Stay on the phone with me, Jayne. There's a patrol two minutes from your house. They'll be right there."

"Okay," I whispered. I didn't say another word, just breathed into the phone, ears perked for footsteps on the stairs. So far, nothing. But it wouldn't take long. If he was looking for me, he would correctly assume the bedrooms were on the second floor.

I heard a knock at the front door.

"Jayne, I've been notified that the patrol is at your house. Now I need you to go downstairs and open the door."

The thought of moving petrified me. "Really? What if he attacks me when I do?"

"The police aren't leaving until the door opens. I can have them announce themselves. Or I can tell them to force an entry, though it might damage your door."

I imagined my mom being more upset over the damaged door than a dead daughter. No, that was unfair. "Have them say who they are and I'll open the door."

"Fair enough."

A moment later a voice outside shouted, "This is the police. Open the door or we have permission to force an entry."

I gathered my courage and stood up. Then I ran down the stairs, phone still clutched in one hand, and opened the door.

Two officers stood there, weapons drawn. I blinked in the sunlight, unable to focus on their features.

"Jayne?" one asked.

I nodded.

"Stay out here with me while we search the house."

His partner ducked inside, weaving around corners with his gun just like in a cop show. I took gulping breaths of air, trying to calm my heart.

A moment later the man returned. "I didn't find anyone. Why don't you come in with me and we'll all look again, together?"

I nodded. Now that the mind-numbing panic had passed, I felt tears burning behind my eyes. I'd heard a door slam shut. Had he snuck out the back door?

We combed through the house, checking every closet, pantry, under the beds, behind doors. My terror subsided bit by bit.

"Ma'am?" The officer who had searched my house motioned me over to the laundry room. A cool breeze blew in from a cracked-open window. "I opened this door when I came through the first time, but just now it was shut again. Do you think the wind might have blown the door closed, and that's what you heard?"

As soon as he said it, I knew that's what it was. I closed my eyes, feeling like the biggest idiot on earth. "Yeah. That could've been it."

He looked over my shoulder at his partner.

"Premises are secure," his partner confirmed.

"We're going to leave you now," the first officer said to me, placing a hand on my shoulder. "Keep the doors locked and don't hesitate to call if you hear anything else."

"Right," I murmured. I escorted them to the front door and fastened all the locks. Then I sank down onto the tile floor, wrapping my arms around myself.

CHAPTER SEVENTEEN

I SAT ON the cold tile floor until the fear washed out of me. Why me? Why did I have to See that girl's death and then meet the killer at a stupid high school game? Why did I have to See, anyway?

When had I started Seeing? How old was I when my life spun away from me? I clearly remembered Seeing when I was thirteen. I was twelve when I saw Joshua's death. I could remember as far back as when I was eleven. Before that, though—I couldn't recall.

The phone in my hand rang, startling me back to present day. Immediately my heart started a staccato pounding, and I held my breath when I picked it up. Aaron. I exhaled. Running a hand through my wildly wavy hair, I pulled my legs up and hugged my knees. "Hello?"

"Jayne, thank goodness." His British accent danced across the air waves, bringing a warm feeling of comfort and security to my chest. "You never called me last night. I've been calling all morning. You aren't at school. Are you ill? I've been so concerned."

"Oh, Aaron, I'm sorry. It's been… a bit of a rough morning."

"I'm coming over."

I could think of nothing I would like more than someone else here in the house with me. "Um." I stood up and worked my way into the hall bathroom. I shot an alarmed glance at my reflection. "That's all right. I'm fine, really. Just tired."

"Are you sure? I've got half an hour."

"No, really." I kept my voice calm. "By the time you got here you, school will have started."

"Well... if you're sure."

I wasn't at all, but I couldn't let him know that. "You made it to school, huh? No problems waking up?"

"Not to say I wasn't tired, but I had hoped to see someone."

Did I detect a note of teasing? "Oh? I'm sure Ms. Siegfried was happy to see you, too, but she probably didn't jump out of bed over it."

"I'm sure she was quite happy to see me."

My thoughts jumped away from my current dilemma, remembering I had a life outside of my paranoia. "What about Dana? Is she there?"

"Definitely not. I doubt she has recovered yet."

I nodded. She had been pretty drunk. "Yeah. True that."

My phone beeped at me, and I pulled it away from my ear. Uh-oh. Mom was calling. "Hey, Aaron, I have to go. So sorry."

"Not a problem. I'll call you later."

Taking a deep breath, I clicked over. This was not going to be good. "Mom?"

"Jayne, I just got a call from the police. Are you okay?"

I exhaled, hoping to stay on her concerned side. "Yeah. Yeah, it was nothing. I heard a noise and got scared."

I shouldn't have said that. Her tone changed immediately. "What were you doing home? When you said you were going to school late, did you really mean not at all?"

I winced. Mom sounded really angry, an emotion I usually saw displayed toward my sister. "Mom, I'm so sorry. I was really tired, I couldn't get myself moving—"

"Is that because you're hungover? Or was it only Dana who landed herself at the police station?"

Whoa. Now how on earth did she know that?

My silence was telling, and Mom said in a rather smug voice, "Dana's father called me. Right before the police did, actually. He thought I should know what happened last night."

Thanks, Mr. Sparks. I decided now wasn't the time for belligerence. "Mom, I didn't have anything to drink. I swear. I just went to hang out and have some fun."

"Jayne! You could've been arrested! You could've been killed! What if you had been in the car with Dana?"

"But I wasn't, Mother. Calm down. No one was going to arrest me. I didn't do anything wrong—"

"You were in the wrong place, Jayne, and that's enough. You're not going in to work tonight. Just sit your tiny butt down and wait for me to get home. We're going to discuss this."

I hung up on her, a sick feeling in my stomach all over again. Discussing things was never a good thing with my mother. And I hated it when she called my butt tiny. I didn't care what she said. I was going in to work.

No, I wasn't. I exhaled and called JT's. Tom didn't handle it all that well, and I worried I wouldn't have a job when I walked in again.

I went up to my room and tried to sort through my feelings. Sometimes it helped if I wrote them down. I pulled out a notepad and jotted:

Anger

That was the first thing I felt. I added:

Mom. Not understanding, bossing

But beneath that anger was another current of emotion, strong enough to keep my leg bouncing up and down even when I was angry. I wrote:

Fear

No reason to expound upon that one.

It wasn't the last emotion, either. I felt one more that refused to be smothered even by my fear. In fact, the juxtaposition of the two other emotions made this one even more poignant.

Excitement

I paused, my pen hovering over the paper. It was more than excitement. It was giddiness, anticipation, hope.

Writing helped. Feeling significantly calmer, I pulled out my green file folder. My people folder. Hesitantly, I opened it. My eyes scanned down the rows of names, visions, and deaths, for the occasions when I could verify the death had occurred.

Aaron. Murdered by ex-wife.

I paused, looking over my words. I never forgot the face behind the names, but I knew this one would haunt me for a long time.

Harold. Dies in fire.

That was the last one I'd updated. Memories of the heated house, of him trying to protect his little sister, brought a sob to my throat. I shook my head and started writing on the next line. "Hank. Dies in car accident, drunk driving." I closed the file and put it back in the bottom of my desk drawer. I felt a little guilty for not being more upset about the guy's death, but honestly, I was just happy that he hadn't taken Dana with him.

Downstairs the front door opened, and I put my hand on my desk, forcing myself to take several deep breaths. Nobody should be home right now. Was it the wind? Had I left the door unlocked?

"Jayne?" My mom's voice carried up the stairs, followed by her footsteps.

I closed my eyes and admitted to myself that I was paranoid. "I'm here." I stepped out of my room and waited on the landing. Mom's eyes were clear but her nose was red, a sure sign that she had had an emotional episode. "You're home early."

"I wanted to talk to you now."

"Mom, I—" I took another deep breath. I needed to stay calm if we were going to work this out like adults. "I know you're mad. But grounding me from work? Come on."

"You can go back tomorrow. Today, however, you're grounded from everything. We've always trusted you, Jayne. And this is how you repay us? Skipping school, going to a bonfire on the beach where *alcohol* is being served—"

"But I didn't drink any," I interrupted.

"How can I believe you?" The tears were welling up in her eyes again. "Your best friend was drinking. She was in a car accident. It could've been you, Jayne. You could've been killed!"

Her tears made me feel even worse. "But Mom, I wasn't. I didn't get in the car with a drunk driver. I'm smarter than that."

"You shouldn't have even been there, Jayne! Avoid the appearance of evil! Now go on back in your room. We'll discuss this again when your father gets home."

I pushed myself away from the banister, rolling my eyes. She was being irrational. I'd have to try to reason with Dad.

"Oh, and give me your phone. You're grounded from friends."

"Fine." I pulled my phone out from my pocket and slapped it into her hand. Then I stepped back into my room and closed the door tight.

※

My father was much more understanding. While Mom cried and wailed about what could have happened, trying to get me the death sentence, Dad pointed out all the negative things that I didn't do.

"But in the end," he finished, "Jayne, you shouldn't have skipped school. And as soon as you saw there was alcohol at that party, you should've left."

I leaned back in my chair, folding my arms across my chest and staring at them. I was in high school, for goodness sake. Did they not know what went on in the sanctity of the school hallway during daylight hours? "Right. I'll keep that in mind for the future."

"Good."

Mom opened her mouth, and I knew she was trying to think up a way to make Dad's verdict more threatening.

"However," Dad continued, "since you did break the law and violate our trust, there's going to be a punishment."

Oh boy. "Yes?" I arched an eyebrow. No point in mentioning that I didn't actually break the law. I'd already been sentenced.

Dad glanced at Mom. "I have a project for you."

"A project? For real, Dad?" No way. I felt my mouth drop open. When Beth and I were young, Dad always had a list of "projects" that he used as punishments for us. Something he wanted tackled but didn't feel like tackling. Thus he would give the job to us. But I hadn't been assigned a project since I was, like, thirteen!

He lifted a hand. "Jayne, this is very serious. I understand that you were just in the wrong place at the wrong time, but you need to think very hard about what you do. Your first wrong choice was to skip school. That one bad decision led you down this path, and here's your stop."

"Whatever." And they say teenagers are dramatic. I put my head in my hands, seriously annoyed. "What's the project?"

"It's at a house I'm selling," Mom interrupted, looking triumphant. "The owner's in the hospital and asked me to tidy up the spare bedrooms. This'll be perfect for you."

"There," my father said, nodding. "You can accept the project or be grounded to your room for the next two weeks with no car privileges."

Clean out some old house. That wasn't so bad. How long could it take? Just a few evenings, maybe a Saturday. "I accept."

My dad extended his hand, and I shook it.

"Congratulations, Jayne. The project is yours."

CHAPTER EIGHTEEN

"Beth! We're leaving now!" I slammed the front door, impatient to get to school. I was in a bad mood. I'd slept through my alarm—again—and there'd been no hot water in the shower. My breakfast was a cherry pop-tart, still wrapped in the crinkly foil. Today was not going to be good.

My phone jangled in my bag, and I yanked it out. It was Aaron. I paused by the white patio bench, giving Beth a moment to catch up. "Hello?"

"Jayne, hey, it's Aaron."

What, did he think my cell phone didn't have caller ID? "I know."

"How are you today? Will you be in school?"

I shifted my bag from one hip to the other. "Planning on it." The front door opened, and Beth slipped out, twirling lightly in a lime green sundress, the lemon scent drifting off her like a matching cologne.

Wasn't it Aaron's fault I'd been at the bonfire? "I've got to go." He started to say something, but I hung up. I was being irrational, petty, and spiteful, but I didn't feel like changing my attitude just yet.

Mom had taken me over to the house last night, which was just two blocks from ours. It was a disaster. It didn't look like the old lady had thrown anything away in years. A hoarder, maybe? Last night I could hardly walk through the mess of boxes, some open, others closed and making tall leaning towers of potential catastrophe. It was almost midnight before I got home.

Beth stood by my car, examining my windshield.

"Beth, let's go!" I said, slipping my sunglasses on. "I can't be late today!"

She turned around. "Someone left something for you, Jayne."

I ducked my head in one smooth motion before she met my eyes. My gaze landed on her hands, where she held up a single white rose.

I quickened my pace down the driveway. "Thanks," I said, taking the rose from her.

A small piece of paper was taped around the stem. I pulled it off and opened it.

Missed you in school. Want to talk.

Aaron

Just like that, all my anger wiped away. I was never very good at keeping grudges, anyway. The sunshine felt warmer, the day cheerier. I allowed a small smile to cross my face.

"Is it from your boyfriend?" Beth asked, still standing there, her lemon smell drifting past me on the breeze.

I took a deep breath, but not even her scent could dampen my sunshiny day. "I don't have a boyfriend," I said, but I couldn't keep a smile from tickling my lips. I climbed in, placing the rose carefully on the dash.

I dropped Beth off at the middle school, then parked quickly and hurried to my locker. I felt anxious and jittery. Was I on speaking terms with Dana? I waited for her to call me yesterday, but she never did. I considered myself lucky that I'd gotten my phone back from my mom this morning.

I glanced around as I pulled out my books, tucking a strand of wavy hair behind my ear. No sign of her.

No Aaron either. My heart rate slowed as disappointment replaced excitement. The tardy bell rang. Sighing, I spun the combination and pulled out my Spanish and calculus books.

Dana wasn't in second period. In fact, there was no sign of her or Aaron all morning, and I was starting to think I'd imagined the rose. Were they both angry with me?

I noticed Aaron right when I walked into English class. He sat on the edge of a desk, leaning in toward Poppy and laughing. I froze, feeling like someone had just punched me in the gut. I tried to sit down quietly in the back, but dropped my book with a thud. The giggling stopped, and I knew they were watching me. My heart pounded as I retrieved it. Had something changed?

Mrs. Siegfried came in and launched into a discussion about our upcoming exam. Her words barely registered. I couldn't take my mind off Aaron. I heard Poppy fold up a piece of paper and slide it across the desk toward him. I resisted with all my might turning toward them. Then the paper went back to her and she giggled loudly.

Mrs. Siegfried paused and looked at Poppy. "Did you have an example to share with the class?"

"Hm?" Poppy widened her eyes. "Oh, no. Sorry." The class snickered, and I felt a tiny bit better.

I wasn't given much time to relish in Poppy's discomfort before Mrs. Siegfried's eyes turned to me. "Jayne? How about you? An example?"

My cheeks grew hot. Of course, when I had no idea what she was talking about. I tried to bluff my way out of it. "I'm not sure if you want me to give a literal example or a figurative one."

"How about just give one from our reading assignment? Such as, 'although Othello showed great strengths as a military strategist, his lack of confidence in his personal life and friends brought about the destruction of the relationships he held dearest.'"

Sounded like a thesis. Taking a guess that we were discussing theses in general and Othello in particular, I said, "Othello was able to be deceived because he slowly let himself fall prey to Iago's villainy, allowing Iago to enter into a more intimate position than even his wife."

"All right, let's talk about this example." Mrs. Siegfried turned to the white board and began writing.

I heaved a sigh of relief. Certainly not the best thesis I'd ever come up with, but it got the attention off of me.

My thoughts turned back to Aaron. I swallowed hard, surprised to feel a lump in my throat. My eyes stung and I pressed my palm against my forehead. Our relationship had barely gotten started! It couldn't end yet!

What was I supposed to do after class? Linger by my desk in the hopes that he stopped to talk to me? Flee as quickly as I could so he wouldn't see how he affected me? March up to him and fling his white rose at Poppy?

I cringed at the thought. I could just imagine Poppy's tinkling laugh. Besides, I'd left the rose in the car.

The bell rang and I jerked in my chair, my undecided plans taking flight. I grabbed my bag, shoved my book under an arm, and made a beeline for the door.

"Where are you going?"

An arm blocked my exit. I blinked, wondering how on earth Aaron had made it out before me. "Not even going to say hi?" He cocked an eyebrow, that cute boyish grin crossing his chiseled features.

"Well." I wanted to sound blustery and indignant, but the word came out mild. I gestured behind me. "You looked occupied."

He dropped his arm and stepped from the room, his eyes on me. "Don't tell me I'm not allowed to talk to other girls?" He sounded amused.

I blushed and followed him, feeling beyond flustered. "You can do what you want. I don't own you." I quickened my pace and pushed past him.

Aaron caught up with me, taking my arm. "We were just talking. And she's a cute bird."

I scowled. "Fine. Let me stay out of the way so you can keep chatting with your 'bird.'" I yanked my arm, but Aaron didn't let go. He leaned over me, eyes boring into mine.

"Why so angry, Jayne?" he whispered, his gaze probing. "Is everything okay? Didn't you like your rose?"

The rose. Confusion battled against my anger, and I relented. I lowered my eyes. "I loved the rose. I'm just a bit confused—I thought you'd be waiting to talk to me, to sit by me, I don't know." I shut my mouth. I sounded like a lovesick idiot.

"Ah," he said softly. "I wasn't sure what you wanted from me." He lowered his head, and I realized what he was going to do a half second before he did it. His lips brushed mine, and then pushed harder, warm and demanding. I clutched my book to my chest, feeling something ignite in my navel. Aaron pulled back, his eyes darker than usual. "Can I sit by you at lunch?"

I sputtered. There was no turning back now. I'd fallen, heart and soul. "What makes you think you're invited?" I asked, trying to salvage some control.

He smiled, the dimple in his chin showing. "Because I like you." He took my hand and I let him pull me along behind him, trying to ignore the tingles caused by his touch.

I led Aaron to our usual spot, waiting for Dana to join us. When she didn't, I tried calling her, but she didn't answer her phone either. Aaron watched me while he unwrapped a whole-wheat sandwich with sprouts poking out of the sides. Somehow I doubted his mom made it for him.

"Are you looking for Dana?" he asked, opening a bottle of orange juice.

"Have you seen her?" I furrowed my brow. "You said she wasn't in school yesterday. I didn't expect her to miss today too."

"I don't think she's here." Aaron peered into the orange juice, and then looked at me, his expression somber. "What does she think of you seeing the future?"

I inhaled. Oh please, we weren't really going to talk about this here, were we? "It's not something we discuss very often."

"What else do you know?" Something burned behind his eyes. Curiosity. Hunger. The need to know.

I turned away from his gaze. "Is this why you're suddenly interested in me? Because of my ability? How cool is that, to be with the psychic girl?"

"Jayne." He took my hand, gripping it tighter when I tried to pull away. "I've been interested in you since the moment I saw you. Yes, you have a unique ability that fascinates me. But it's you that interests me."

"And my ability," I couldn't help saying.

"Everything about you," he replied.

He couldn't have rehearsed a more perfect response. I softened. "It's not an ability I'm glad to have. I hate it. It's awful to know when people are going to die, to know how, and not be able to stop it."

He leaned back, rubbing the dimple on his chin. "You've never stopped a death."

"I've tried," I snapped, suddenly defensive. "I try every time. Every. Single. Time. It never works." I felt a headache coming on and rubbed my temples. "Can we just pretend like I'm a normal girl? Just be normal people?" My throat choked up and I shook my head, hot tears rushing to my eyes. That's what I wanted, more than anything.

Aaron leaned over, putting his forehead against mine. "You are a normal girl, Jayne. I just want to get to know you." He pressed a kiss to my cheekbone. "Really well."

I really needed to stop spazzing. "Yes. That sounds great. So let's not talk about this anymore, okay?"

"Okay." He offered me his orange juice. "Drink?"

I had to laugh. Like orange juice would make me feel better. "Sure."

~

"So who is your boyfriend?" Meredith's wide brown eyes stared at me from behind her glasses when I got to journalism seventh hour.

My face warmed. "I don't have one."

"That's not what I heard. Everyone says you were making out with the new kid in the hallway."

"What?" I gasped, fanning my face. I hadn't noticed any gawkers. "There wasn't anyone there!"

Meredith threw back her head and crowed. "So you were! Everybody saw, Jayne!"

The tardy bell rang just as Ms. Montgomery clicked into the room. Her red hair was pulled into a smart French bun with a ball point pen poking out of it. "Edits, class. Paper goes to press on Monday."

I pulled out the three sport columns I'd written, two lengthy ones that gave a detailed play-by-play of the games, and a short one with highlights to be printed on the front page. I hooked my camera up to the computer in front of me and began uploading pictures. "What movies did you review?" I asked, hoping to get the attention off me.

"Nothing so interesting as your love life."

I rolled my eyes, but Meredith wasn't done. "Are you trying to get

Stephen back? Or do you really like this guy?"

I stopped and turned to stare at her. "Excuse me? Stephen? We are so done. This is about me and Aaron, not me and Stephen."

"Sorry. Aaron. I guess you do like him."

I remembered the way his lips brushed mine, so soft at first and then with a greater intensity. Sadness washed over me. I was falling in love with him. "You could say that."

"Is that why you missed school yesterday?"

"No. I was out too late. Did you go to Spanish club?"

"I did, yeah. I'm going again today. We're having a *Cinco de Mayo* party next week, and I'm helping prepare for it."

"I'll come with you. I feel bad for missing yesterday."

We drifted into silence, and then Meredith said, "Stephen was pissed."

That caught me off-guard. "What?"

"I was by his locker when Troy told him about you kissing Aaron. He punched the wall. I don't know, maybe he still hoped you'd get back together."

"Bad timing on his part. He cheated on me. I moved on." I glanced over my shoulder.

Ms. Montgomery was checking someone else's layout and not paying attention to us. I stealthily opened a web browser and pulled up the local paper. A quick scan revealed nothing new about the murders. I heard Ms. Montgomery's heels behind me, and I closed the browser. I began arranging my uploaded pictures next to my articles.

"How's it going?" she asked, leaning in between Meredith and me to check out our work.

"Just fine," I said, clicking on a picture and expanding it. "Just trying to see things from the right perspective."

I didn't see Dana the entire day. She wasn't in sixth hour, or any of her classes, and I know because I stalked them in between my own classes. I became increasingly more anxious. Was she sick? Skipping? Did she blame me somehow for what had happened? I thought for sure she would've wanted to talk to me.

I waited around her locker when school got out, but she didn't show.

I was just about to leave when Aaron walked up, one hand hooked around the shoulder strap of his backpack. "Hi."

"Hey." He nodded, a slight smile about his lips. "Where are we?" He glanced at the locker behind me.

"Dana's locker. But she's not here today." I felt a pang of guilt. I should've called her. "I better go." I pushed past him, a rush of heat moving through me where my shoulder brushed his arm.

"Are you going to her house?"

"I will after work. Right now I have to get to Spanish club." It wasn't like there was a tardy bell for after-school clubs, but it was only fifty minutes long, and I didn't plan on staying for all of it. I didn't want to waste any time. Besides that, I was falling for Aaron, and I was falling fast, and for some reason it made me want to run and hide.

"I'll come too."

I stopped. "To Spanish club? You speak Spanish?"

He shrugged, his deep blue eyes peering into mine. "No. I'll just sit and do homework."

I pictured him in his Oxford coolness, sitting around my dorky Spanish club. I cringed. "It's kind of a private club, you know?"

He stared at me a moment. "You don't want me to come?"

"No, no," I said quickly. "Well, you just might feel out of place... it's not your usual crowd."

"All right, Jayne." He took a few steps back, then turned and walked away.

My gut twisted, watching his figure disappear down the hall. He'd taken that wrong, I knew it. I opened my mouth, ready to call him back, but stopped myself. I'd call him later tonight, after I talked to Dana. Shrugging off the disturbing unease in my heart, I hurried to Spanish club.

CHAPTER NINETEEN

A LOUD RINGING sounded in my ear. I tried to open my eyes and bat at the alarm clock. The noise moved out of range and then blasted loudly in my other ear.

"What the—?" I sat up to find Meredith holding my ringing cell phone in front of my nose. "Meredith? Oh." A quick glance around the classroom revealed several other members from Spanish club.

Meredith giggled. "Thinking about boys makes you tired?"

"Yeah." I grabbed the phone from her and answered it before it could go to voicemail. "Hello?"

"Is this Jayne?" a no-nonsense male voice asked.

I pulled the phone back to check out the caller ID. Unavailable. Great. "Who's this?"

"This is Lieutenant Bailey from the Lacey Township Police Department."

"Oh!" I stood up, hitting my thigh on a desk before exiting the room. I glanced back in the classroom. Nobody was watching me; they were all busy planning the party for next week. "Yes. This is Jayne."

"We need your help, Jayne. We need you to come and try to identify the killer from a line-up."

A knot formed in my stomach. "A line-up?"

"Yes. We know you only have the description Hannah gave you, but you could be a key witness if you can choose the same person another witness identifies. Will you come?"

"Yes." The words were out before I even thought about them. I wanted this guy caught. "But I have to work tonight. What time is the line-up?"

"It's at seven o'clock. Can you make it?"

I scowled. My shift started at five-thirty. My manager would not be happy about me leaving during work. Maybe Matt would be running the store tonight. He was much more understanding than Tom. "I'll be there."

I went back into Spanish club and tried to focus on our extracurricular activities. I twirled my pencil between my fingers and studied my desk. My mind kept going back to the phone call, though. How much confidence did the police have in me?

Then my thoughts drifted to Aaron, and I tried to keep from having a panic attack. Was he mad at me? Did he think I didn't want him around? I pictured him calling Libby now, seeking someone else to build a close relationship with. Why should that surprise me? I knew it was going to happen anyway.

A shadow crossed my desk, and I looked up at Mr. Livingston. "How's your prep work going, Jayne?"

I gave him a woeful smile. "It's not." I couldn't even remember what I'd been put in charge of.

He squatted next to me. "Language issues?"

"Communication issues, for sure." I tried to laugh.

Mr. Livingston frowned, his light eyes registering concern. "Is there anything I can help with?"

I was aware of Meredith leaning forward, listening to every word. "I don't think so. I just have an appointment after this that's making me nervous."

"Oh." He smiled knowingly. "Doctor?"

I lowered my voice. "Police."

His brow knit together tightly, marring his handsome face. "Are you in trouble?"

I winced. So he remembered seeing me at the police department last week. For sure he thought I was going down the wrong path. "No, it's not me. It's about the serial killer. You know, the one that's been hitting the towns around here?"

"Jayne. I told you to leave that alone."

I whispered so no one else would hear, including Meredith. "Well, the police think I might know something. They have questions for me."

"This is very dangerous. I think you should stay out of it."

"I'd love to." I sighed and wiped my hands on my skirt under my desk. "But I have an obligation to tell what I know. You know?"

He shook his head. "No, you don't. You have the right to protect yourself. In a situation like this, you shouldn't do anything to draw attention to yourself. Let me call the police. I'll give them an excuse for you."

I exhaled, appreciating his gesture but feeling more certain than before. "Thanks, Mr. Livingston. But I'll be okay. I can do this."

He straightened. "I still don't think it's a good idea."

"Duly noted." I saluted him and then turned back to my work, trying not to think about my upcoming task.

&

Miracles were real. I still had a job.

Tom, my manager, glared at me but said nothing else, and I quickly put on my apron and set to work in the kitchen. My heart hammered in my chest, and I could feel an anxiety attack coming on at the mere thought of asking for time off to go to the police lineup.

"Hairnet!" Gabby yelled from the drive-thru window, snapping one at me. I grabbed it and scooped it around my head. She grinned, blowing a huge pink bubble. "You lucky you still gotta job, girl."

"Yeah, yeah." I sighed.

"Hey." Matt came over with a tray and piled on the bagels I'd just formed. "So tomorrow night's Friday night, right? And a group of us are heading to the amphitheater for a big band show. So normally I'd play in it, but I'm not this time, so I thought we'd go watch together. What do ya think?"

"I'll come!" Gabby hollered, moving the mic from her mouth and poking her head around the corner.

"That's sweet of you, Matt." I grabbed another lump of dough and punched it down. "But I'm grounded."

"You?" Gabby left her post to sidle up to me. She looked me up and down. "Miss Goody Two-shoes?"

"Yep, me." I elbowed Matt. "You better get those into the oven."

"Right." He disappeared with the tray of dough, only to be back a few moments later. "Your boyfriend's here. Wants to talk to you." He lowered his voice. "Don't let Tom catch you. He's p-oed with you right now."

"I don't have a boyfriend." The words were automatic. Aaron's face entered my mind, the way his eyes had flickered over mine seconds before his mouth pressed against my lips. I gave a little shiver and hoped no one else noticed the pink tint on my cheeks. Him being here had to be a good thing, though. "Tell him I'll be right there."

Matt went back out but reappeared seconds later.

"That was fast," I said, grabbing a paper towel and wiping bread from my fingers.

Matt shook his head. "It's a no-go, girl. Tom's sitting by the register watching. I think he knows it's your boyfriend."

"Oh." I deflated against the counter. "Will you tell him for me? Tell him I'll call him later." I peeked around the corner and spotted Aaron leaning against the the wall, hands in his pockets. I gave a small wave, but he wasn't looking.

"Hang tight." Matt pulled his hat lower on his head and scooted out of the kitchen.

Maybe Aaron wouldn't leave. Maybe he would insist on waiting until I finished.

Matt came back, a folded yellow paper in his fist. "Here." He rolled his eyes. "And don't even think of using me to send a reply."

I wiped my hand on my forehead, staring at the note. My stomach knotted up. Was it a love note? Or a break up note? I took it reluctantly and turned away from Matt's curious gaze. The paper crackled as I opened it.

Call me when you go on break.

Aaron

I exhaled in relief, and then my stomach twisted up again. I hadn't necessarily dodged a bullet. He was going to break up with me, sooner or later. I was only delaying the inevitable.

The suspense was too much. I couldn't bare it. I pushed past Matt and made my way over to the coat rack. I sifted through my bag until I found my phone, then I scrolled through my contacts until I found Aaron's number. Highlighting it, I pressed the delete button. There. It was done. I'd never have to hear him break up with me. Or not break up with me, as per the vision.

I returned to the bagel dough, where Gabby and Matt were both staring at me. I ignored them, shaping two more bagels before the enormity of what I'd done hit me. I couldn't call Aaron. What had I done? I wasn't ready, I wasn't ready for it to be over!

Tom came into the kitchen, clipboard in hand. "Jayne's on kitchen duty and floors tonight, Gabby's on drive-thru—" he leveled his eyes at her, and she scampered away. "Matt, you're on registers with Theresa. You and Jayne close. I'm off."

I waited until Tom's car was gone to ask Matt about sneaking out. Spring was rapidly turning into summer, and it was getting hot. Even hotter in the kitchen, with four ovens going. My palms were sweating with anticipation, but this was the best chance I'd get.

"Let me get this straight." Matt pushed his baseball cap back and ran the towel over the sweat on his forehead. "You need to leave in an hour?"

"It's very important, Matt." I drummed my fingers on the counter, trying not to appear impatient. "I'm meeting with the police." I needed him to think I was begging, not demanding.

"Yes, you said that already." He cocked his head at me. "Didn't Gabby say that's where you went on Saturday?"

I felt the blood drain from my face. "She mentioned that?" I stuttered, furious at myself for saying anything to her.

"Sure, she covered for you when you were late. Did you think we wouldn't wonder?" He squinted his bluish-green eyes at me. "Are you in trouble, Jayne?"

"No!" Just as quickly as it had left, the blood rushed back into my cheeks. I waved my hands at my face. "I'm helping them."

"You're helping the police?" He raised an eyebrow quizzically.

"Yes." I didn't want to explain any more than that. He didn't move, so I added, "They think I might know something about the serial killer."

Matt still stared at me. *He's not going to let me go*, I thought.

He shrugged and turned around. "Make sure you clock out. And go quickly. If Tom calls and asks where you are, I ain't lyin'."

☙

"Do you recognize any of these men?"

Lieutenant Bailey stood behind my right shoulder. Another officer sat by a computer, clicking through programs. The window and the computer screen gave the only light in the darkened room.

I squeezed my purse between my fingers and exhaled. My skin crawled as though the men I stared at could see me, even though I knew that all they saw was their own reflection.

"It's hard to say," I murmured. The face that had been so easy to recall now seemed less defined. Or was I just afraid of making a mistake? I studied the five men in front of me, each with similar characteristics. My gaze paused on the last man. He held the same stance as the other four, feet apart with his hands handcuffed behind him. He tossed his head back and stared at the ceiling, an expression of utter boredom on his face.

His neck. If his head hadn't been tossed back, I would've missed the scar running along the side of his neck. I flashed into Hannah's mind for a moment, the dull perception she had of her own impending death as she stared at that neck leaning over her. I shuddered and fought back tears. "It's him." I pointed. "On the end. Number five."

Papers shuffled behind me, and Bailey conferred with another officer. "Are you sure?"

"Yes." I nodded. "The scar. I remember the scar." I searched my memory, trying to remember if I'd drawn a scar on the paper I'd given him. Surely I had.

"All right, Jayne, thank you," Bailey said, turning around. He didn't look at me, but straightened several folders next to the computer. "I'll be in touch if we need you again."

"What happens now?" My heart pounded in my throat, and I glanced back at the man. "Will he be arrested?"

"He already has been," Bailey said softly. "That's why he's here."

My shoulders slumped with relief. "Thank goodness."

Bailey faced me, his hazel eyes probing my face. "But we have to let him go."

My back stiffened. "Let him go? Why? But I identified him!"

"But you were the only one to do so." His voice was so soft that I strained to hear him. "And you are the least reliable witness. You only know what Hannah described to you before she died. It's practically hearsay." His gaze intensified. "Unless you have another means of identifying the perpetrator?"

I clenched my purse, taking deep breaths to steady myself. I knew what he wanted. "I know that's him. I saw him at the high school game."

He nodded his head. "But that doesn't make him the murderer."

How could I offer proof? I knew that if I told him I'd Seen him in a vision the night before he murdered Hannah, he would no longer take me seriously. I searched my mind, trying to fabricate a story that would satisfy his logical reasoning while also persuading him that this really was the guy. "Hannah pointed him out to me," I blurted out.

The other officer glanced up from the computer. Bailey leaned back against the desk, folding his arms across his chest. "When did she do this?"

"Right before she died." My hands shook. Even my purse couldn't hide them. I tried to weave in enough of the truth to make the story believable. "She came to my work. She wanted to talk, so we drove around town in her car. We saw him come out of an alley. She stopped the car, turned off the lights, and pointed him out to me. We watched him from across the street. She was spooked, but she had places to go, so she took me back to work." I knew my story must be riddled with holes, but all I needed was for it to hold up enough to book the man.

"So you saw him. Why didn't you tell me this before?"

One lie leads to another. "I didn't see him up close. But then when I saw him again, at the basketball game, I recognized him." The words poured out of me in a rush, as if by saying them quickly, he wouldn't realize how mixed up my story was. "He fit her descriptions and the man we'd seen. That's when I noticed the scar."

Bailey stared at me, making a clicking sound with his tongue. "This all would have been important to know before."

I blushed. "I'm sorry."

He glanced at his watch. "I want to get your testimony, but I have an appointment. Just repeat everything to Officer Daniels," he patted the other man's arm, "whenever he's ready."

"So will you lock him up now?" I blurted out. I hated the idea of him out on the street again.

"It's still circumstantial. You only have Hannah's word, and this was before a crime had been committed against her. But it might be enough for us to get a search warrant on him."

I licked my lips and wished desperately for chapstick. "What about DNA testing? Couldn't you check to see if any of his cells were found on Hannah?" I blanched even as I said the words. What a morbid thing to say.

"He didn't agree to testing, and without a search warrant, we can't force him. I really have to go now, Jayne. Tell me the instant you remember anything else."

I looked at Officer Daniels, who had a recorder ready and was waiting for me to repeat my hurried story of lies. I rubbed my temple, feeling suddenly drained of energy. I couldn't even remember what I'd prattled off. Not that it mattered. My testimony hadn't even been enough to keep the guy locked up. "I have to get back to work," I said to him. "Thanks." I walked out the door without waiting for the guy to comment.

CHAPTER TWENTY

By the time I got back to work, it was eight o'clock. Matt barely spoke to me. That suited me fine. My mind was elsewhere.

I helped close up and then headed out the door. I needed to talk to someone. I had actually told Aaron my secret power. Maybe I could confess my dilemma with the police and Hannah as well. I got as far as pulling my phone out before I remembered I'd deleted his number.

"Stupid, stupid Jayne!" I cursed myself. I sat in my car for ten minutes, fishing through my backpack, looking for that slip of paper Dana had given me just a few days earlier with his phone number on it.

Nothing.

I put my head on my steering wheel, feeling like an absolute idiot. Why had I done that? Such a spur of the moment decision, trying to save myself from future pain. And now I felt so much worse. What was Aaron thinking?

Maybe, just maybe, Dana had his number. I needed to talk to her anyway. I called Dana on the way to her house, but she didn't answer. It was almost eleven at night, but I still expected her to be up and about.

I let myself into the house, trying to be surreptitious. Voices murmured from the kitchen. I climbed the winding staircase up to Dana's room, hoping to go unnoticed. Her door was closed. I knocked once and let myself in.

Dana sat cross-legged in her chair at the vanity, bloodshot eyes staring at her reflection. Her window was open to the night sky, and a mild breeze blew the green curtains into the room. Her eyes met mine in the mirror. Dark shadows made her face look thin and gaunt. Her normally perfect hair was ratty and limp.

"Are you okay?" I asked softly, crossing the room to her. "You haven't been in school for two days. I've been trying to call you."

She reached over and took a sip from an orange cup. "You called once." Her voice was hoarse and emotionless.

Twice, if she counted just now. Which it didn't look like she did. I tapped my fingers on my jeans, trying to feel this one out. "What can I do for you?"

She lifted a shoulder. "Nothing. I'm fine. I'll be in school on Monday."

"Are you in trouble?"

She gave a short laugh that sounded like a bark. "Um, yeah. I got in a car with a drunk driver who got himself killed." She swallowed, moisture pooling in her eyes. "Not to mention that I was drunk."

I nodded. "My parents grounded me. Nothing but work and school."

"Hm." She gave a disinterested grunt.

I checked my watch. It was late, and this conversation was going nowhere. "I better get home. But I can get your homework for you."

She waved a hand. "Just go."

I hesitated, wanting to say something more, but having no idea what. She was obviously unhappy with me. "I'm so sorry, Dana. Call me if you need anything, okay?"

She sighed and put her head down on the vanity. "Yeah. You're a fabulous friend."

I started home, a heavy weight in my heart and a bad taste in my mouth. Not that my life had been great before, but when had it become so dismal?

Blue and red lights flashed behind me and I froze. What now? I pulled to the side of the road, my hands clammy, and the cop pulled around me and drove into the distance. I exhaled in relief. He wasn't actually after me.

I merged into traffic, the flashing lights still blinking in my mind. Why did that feel familiar? I couldn't remember the last time I'd been pulled over. I turned my radio off, trying to focus.

Dark, gray walls. Nighttime. Red and blue neon lights.

Hannah. A night club with red and blue lights.

I pulled over again, my mouth dry at the sudden realization. Of course the police already knew where Hannah had died, but nobody had told me. I sifted through the night clubs I was familiar with, hoping I would recognize one with blue and red lights. Not that I'd ever been to one, but I'd seen them often enough.

Two came to mind: Estella's Dancing Bar and The Electric Cowboy. The Electric Cowboy was in Forked River, while the Dancing Bar was in Barnegat Bay. Since that was where Hannah died, I decided to try there first. I turned my car around, not sure what I would find, if anything, but determined to look.

When I reached the club, all kinds of doubts filled me. There must be dozens of other night clubs that I wasn't familiar with. Maybe they all had red and blue lights. The chances of it being this one were minuscule. And even if it were, I should've come in the daytime, when I might actually be able to see something.

But I was here, so I may as well look. I climbed out of my car. Loud music blared from the club, the smell of alcohol and cigarette smoke leaking out the door.

Sure enough, there was an alley behind it. I took a few steps into the alley, shivering as the temperature dropped. The flashing lights from the club lit the wall of the building beside it, strobing red and blue across the bricks. The smell of rot and refuse filled the small area.

I walked toward the dumpster in the back and the vision popped into my head as clearly as Seeing it again. I spun around and studied the pavement. This was it. This was where she had died. Mottled spots stained it, but they could be from anything. I knelt and pressed my fingers against the stains. A sigh escaped my lips. What did I hope to accomplish here?

Feeling like an absolute idiot, I headed back for the parking lot, streetlights beckoning to me at the entrance of the alley. The warmth hit me when I exited and I inhaled with relief.

My phone rang, startling me. I glanced at the name. Mom. "Hello?"

"It's late, Jayne. You should be home by now."

I scowled and bit back a reply. I didn't need another project, and I knew she'd happily find a reason to give me one. "I'm almost there. I'm driving." Which wasn't true at all. I would just tell her the traffic was bad and that's why it took so long.

Oh, the days when I never lied to my parents appeared to be long gone.

CHAPTER TWENTY-ONE

I DIDN'T SLEEP well that night. I checked my phone a dozen times to see if I'd missed any calls. I kept thinking I must've accidentally turned it to silent. But no, no calls. Not from Dana. And not from Aaron, whose number I'd forgotten to retrieve from Dana.

As soon as I got to school, I looked for Aaron. I debated in my mind how to play this. Should I stand by his locker and act like nothing had happened? Write him a note and apologize?

I spotted him before first hour, going the opposite direction as me. I smiled and waved, but he didn't see me. "Aaron!" I called.

He glanced my direction, then checked his watch and walked away. My smile dropped from my face. Had he seen me? Surely not. I stood there as students crashed into me, oblivious to the tardy bell. Then I shook it off. I'd talk to him in fourth hour, tell him what happened at work. No need to mention deleting his number.

I saw him again in the hallway in front of me before English, too far away to call out to. Aaron didn't stop to joke or act macho with the football jocks in the hallway. He didn't saunter like the other rich kids, but there was a definite classy air about him. He held his head high and walked with a straight back, much the way I imagined someone at a prep school would do. His hair was neatly combed, white shirt pressed under the navy sweater. He was so past the high school stage.

I quickened my pace and entered just behind him, breathless. I assessed the seating arrangements. Aaron wasn't sitting by Poppy, at least. He sat at the table I'd sat at yesterday, just behind her. Poppy had her back to him and was gaily chatting with a blond bimbo who giggled at everything she said. She hadn't noticed Aaron, but I knew that wouldn't last long.

I started for the seat next to Aaron before noticing the backpack occupying it. I faltered. Was he saving it or blocking it?

The bell rang and Ms. Siegfried closed the door. "Jayne, please find a seat."

Find a seat. My ears burned and I swiveled around. Shouldn't be so hard, right?

The seat next to Poppy was empty.

I dropped into the chair beside her, resisting the urge to fan my face. Poppy stopped talking and gawked at me. I kept my eyes forward, pulling out my notebook and "Othello."

Why did things have to be so awkward? Why couldn't I just act casual and normal, grin at Aaron and say, "Mind if I sit here?" Giggle flirtatiously and move his bag?

Instead I felt so confused. I didn't know where I stood. Never mind that he kissed me yesterday. I didn't have the confidence of a girlfriend. What were we?

I tensed as the end of class neared, my heart rate increasing at the prospect of Aaron coming over to talk to me. *Talk to him first, Jayne,* I told myself. I swiveled in my chair, ready with my smile, just as Aaron gathered up his books and walked out.

I stopped breathing. He just walked away. That was it. The disappointment was poignant. It stabbed my gut like a sharp, twisted knife.

"Did you guys, like, fight or something?" Poppy was frowning at me, tapping a pencil on the desk.

"Oh, No." I exhaled, trying to play it cool. "We're just giving each other space."

"Oh." Poppy smiled brightly. "Isn't that nice?" Getting up, she flounced away.

There were still a few people in the room, but I felt very, very alone.

⌘

Dana's reception hadn't been warm the day before, but I didn't know who else to talk to. I didn't really have any other friends; I didn't have time for anyone except Dana. She was kind of a full-time job.

Dana was out in the yard playing baseball with her little brother, Zach. She wore beige capris that tied at her calves, and her curly blond hair was pulled through a baseball cap. She stopped playing and watched me pull into the drive.

I licked my lips. Maybe this was a bad idea. I grabbed my chapstick from the dash and swiped it over my mouth. It was slightly melted and came off in clumps. I stepped out of the car and moved toward her. "Hi, Dana."

Dana handed the ball to Zach. "Game's over, kid."

"Hi, Zach," I called out.

"Hey, Jayne," he replied, already moving off, tossing the ball in the air to himself.

Dana folded her arms across her chest and walked over to me. The color was back in her face, though her lips were pressed into a stern line.

"You missed school again," I said, not sure where to start.

"I know."

"So." I pushed a hand through my wild hair. "You're still mad at me. Though to be honest, I'm not really sure why."

She sighed and dropped her arms. "I don't even know where to begin, Jayne. It's like I don't even know you." She turned around and walked back toward the house.

I followed her to the porch, where we both sat on the concrete steps. Where was this coming from? What exactly had I done to make her so mad? Was it because I had called her father? "What's this about, Dana? Is it about the bonfire?"

She picked up a quartz rock and smoothed her fingers over it. "Not really. I guess." She blinked and met my eyes, light-blue and unwavering. "What are you playing at?"

"Playing at?" My palms were sweaty with anxiety.

Dana dropped the rock with a clink. "Aaron called me yesterday."

"Aaron?" I echoed, my mind spinning fast to put the pieces together. Had he told her he'd kissed me? Was she upset about finding out from him? It wasn't like Dana to be so dramatic, but I didn't know what else to think. "Listen, Dana, I was going to tell you."

"Tell me what?" she interrupted. "Either you fed him a bunch of BS, or you've been holding out on me since—well, for as long as I've known you!"

Now I was really confused. "I'm lost."

She sighed again. "Aaron spouted off a bunch of nonsense about how you're acting weird, and he wanted to know if it had anything to do with the fact that you're *psychic*." She glowered at me. "Obviously he thought I would know, since I'm your *best friend*. I wasn't sure if I was supposed to laugh or play along. So I just told the freaking truth—that I didn't really know. And then I hung up." She leaned back on her elbows. "So, Jayne. What's going on? If you're just trying to scare Aaron off, I'm sure there's an easier way to do it."

This was more complicated than I'd imagined. I took a deep breath. "Well… Aaron's right. Sort of. Sometimes I can see the future."

Dana crossed her arms and stared at me.

The words flew out of my mouth, certain that my window of explanation was closing. "I saw it that night at the bonfire. I saw you getting in the car with that idiot and him dying in an accident. That's why I was so adamant about you leaving with me."

Her expression softened, but she didn't drop her arms. "Keep talking."

What more was there to say? "It's been happening for years. But it's not fun. I always see when people die. I hate it. It makes me want to hide in my room and never look at another person again."

Dana unfolded her arms and leaned against the white pillar. "Why didn't you ever tell me?"

I exhaled, so relieved she hadn't laughed at me. Or worse, told me I needed help. "When I'm with you, I can pretend like I'm normal. Besides, what if you thought I was crazy?"

"Jayne." She grabbed the back of my head and pressed her forehead against mine. "You're my best friend. I've known you for *ages*. I know what kind of person you are, I know how weird you can be, and I know when you're acting strange. Don't you think I would know if you were crazy?"

"Maybe." I cracked a smile. "Maybe not. You're halfway there, yourself."

She released my head. "Okay. Cat's out of the bag. You're really psychic." She tapped her lips with her finger. "It's going to take me some time to fully appreciate that fact. So what's in my future?"

"I've never seen your future." It felt so strange to be talking about this with Dana, as casually as if discussing the weather.

"Oh." She looked disappointed. "But you saw my future at the bonfire."

"No." I shook my head. "I saw his future, and yours intertwined with his. But I've never seen yours. I don't see people's future's, Dana. I See their deaths."

"*All* people? You see everyone's death?"

I pressed my lips together. "No, it's kind of random. I seem to see only the awful deaths." I thought of Herold, of Hannah, and shuddered.

"Interesting," she murmured. "So, uh, what's the deal with Aaron?"

I leaned forward, glad she'd approached the subject. "What did he tell you?" *And can I get his number from you?*

"Not much. He sounded a little confused. Like he was trying to figure you out and hoped I had some clues."

"Sounds like something a girl would do."

Dana laughed. "Either that, or a guy who's really trying to win someone over. So what gives? I know you like him."

"I don't know what's going on. He didn't talk to me all day." I sighed. "It won't work out anyway. I keep thinking it's better just to let him go, but..." I shrugged. "I can't seem to do it."

"Who says it won't work out? Just because he's rich and English and extremely attractive doesn't mean he wouldn't be the absolutely perfect fit for you."

"I know it won't work."

"How can you possibly—oh." Her eyes widened slightly. "Really? You saw his future?"

"Yes."

"And?" She leaned toward me, clasping her hands together. "What, he wasn't with you?"

I bit my lip. "He left me for his ex."

"That scumbag! Wait. It hasn't happened yet."

"No, but it will." Sooner than later, at this rate.

"Now that, Jayne, you can't know. I'm sure we could—"

"Dana. I've tried." I fixed her with my most serious expression. "It never works. You're proof. Even telling you the truth at the bonfire, I couldn't keep you out of that car."

"That's just one example. I'm sure at some point—"

I was already shaking my head. "I always try." Joshua came into my mind, his vibrant smile, the excited exuberance of a four-year-old boy.

"Joshua was the first person I tried to save," I whispered. "I was determined to save him after I saw his death. I memorized his outfit. When he wore it, I offered his mom to babysit him all day. My goal was to keep him off the street, where I knew he got hit by a car. We played all day. Then I took him home, so pleased with myself for having staved off the tragedy.

"But Joshua slept in his clothes. The next day a car hit him while he rode his bike." I closed my eyes. "That was the day I learned I can't stop destiny. I can't change our fates. I was twelve. I always try. But I've never succeeded."

Dana leaned back against the pillar. "Well, damn, girl. That's about the saddest thing ever."

I smiled wistfully. "Yeah. No kidding."

"Dana." Mr. Sparks stepped out of the house. He nodded at me. "Hello, Jayne. Dana, I'm leaving now. I expect you to go inside and stay there until I get back."

She nodded, rolling her eyes at me behind his back. "I'm grounded," she said as he walked away. "Can't go anywhere."

"Not even school?"

She shrugged. "I included that in the grounding. I'll be back on Monday."

"I'm in trouble too. My dad assigned me a project."

She raised her eyebrows and whistled. "A project? Wow, he hasn't given you one of those since like, fourth grade."

"Eighth, I think," I clarified.

Dana frowned. "But why are you grounded? You didn't do anything wrong."

"Yeah, well..." I pushed myself to my feet. "I guess in their eyes I did."

"That's my fault, huh."

It might be her fault. She was the one that wouldn't come with me, after all. "Never mind, Danes. Could be worse." I thought of the wreck, of that dead boy.

"Yeah," she said softly. Then she shook herself. "Tomorrow I have permission to go to the mall with my mom. So we can talk about my future. Want to come?"

"Can't. I'm still grounded. I have my project. Will you be at the lacrosse game tonight?"

"I thought you weren't going to go to those anymore?"

When Stephen and I first broke up, the thought of watching him play without being his official supporter gave me indigestion. So I'd requested another reporter to go to the spring games. "I don't care anymore. It's the tournament. I'm going."

"Then, yeah, if I can convince my dad to let me go. I'll see you there."

ಬ

After a busy evening at work, I could hardly wait to get into the fresh, open air of the lacrosse game. The only reason my mom was letting me go was because she thought I had to report on it. Not about to give that away, I attached my recorder to my belt. I carried my journaling notebook under one arm and started for the bedroom door.

Just as I went to open it, my phone rang. I put my stuff down and grabbed it, thinking it might be Dana.

Unavailable.

I answered it. The cops always called from a restricted number.

"Jayne?" The deep male voice had an uncanny timbre to it that sent goosebumps down my arms.

"Who is this?" I asked, my fingers tightening around my bedroom doorknob.

"Will I see you at the game tonight, Jayne?"

It was *him*. Scarface. I was certain of it. My hands began to shake. "Why are you calling me?"

"Why have you been meeting with the police, Jayne?"

"Stop saying my name!" I shouted. If he was trying to unnerve me, it was working.

"They called you in at the line-up. Why? What do you know?"

There was no way he could know that. I knew the police kept us witnesses hidden from them. He couldn't see through the mirror. He didn't have video cameras watching the police building—did he?

Maybe he had an accomplice.

It was the journalist in me jumping to conclusions, but my skin prickled. I hung up, thoroughly spooked and no longer interested in the game. What if there was someone working *with* him? The police weren't looking for two. Just one.

I closed my bedroom door and locked it. With shaking hands, I dialed Lieutenant Bailey. He might not take me seriously, but I had to let him know what I thought. Then I needed to call Dana to make sure she knew I wouldn't be at the game. The drive out to the Lacrosse fields was relatively uninhabited, with farmlands and pastures on either side. The thought of running into him out there made me shudder. In fact, it was better if Dana didn't go either.

If only I could See the future at will.

Neither Lieutenant Bailey nor Dana answered. I left them both detailed messages and waited for them to call me back. No one called.

I turned the light out early and crept under my blankets, still fully dressed. It was the first night in years that I was tempted to go sleep in my sister's room. Every time I closed my eyes, a creak in the house sent them flying open again. Exhaustion finally won out, but I was so tired I felt nauseous by morning.

The lemony Febreeze smell woke me, but I wasn't sure where it came from until I opened my eyes.

And found Beth in bed next to me, curled on one side and staring at me.

"No!" I cried, squeezing my eyes shut again.

Beth puts on another black stiletto and smiles at her reflection. Her long brown hair is curled stiffly like a helmet, making her look forty instead of twenty. Her eyes crinkle with the force of her smile, but the mirth doesn't reach her tired eyes. The smile falls from her face.

"Ready?" A curvy red head wearing a corset walks in and takes Beth's arm. "First one to break a thousand bucks buys drinks."

"You're on." Beth takes her dressing robe off and walks onstage, assuming a position around the pole. The crowd jeers and whistles.

Then Beth walks into a dirty apartment reeking of rotten fruits, and dumps a wad of cash on the table. Her emaciated face is thick with make-up. A fat and unshaven man stands up.

"What's that?" he thunders.

"That's what I got," Beth retorts. "Take it or leave it." She turns to walk away, but he grabs her and punches her face. Beth cries out and huddles on the ground, protecting her head with her arms while he kicks her side. She jumps up and runs out the door while he sends curses at her.

Beth returns to the club, this time as a customer. A strobe light flashes brilliant colors around the room. Music plays loudly. Beth nods along to the words of the man next to her, then takes the syringe he hands her.

"Three doses," he mouths, handing her a small bag filled with white powder.

Beth nods again, her eyes sunken and dull. She hands him a wallet and watches him walk away. Opening the syringe, she dumps the entire contents of the bag inside. She sits at a table and injects it into her arm. Then she sighs and leans back in her chair, eyes closed. Silence overwhelms her, just as she hoped it would.

The end. It was finally over. I lay on my bed crying, with Beth shaking me. "Jayne? Jayne? What's wrong?"

I wanted to tell her everything. I wanted to warn her about that awful man, about the drugs, about the life she would take.

But she wouldn't believe me. Not yet, anyway.

"Nothing." I wiped the tears from my face. "Bad dream, that's all." I put my head in my hands. Why did I always See such awful deaths? Never the gentle, dying-in-your-sleep kind.

"Oh, Jaynie. Because of prom?"

Prom? What did that have to do with anything? Then I remembered that prom was next weekend. If only that were the extent of my problems.

"No, I'm fine." I needed some space. "If you stick around, I'm going to assume you're volunteering to help me with my project."

The bed trembled as she slid off. She didn't smell like lemons anymore. I'd Seen all there was to See. I waited until she had gone, and then I lit my sweet pea scented candle. The clean smell filled the room, and I let it carry the images away. I added Beth to my green folder, wrote down her death, and filed it to the back.

I swallowed past the lump in my throat. What did it mean for her current life? For her ambitions? Should she just give up now? It was all pretty pointless, right?

I wondered what I would do, if I knew I would die in four years from a drug overdose. There had to be a way to stop it.

I paused, pressing my pen to my chin, and looked out my window. Fluffy cotton clouds floated in the azure sky. My eyes dropped to the white flowers popping out all over the dogwood tree in the yard.

And there she was, light blond hair flying around the branches of the tree. Our eyes met.

"What am I supposed to do?" I cried, staring at her through my closed window. "There must be something! Give me a better hint!"

She lifted a hand to her mouth in a gesture that looked like blowing a kiss. Then she turned and walked around the tree, her feet several inches off the ground. She never appeared on the other side, but out of nowhere a swan flew out of the branches, taking flight into the dark sky.

CHAPTER TWENTY-TWO

MY MOM escorted me to the house she was trying to sell. She settled at the kitchen table with an armload of paper work and sent me off to clean. As much as I hated being grounded on a beautiful Saturday morning, her presence made me feel safe. I started in the master bedroom, sorting through boxes of old clothes, waiting for Lieutenant Bailey to call me back. Around ten in the morning, I joined my mom in the kitchen.

"These are probably Salvation Army." I thumped a box of undesirables on the kitchen table. "Some of these clothes she may want to keep."

"Get that off the table," Mom demanded. I obliged her before she could swat the box. "I'll ask her when I call her again. I don't think she wants most of this stuff." Mom lowered her voice. "You know. She's coming to the end."

Yeah, I knew all about that. "I'll donate them for her if she wants."

Mom nodded. "Ready to go home?"

"Yes."

My mom and I walked the two blocks home. I pulled my hair out of my ponytail and hurried up the landing, letting the waves cascade around my shoulders. My fingers were chapped and my clothing caked in dust. I definitely needed a shower.

My phone rang twice while I showered, but I wasn't about to break my standing rule that I not use the phone in water. Some people might manage it, but I'd fry the battery, for sure. When I finished, I wrapped the towel around me and checked out the missed calls. Both from Dana.

I ran gel through my hair and called her back. "Dana? I missed a couple of calls from you."

"Hmm?" She sounded distracted. "Oh, yeah. It's nothing."

Why had she called twice, if it was nothing? "Oh?" I said, playing along. Whatever it was, she would spill it.

"We won the game last night."

"So you went?"

"No." She sounded insulted. "You tell me not to do something, I'm not questioning. Besides, what fun is a game without you?"

A sense of relief washed over me. "Thanks, Danes."

"We moved on in the tournament. There's another game tonight. You coming?"

Was I? Would *he* be there? My skin crawled at the thought. Lieutenant Bailey hadn't called me back. I didn't really like the idea of being stalked.

"Jayne?"

"Oh, yeah. I'm working until close."

"Can you get it off?"

I probably could. The question was, did I want to? Then I had the craziest idea. What if I didn't wait for him to stalk me? What if I stalked him instead? "I'll see what I can do."

"I'll save you a seat."

Something in her voice was off. "Everything okay?"

"Huh? Oh, yeah, great. I'm ungrounded. I'll talk to you later, okay?" She hung up.

I stared at the disconnected phone, feeling a twitch of uneasiness. That had been really weird.

Not to mention that I didn't want her to save me a seat. I wanted to sit in the car and spy on others entering the game field. I debated calling her back and decided to let it go. We'd talk when I got there.

The spring air had turned rather nippy. Forecaster said we might even get a late frost that night. I put a knit cap on my head, grabbed my jacket, and hurried out the door.

8

"You're seriously asking to leave early?" Matt laughed out loud. He reached up and adjusted his baseball cap, giving me a quick peak at his light brown eyes. "You don't want this job, do you?"

I felt the blood rush to my cheeks. "I want the money," I said. At least it was an honest answer.

Matt shook his head. "You can have it off if Gabby will close for you."

I looked over at Gabby just as she popped a big green bubble. For a second I thought it would get stuck on her nose ring, but it didn't. "Didn't you open, Gabby?"

She finished wiping down the counter. "Yeah."

"You know what, it's not that big of a deal." I put on my hairnet, trapping my wavy brown hair. "Don't worry about it."

"No, it's fine," Gabby said, grinning at me through her black lips. "I want money too."

"There you go." Matt handed me my clipboard with my duties on it. "You can leave at five."

Too perfect. Depending on traffic, I might actually make it to the game early. I felt the first stirrings of excitement. Maybe Aaron would be there.

I caught myself. I'd willed myself not to think about him all day, turning the thoughts in a different direction every time I wondered why he hadn't called me yet. His face popped into my head unbidden, those crystal blue eyes, strong jaw, dimpled chin. I sighed, remembering the feel of his lips on my mouth. No use now. I lost myself in the daydream, enjoying the memory.

I got to the field early, parking next to Dana's yellow Beamer. Dana didn't answer her cell phone. Typical. I sat in my warm car, surveying the gray sky and debating my choices. Almost no one else was here yet. Chances were I could sneak in and grab Dana before anyone spotted me. Turning off my car, I hurried through the gates.

The coaches were setting up. Dana sat on the front row of the metal bleachers, a thick blue and purple blanket wrapped around her knees. She handed me a thermos of hot chocolate when I sat down.

"Expecting the Ice Age?" I teased, taking a sip.

She gave a fleeting smile that died before it reached the corners of her mouth. "Yeah."

Something was up. I considered probing, but really, she'd tell me when she was ready. I had more important things on my mind. "Can we watch the game from my car?"

She gave me a long stare. "Why?"

I shrugged. "I'm cold?"

"You can share my blanket. And I just gave you a thermos of hot chocolate."

I gave up. Lowering my voice, I said, "There's a man stalking me. I think he'll be here tonight, and I want to catch him."

"Jayne!" she hissed. "Have you called the police?"

I pulled on my fingers, resisting the urge to pop them. "I did yesterday. They must be busy."

Dana stood up, gathering her blankets around her so she looked like a quilted mermaid. "To your car, Jayne. And you better tell me everything."

We got the heater going right away. I shivered a bit and waited until I felt sufficiently warm. How much should I say? I didn't want to freak Dana out. "You know the serial killer that's been out here?"

"Yes..." Dana drew the word out. I saw her check the locks on the doors.

"I found him. And he knows I did."

She inhaled sharply. "Do you have proof?"

I shook my head. "That's the problem. I've given the police a lot of information, but without proof, I think they are starting to dismiss me."

"And now he's stalking you?" Dana whispered.

I nodded. "I think he might be here tonight. Rather than sit around like a duck, I thought I'd try and beat him at his own game."

"You're the journalist." Dana settled back in her seat, but she didn't look relaxed.

I studied each man that walked through the gate. Fifteen minutes into the game, only an occasional straggler came through. I frowned. I had his profile memorized, but hadn't noticed him arrive. Had I missed him?

"Look at that girl over there." Dana nudged her head to her left. It was the first thing she'd said since the start of the game, and I leaned forward to peer out the window.

A skinny blond with straight hair and long fingers sat huddled on the edge of the bleachers, the tips of her fingers touching while she contemplated the figures in front of her. I knew her.

"Stephen," I murmured.

Dana gave me a startled look. "Yeah, I was gonna tell you. She came with Stephen. How did you know?"

"Oh, um—" and then I remembered that Dana knew my secret. It still felt weird to talk about it casually. "I Saw him with her. In the future."

Dana gaped at me. "See, those are the kinds of things you should tell me about."

"Yeah, well." I shrugged. "Now you know why I turned him down when he asked me out. I knew there'd be another girl." Dana's odd behavior made sense now, too. "It's okay, Dana. I'm really over him."

Her eyes flicked from side to side, and she appeared more uneasy. "Yeah. But only because you fell for someone else."

"Yeah." The word escaped my lips in a sigh, and once again my thoughts turned to Aaron. We'd make it right on Monday, somehow. If he'd let me talk to him.

She looked at me directly. "Is that over?"

"No!" I hesitated. "Well, I don't think so. Not yet, anyway. But we haven't talked. He was really weird in school yesterday. He hasn't called me, either."

"You could call him."

I shrugged, a bit embarrassed to explain why I didn't have his number. "I deleted his number. I guess I've been expecting him to dump me and I couldn't bear the suspense."

She exhaled. "That's good. At least it's better than if you weren't expecting it. Girl, I saw him at the mall today."

I waited, my stomach twisting in dread. Just because I'd been expecting it didn't mean I'd given up hoping. "And?"

She gave a small cough and looked toward the bleachers. "He was with that other girl. You know. The one from England."

Libby. I sucked in a deep breath, surprised at the pain I felt. She was here? Already? Then that meant it really was over. Aaron had already moved on.

CHAPTER TWENTY-THREE

"THAT'S FINE." I returned to my vigil, trying hard to remember what I was watching for. "I'm glad he's happy." Who cared about Aaron, anyway? Or his smile, or his kisses? That stupid accent?

"You don't sound so glad." Dana's eyes watched me beneath her purple cap.

I shrugged my shoulders, knotting my hands into fists to keep them from trembling. Hot tears stung my eyes, and suddenly I didn't care about the serial killer anymore. "Let's get out of here."

"What about the game?"

I gave another shrug. The tears escaped my eyes and ran steamy trails down my face. I sniffed and passed a hand over my eyes.

Dana leaned across the car and wrapped her arms around my shoulders. "Hey. Let's go Karaoke."

"I can't." My heart ached. A physical pain stabbed my chest. "My mom said I could go to the game and then come home."

"Well… the game barely started. No one is going to expect you home just now."

"What about my stalker?"

"You really want to hide out in your car and track down a creepy murderer? Or go to a crowded pizza bar and chow down on some melted cheese?"

I glanced at Dana, at her sly smile, and had to smile back. "All right."

"Fabulous!" She hugged me. "That's my girl! Let's cheer up!"

The only Karaoke bars open at six o'clock are the family ones. Dana squeezed my arm and winked at me. "Let's pretend like we're drunk."

I frowned and studied the moms and dads in the diner. "But we're not."

"But they won't know that."

"I don't even know what drunk feels like."

"Then follow my lead." Dana grabbed my hand and marched up to the box. Dancing on the balls of her feet and swaying to an eight-year-old girl's off-key rendition of a pop song, she made a selection. "Come on!"

I staggered after her, tripping over chair legs in an effort to keep up. Dana turned to me and kissed my cheek loudly. "This is going to be fabulous!" she shouted.

I flushed. "Yeah. Great."

Dana noticed a guy watching us. She leaned over and yelled in my ear, "That's not your stalker, is it?"

I shook my head. "Definitely not." Way too cute. He caught my eye and flashed a grin.

Dana smiled and waved. "Hi! Hello there!"

The people waiting in front of us glanced back at her. A few people scowled.

"Don't mind her," I said. "She's just loud."

Dana giggled and wrapped her arms around my neck. "There's a whole lot more to me than just loud."

I knew from the heat that my face was red. I fanned it with my hands. Would it never be our turn?

"Hey." The guy who had been watching stopped in front of us. He had his thumbs looped through the pockets of his tight gray denim pants, a fitted maroon and black striped sweater on his broad shoulders. His stance so reminded me of Aaron.

But he wasn't Aaron. He had a friendly face, light brown eyes and sandy brown hair, chapped and tanned from sunshine and ocean breeze.

"You girls up next to sing?" he asked, jerking a thumb over his shoulder.

"Yes," Dana squealed, latching onto his forearm. "Want to sing too?"

He managed to free his arm from her grip. "That's okay. But I'll cheer for you." His eyes didn't leave my face the entire time he spoke.

Dana glanced back at me. "Oh, she's not singing. Just me. You can both cheer for me."

"Dana—" I began.

And then it was our turn, only she walked up without me, leaving me standing with Surfer Dude.

"I'm so sorry about that," I said, turning and shaking my head. "She just gets a little carried away sometimes."

"Don't sweat it. I've got friends, I know how they are. Though it's a bit early in the evening to be—" he pantomimed taking a drink.

"Oh, she's not." I pulled on my sleeve. "She's pretending. We don't drink." And now I was rambling. I closed my mouth.

"Ah. And your name is...?"

"Jayne. I'm Jayne."

"I'm Dallas."

"Dallas," I echoed. He smiled at me and I grinned back, and for a moment, Dana's plan worked. I felt carefree, attractive, likable.

"Do you want to sit at a table?"

"Oh, no." Just like that, the moment passed. I remembered Aaron, quickly forgetting me in the arms of his true love. "No, we were just leaving." I would make sure of it. Dana descended from the steps. I didn't even know what she'd been singing. I stepped up to her, grabbing her forearm. "All right, you've had your fun. Let's go."

"Already?" She glanced around. "Don't you want some pizza?"

"No." I wanted my bed. I wanted my pillow. I wanted to cry.

She pursed her lips and shrugged. "Okay. Nice to meet you, bye-bye." She waved to Dallas.

"Well—can I at least get your phone number?" Dallas followed us to the door.

I paused. "I'm not really much fun right now, Dallas. Don't waste your time."

"Oh, phooey." Dana grabbed a napkin off a table. "Here's her number. There. And yours?"

Dallas wrote his number down and handed it to me. When I made no move to take it, Dana did. "Bye," she said, shoving me out the door.

"Seriously, Jayne," she exploded as soon as it closed. "Did you have to blow him off? What if he was the one to heal your heart, huh? Or did you see something about his future?"

"No," I admitted. "I just don't feel ready."

"Well, I think you should call Aaron and confront him."

"What for? She's the one he's going to be with. I should just let nature play its course."

"But Jayne, what if you made it happen? Maybe you didn't show enough interest, so he went back to her!"

That was definitely possible. "It doesn't matter what I did. Nothing would've changed it."

"But how do you really know that?"

"Because I've tried!"

"With everyone?" We stopped outside my car, looking over the roof at each other. "Because if you don't try every time, you never know if that might be the one you'd succeed with."

"Dana." I opened the door and sat down. "Don't do this to me. I just need to let him go."

She joined me. "Okay. Okay. I'm sorry. I just keep thinking, there must be something that could be done."

"Let me take you to your car," I whispered.

We traveled back to the field in silence. The game wasn't even over yet. Good thing I wasn't covering this game, or I'd probably be looking at getting fired—again.

I drove up to Dana's car. It had begun to rain, a cold mist that longed to be snow. Dana climbed in and rolled down her window.

"I'll come over tomorrow and help you with your project, okay?"

I turned my heater up and squinted at her. "You don't have to."

"Yeah, I know. But it's kind of my fault you're in trouble."

What she really meant was that she wanted to keep me in high spirits tomorrow. I rubbed my hands in front of the vent, wishing it weren't blowing cold air. "Sure. Thanks."

I followed Dana out of the parking field. We were the only cars leaving. She waved as her car turned left, and I waved back. Another set of headlights in the parking lot turned on behind me. I made my right turn and the other car swung out. I kept one eye on the road and the other on my rear view mirror. It wasn't unusual to have another car on the road. However, to have another motorist sitting in their car watching the game and deciding to leave at the same time I did—I found that slightly questionable.

The car followed my every turn halfway to my house. Just as I started to get nervous and consider calling the police, it sped up and passed me. I stared at the out-of-state plates on the black car and breathed a sigh of relief. Belatedly, I wished I had glanced at the driver.

No, I told myself. *It wasn't him.*

I drove the rest of the way in relative calm. Turning on to my cul-de-sac, I slammed on the brakes and stopped my car. Sitting in my driveway was a dark vehicle. It faced the road, headlights on. I glanced at the clock.

"Relax, Jayne," I murmured. "It's not even eight o'clock. Maybe someone is visiting Beth." But why would they back into the driveway?

I willed myself to keep driving, but my foot refused to push on the gas. Sighing, I grabbed my phone and called the house line. My heart began to pound with each ring, and I rubbed sweaty palms on my leg.

"Hello?" Mom's voice answered, and she sounded groggy.

"Mom." I almost cried with relief.

"Jayne? Are you okay?" A light turned on in the living room.

"Yeah, I'm fine. I'm almost home and there's a car in the driveway. I don't want to block it in. Who's there?"

"Oh?" The blinds flickered and I imagined my mother peaking outside.

In front of me, the car slowly rolled down the driveway. It gunned the engine and drove away quickly. I turned my head as it passed, but the windows were too dark to see inside.

"Must've been someone turning around. They just left," Mom said.

"Right," I whispered. My hands were shaking, and I had to admit I was terrified. "I'll be right in."

∞

"So what are we doing in here, anyway?" Dana asked from behind me as we entered the spare bedroom of the old lady's house.

I paused to straighten a picture frame on the vanity. I'd never met the owner, but I had her face memorized now. "Organizing." I did feel more refreshed today, or maybe just drained. That could have something to do with being up at eight in the morning on a Sunday. I tried calling Lieutenant Bailey again this morning, but no one answered. I left another voicemail and hung up, feeling like I was getting the run around.

Dana lifted one brow. "You look tired, hon. Didn't sleep well?"

I ran my fingers along a shelf, sending dust particles flying into the air. "Yeah, not so well. Too much on my mind." Like being stalked. Every time headlights had flashed on my back wall, my eyes jerked open.

"I'm sorry about Aaron." Dana touched my forearm.

I looked at her and blinked, not drawing the connection between my tiredness and Aaron.

She frowned. "You're not upset about him? What is it, then? Stephen?"

It took a full two seconds for her words to trigger the memory of last night. And then I gasped, the hurt of Aaron's betrayal socking me in the stomach. With Libby. Already. As if he hadn't ever kissed me, as if nothing had ever happened between us.

"That jerk!" I cried, unable to stop the anger that built inside me. "He practically cheated on me!"

"He's an idiot, Jaynie," Dana said, just like a good best friend should. "That he would choose that red-headed bimbo over you proves it."

I laughed, though it came out more like a sob. "Yeah." I pressed on my chest and shook my head. "Let it go. This is just the way it is."

"It's probably a bad idea to mention that prom's next weekend, huh."

I thought of that beautiful pink dress in my closet. "There's always next year." The words felt hollow.

Dana's eyes wandered around the guest room, her hand still lingering on my arm. She let out a low whistle. "Wow, girl. You're never going to finish this."

"Yeah. This is worse than the master bedroom," I sighed. Half-opened boxes of papers, kitchen ware, records, shoes, and other random knick-knacks lay scattered around the room. Somewhere under all this was a bed.

Dana knelt by a black garbage bag that lay on its side, books gushing out. "Do we keep these things?"

"Judgment call." The owner—what was her name? Adelle?—had given permission for us to dispose of anything impersonal or older than seven years. I opened a cardboard box of papers. "If it's got a name on it, keep it. If it's less than seven years old, keep it. Otherwise, trash."

She righted the bag and twisted it closed. "Well. More trash here!"

I laughed, feeling a jolt of warmth. I appreciated the atmosphere of normalcy that Dana brought with her. "Why don't you look through it? You might find a book you like."

"Doubt it," she muttered. But she obliged me and sat down.

I made my own trash pile. Lots of old school papers, yellowed with age, graphite smeared across them. Essay questions about the importance of Prohibition and why the stock market failed. Interesting, but not enough to keep.

I picked up a postcard from Germany with a picturesque castle on the front, addressed to Adelle. The words on the back were brief: "Lovely countryside. Miss your beautiful hands. Join me."

I put the postcard aside, but my curiosity was piqued. What if there were more? I sifted through the papers with more purpose, wondering about Adelle's lover in Germany. I found folded up notes, of the variety that girls passed around in the halls at school. Apparently that began many years ago.

The notes went back in time, to her junior high days, girls asking about hair styles and making after school dates. Different, but the same. No more postcards, though.

I picked up a wadded-up pink paper and almost tossed it into the trash pile, but then stopped myself. I could see words scribbled on the other side, words that looked hurried and anxious. Curiosity got the better of me and I unfolded the paper.

Snow falling on dirt road. Sled goes too fast. Car

around corner. Collision. Girl dies on impact. Inevitable, no way around it.

Inevitable. The word glared at me from the paper. Goosebumps popped out on my arms. Who wrote this, and why? What did it mean? I put the pink paper next to the postcard and pulled out more papers, no longer idle in my searching. I found another one:

Burning! Barn falls down around him. Pain! The flames! Blackness.

I dropped the paper and took several deep breaths, feeling my heart pound. Either these were story ideas, or someone kept a very morbid account of deaths. Kind of like I did.

I started my search again. I found a paper that had been ripped into pieces. I had nearly emptied the box now, and it didn't take a lot of time to find the other pieces. I put it together. The words were engraved into the page, as though written in fury, desperation.

Not my son. Not my son. The fever, the anguish. I cannot live with this.

Tears pricked my eyes as I imagined the pain she must have felt. Not just her sister, or her lover, but her child. To See his death and not be able to stop it... my heart wrenched with sympathy.

There was no doubt about it; she could See.

"You okay, Jayne?"

I blinked back tears and looked at Dana. "She could See. Adelle could See."

"Did you think she was blind?"

I shook my head in impatience. "Like me, Dana. She could See the future."

"Oh." Her mouth formed a perfect "o." "How do you know?"

I gathered up the evidence and laid it out for Dana. She pressed her lips together and studied them. "So her son died?"

"That's what she Saw." I tucked the papers into my jeans pocket and stood. "I need to talk to her." I didn't wait for Dana, though I knew she would come behind me.

"Wait! Isn't she in the hospital?"

"Yes." I paused at the front door, locking the house back up. Dana kept pace with me as I hurried home.

"Hey, Mom?" The aroma of rising cinnamon rolls greeted me, and I paused to take in a deep breath. Dana slid up behind me.

"Don't touch anything, you're dirty!" she scolded, turning around to face me. "It's not lunch time yet. What's going on?"

I toyed with the dishtowel hanging from the fridge door. "I have to go somewhere real quick. I'll be right back. Promise." I deposited the key on the counter. "Can I borrow my car?"

She narrowed her eyes at me. "How long will you be gone?"

"One hour." I put on my best puppy dog face. "Please."

Mom sighed. "Fine. One hour."

I grabbed my keys, giving Dana a triumphant smile before hurrying out the door.

CHAPTER TWENTY-FOUR

"LET ME get this straight," Dana said as I backed out of the driveway. "We're going to the hospital to visit Adelle, the owner?"

"Yes," I agreed.

"And what is it you think she'll be able to tell you?"

I faltered. "Well. About my Sight. Maybe she knows how I can change the future."

It took only moments to find Adelle Gregory at the hospital. My heart sank when we entered the oncology ward. This woman wasn't just sick. She was dying.

"I hate the smell of hospitals," Dana whispered beside me, as uneasy as I'd ever seen her.

I stopped outside room 551. I gave a light knock on the door and poked my head in. The old woman on the bed with curly purple hair snored quietly, her mouth gaping open.

I sank into a chair next to her, itching to ask my questions but not wanting to wake her. Dana sat down beside me and picked up a magazine from the bedside tray.

After twenty minutes, she put down the magazine. "Jaynie, it's almost eleven. We'll have to leave soon. Maybe you should wake her."

Oh, I felt like an awful person for doing that. Still, we hadn't come here for nothing. I stood up and shook her shoulder gently. "Adelle."

She snorted and smacked her lips, but didn't wake.

I tried a little harder. "Adelle."

She groaned and tossed her head, but still nothing.

I counted to ten, then shook her as hard as I dared. "Adelle!"

Her eyes snapped open, large and unfocused. Her pupils scanned the room and came to rest on me. A smile slid across her face. "Declare."

Except it wasn't exactly "declare." My memory had deceived me. "What?" I leaned in closer. "What did you say?"

But her eyes were closed again, soft snores escaping her mouth.

Dana sighed. "I'm sorry, Jayne. We'd better go now. You're mom only gave you an hour, and I need you to not be grounded anymore. We'll try again later."

I nodded, feeling defeated, and followed Dana out of the room. "What did she say, Dana? Did you hear her?"

Dana wrinkled her nose. She reached into her purse and pulled out two Dum-Dums, offering one to me. I shook my head.

"No," she said. "It didn't make much sense to me."

I sighed. I wasn't anywhere closer than I'd been.

We checked in with Mom to get the key. Warm cinnamon rolls sat on the counter, and she turned off the hand-mixer when we came in.

"Just in time," she said. "Want a snack? Help me ice these and you girls can have some."

Dana was already on the move. "Cream cheese icing? I'm there."

The gears turned in my mind as we returned to Adelle's house. "I've got to figure out what she said," I murmured, tapping my chin. "The other woman said it too."

I unlocked the house and Dana stepped in behind me. "What other woman?" she asked.

"Oh." I'd forgotten to mention that part. "There's this girl I see after every vision. At first she just seemed to be watching me, but lately I think she's trying to tell me something."

"She's *always* there?" Dana stared at me, her blue eyes wide. "That's like impossible. Unless she's like stalking you. Or a ghost."

A ghost. I sank down onto the beige carpet. No one could see her except me. She appeared and disappeared at will. She walked in the air. Was she dead?

"Okay, let's start over." Dana sat cross-legged in front of me. "What has she told you?"

"Well, that word. Declare."

She shook her head. "It didn't sound like 'declare' to me. It sounded like something in another language."

I wrinkled my brow. "Well, that's just extremely non-helpful." I stood up. "Adelle knows the answer. I'm sure of it. I need to find her journal or something."

"Right." Dana stood as well. "I'll take the next room over."

I worked faster without Dana to distract me. I organized each corner of the room, cleaned out drawers, pulled junk out from under the bed. Nothing that resembled a journal came my way.

Dana rejoined me, pushing her blond curls off her forehead with both hands. "I didn't come across a journal anywhere. Anything for you?"

"No." I gave a quick shake of my head. "It's okay, though. I think I've found a way to beat this thing."

"Yeah?" Dana bounced on the bed, hugging her knees to her chest. "How's that?"

I stuffed all the junk and homework papers into a giant trash bag. "You know how I Saw Aaron dumping me?"

"You actually saw him breaking up with you? It wasn't just a fizzle out?"

To be honest, I couldn't quite recall. But my plan depended on that, so I said, "Yes."

"Okay."

"So, I'm going to do it first."

"Do what?"

"Break up with him."

Dana blinked. "Wait, that makes no sense. If you break up with him, don't you get the same outcome? I thought you wanted to change things."

"This does change things. It totally mixes things up. There's no way for me to see the consequence of me breaking up with him."

Dana gave me a pitiful look. There's no other way to describe it. "Jayne, honey, I think in his mind, you guys are already through."

That heavy ball rolled around my stomach again. "But we never broke up."

"Did you ever officially go out?"

"No." *But he kissed me.* That meant something. That was more than going out.

"Then why should he officially break up with you?"

Her logic made sense, but I refused to buy it. "No. We're still together."

"When was the last time he talked to you?"

"Just three days ago. Thursday in school." Was it really three days ago? Three days ago that he had kissed me?

"And it's Sunday. Why hasn't he called you?"

She was right and it infuriated me. I jumped up. "Doesn't matter. I want it to be official."

Dana stood up too. "Okay. So you're going to put on a big show and dump him?"

Big show? I wasn't going for dramatics here. "Uh, no. I'm going to call him and tell him it's over."

Dana bit her lower lip. "No, girl. You want to make him hurt over this. You want to make him writhe in agony that he let you go." She jumped up and took my hand. "Let's go."

"Where are we going?"

"Shopping. You have a heart to break."

I had a momentary panic attack. "What about my mom? She'll kill me!"

"We'll be fast. She'll never know you left!"

I glanced at my watch. It was just after noon. "Fine. But we're back here by two o'clock!"

※

I stood with Dana inside a dressing room and laughed at the reflection of my body contorted inside a tiny black dress. It sucked itself to my skin like a mold, making my butt stick out and my hips look angular. "Dana." I shook my head. "There's no way on earth I'm wearing this." I wasn't even sure I could get it off.

"You look hot." She growled and made a clawing motion at me.

"Cute." I tried twice to get the zipper between my fingers but failed. "Use those claws to get it off."

She clucked her tongue. "Shame. What are you going to get now?"

"Something practical." She gave me a stern look, so I added, "And sexy."

She crossed her arms and leaned against the wall. "All right. Let's see what you come up with."

Dressed in my own clothes again, I stepped out and began perusing the racks. I'd never dressed up for Aaron before, so to be honest I wasn't sure what I wanted. I figured I'd know it when I saw it.

It only took me two minutes to find it. A short navy dress with a belted waistline and white chiffon cap sleeves. Totally me.

Dana smiled as soon as I pulled it on. "Fabulous. Now we just need shoes and hair."

I pushed upward on my wavy brown hair. "I already have hair."

"Yes, and we need to tame it."

I frowned. "What's wrong with it?"

"I love your hair, Jaynie, you know I do. But we need something different for this occasion. Something striking. We want Aaron to take one look at you and think, 'Uh-oh. I made a mistake.'"

"Well, one of us is going to think that," I grumbled.

"What?"

"Nothing." I gave her a perky smile. "Carry on."

We picked out a pair of shoes and I bought the whole ensemble, trying not to flinch at the price. This had better be a truly awesome break-up.

"Next stop, salon."

She was way too excited about this. Dana seemed to have forgotten that the whole point to this shopping spree was so I could kill my pathetically dysfunctional love life.

My phone vibrated in my purse. I paused to pull it out, but didn't recognize the number. I opened the text, my eyes scanning the message.

J- thngs didnt work between us. Sorry. Ur great. B happy. A

I gasped. "It's from Aaron." My knees nearly gave out, and Dana guided me to a bench in the mall. "He broke up with me by text," I whispered, numb.

"By text!" Dana echoed angrily. "That scumbag!"

What a charade. I knew better than to try to change things. "It can't be beat, Dana," I snapped, clutching the phone in one hand like a grenade. "For all I know, the only reason he broke up with me so quickly is because I made the decision to break up with him." I stood up, feeling foolish with my bag of new purchases dangling from my fingertips. "I"m taking these stupid clothes back." What had I been thinking? What an idiot. Like something pretty would make him take me back.

My phone trembled in my hand, and I snapped it open without checking. "What?" I bit out, hoping it was Aaron.

"Miss Lockwood?"

I paused, trying to place the voice. "Yes?"

"This is Lieutenant Bailey."

"Oh, of course!" I gripped my bag, thoughts of Aaron fleeing. "I'm so glad you got back to me! I've—"

"Miss Lockwood," he interrupted, and for the first time I noticed that he sounded impatient. "I need to know where you got your information."

"Wh-what?" I stuttered.

"We've gone through everything Hannah owns, from her car to her computer to her phone. She doesn't have any of your contact information. Her brother also states he was with her the same night you say you were, and he has no idea who you are. Either you were secret friends, or you're lying."

His cold accusation fell on my ears, and I shivered. Dana was watching me closely, and I wondered how much she could hear.

"So unless you would like to give us a substantial reason for why we should believe any of the evidences you've given us, your entire testimony will be considered misleading and thrown out."

He was absolutely fed up with me. I could tell. And he no longer took me or my fears seriously. I closed my eyes. Would he believe me if I told him about my abilities?

The worst that could happen is that he wouldn't. He would think I was crazy, laugh at me, and ignore my pleas. Pretty much just like he was doing now.

"I need to talk to you in private," I said. "I'll tell you everything."

Silence reigned on the line. I glanced around, my paranoia returning as my break-up adrenaline faded. Could my stalker be here? Was he watching me?

"Monday," he said. "Be here at seven-thirty in the evening."

"Okay," I said, but I could tell from the way the cell phone didn't reflect my voice that he had already hung up.

CHAPTER TWENTY-FIVE

I PUT MY phone down and sat down on the bench, trying not to hyperventilate. The mall felt stiflingly hot. I took several deep breaths and wrapped my fingers around the bench as sights and sounds swirled around me.

"Jayne?" Dana hovered over me. "Are you all right?"

I groaned and put my head in my hands. Lieutenant Bailey didn't believe me.

Dana took me by the elbow and pulled me up. "Let's get you home."

The plastic bag rustled in my hand, and I shook her off. "I need to return this."

"Not now." Her voice was firm as she guided me through the mall. "You're a mess. Besides, that dress looks great on you. Find some other guy, show Aaron you're over him."

Even the raging turmoil in my head wasn't enough to keep my heart from squeezing when she mentioned Aaron's name. "He won't care. Don't you get it? I know how this story ends."

We were outside of the car now, moving quickly through the parking lot, and I was glad. I couldn't shake the feeling that people were watching us. The police thought I was a liar... some psycho chick wanting attention.

"And how is that?" Dana lifted her chin, a bit of a challenge in her eyes.

It took me a moment to remember what we were talking about. "They go to school together. They get married. The end."

"How does he die, then?"

Death. I shuddered. "She kills him."

Dana gasped. "What? Jayne! You have to warn him!"

I shook my head, tasting bitterness in my mouth. We climbed into Dana's car. She turned it on, and the locks slid down automatically. My shoulders relaxed at the click, then tensed again when she rolled the windows down. "They get a divorce. He won't give her the house, so she has someone kill him."

"Jayne! And you're just going to let that happen?"

"I've done what I can to stop it! I can't!"

"Does he know you can see the future?"

"Yes."

"Then tell him! Tell him what you saw!"

"He won't believe me, Dana." I didn't realize I was crying until I tasted a salty drop on my lip. "He'll think I'm being malicious or manipulative or something, making it up." *Just like the police.*

Dana stopped at the red light and looked at me, her eyes wide and woeful. Then she sighed. "If you say so, Jaynie. But I think if it were me, I would never give up on the man I love."

I sputtered, my face warming to my roots. "Love? Who said anything about love?"

"Then why are you crying?"

I wiped viciously at my traitorous eyes, swallowing several times. "Something in my eye. Can we roll the windows up?"

෩

Dana offered to stay with me, but I turned her down. I wasn't in the greatest of moods, and I wanted some alone time. It was two o'clock by the time we got home. She talked to my mom, distracting her while I deposited my purchases upstairs. I came down, hugged her goodbye, and pleaded a headache to my mom. She let me go rest, but only after threatening to keep me home from school until Adelle's house was ready.

Actually, the thought of burying myself in the house and finishing up my project was rather inviting.

But first things first. I needed to make a list.

I sat down at the desk in my room and pulled out a piece of paper. Starting at the top, I wrote down my feelings.

Frustration. Toward the police for not believing me.

Anger. Toward Aaron for breaking up with me through a text message.

Embarrassment. For spending too much money on stupid clothes.

Despair. Because nothing I do will ever change the future.

Hurt. Hurt hurt hurt Aaron.

The last line brought tears to my eyes, and I flung my head onto the desk, sobbing. I'd tried so hard not to fall for him, but I realized now that had been about as stupid as thinking I could make him stay with me instead of Libby. Falling in love with him had also been inevitable.

Stupid, stupid Aaron.

I took the list and ripped it up, then flung the pieces around my room. Letting my angry energy drive me, I headed downstairs.

"Mom?" For once, she wasn't baking. I wandered into the sitting room. "Mom?"

She paused the movie she was watching. "Yes, Jayne?"

"Can I borrow the key to Adelle's house? I want to finish up the project."

"Sure." She dug around her purse and pulled out a keyring. "Are you feeling better?" She eyed me, probably noticing my swollen face.

"Yeah. A bit."

"Lock it up after you."

"Will do."

I slipped out of the house, wanting to get this project finished up before nightfall. Just in case it didn't go so quickly, I took my car the few blocks to Adelle's house. Had anyone followed me here? I did the deadbolt and the chain. Being alone made me nervous, and I almost gave in to the temptation to call Dana and have her join me.

Don't be a wimp, I told myself. *You're the only one here.*

With that note of encouragement, I threw myself into the task. I organized the remaining papers and restacked the boxes. I found a few journals, but they were empty. I flipped through them anyway, and a loose paper floated out of one and drifted to the ground. I picked it up.

The time has come to pass Dekla on. She no longer needs me.

"Dekla," I whispered, letting the paper slip through my fingers. Not declare, and definitely not de-claw. But what on earth was Dekla?

Time to visit Adelle again. I pushed myself off the carpeted floor, my fingers already hitting the speed dial on my phone.

"What's up, Jaynie?" Dana asked, her words distorted by what I assumed was a Dum-Dum.

"I need to you look something up for me." I locked up the house and slid into my car. "D-E-K-L-A. Google it for me and tell me what comes up."

"On it."

I hung up, content to let Dana do my research. Adelle and I were going to have a little chat. But I had to hurry. It was already three-thirty in the afternoon, which only left me three hours before the game.

Dana called me back when I was two minutes from the hospital.

"What have you got for me?" I asked, stopping at a red light. "Did you find out what Dekla is?"

"Yes," she replied. "Only it's not a what, it's a who. She, actually. Dekla is one of the Latvian goddesses of fate."

"A goddess of fate?" I visualized the tall blond woman. Was she Dekla?

The car behind me honked and I jumped, only then noticing my light was green. "Thanks, Danes." I made my left turn and pulled into the hospital parking lot.

"What's going on, Jayne?"

"I'll tell you at the game. See ya." Hanging up, I hurried toward the doors.

ঔ

I bought a card and two balloons in the hospital gift shop, then took the elevator up to see Adelle. To my infinite gratitude, she sat upright flipping through TV channels when I walked in.

"Hi, Adelle," I said meekly, holding my card and balloon out like some kind of offering.

She turned her attention from the TV, focusing tired gray eyes on me.

I opened my mouth to offer an explanation of my visit, when she whispered, "Dekla. You've come."

That name again. My heart pounded and I turned around, expecting to see the familiar woman in the halls behind me. Nobody. Could only Adelle see her? I swiveled back. "Do you see her? Is she here?"

Adelle held out her hands and gestured me forward. "You've misunderstood. You're Dekla."

The world swirled around me, and I reached out a hand to steady myself. "What? Me? No, I'm Jayne. I'm not a goddess."

Adelle shook her head, a small satisfied smile on her face. "No. You are Dekla. You see the fate of those around you. You walk in their shoes at the moment of their death. You have the ability to change their destiny."

I opened my mouth, about to question how she knew all that, when her final words caught up with my brain. I coughed and sputtered. "Change their destiny? I've tried. I can't."

"Yes, you can." Adelle gestured again, pulling me toward her. "You just haven't learned how."

I came to her this time and settled on the edge of the bed. I set down the cards and balloons, noting how my hands shook. "I'm just a girl."

Her gray eyes widened, piercing me. "Then how do you explain your powers?"

"I don't have any powers. Just a curse." My voice came out bitter.

"That's not true, child. You simply must ask Laima to teach you."

"Laima?"

She nodded. "I know you've seen her. She follows you. The scent of death calls to her, and she waits to see your verdict about their fate."

Her words crashed over my brain like a cold tsunami, taking my wits with them. "What? Scent of death? You mean the lemon smell? Oh! She's the woman I see!" Laima. She had a name.

"You smell lemons?" Adelle smiled again, the wrinkles around her eyes tripling. "Better than me. I smell wet dog. You must ask Laima to teach you."

Too much information at one time, and I didn't know which question to ask first. "Teach me what? What do you mean, my verdict?"

Adelle squeezed my hand. "You are the second goddess. Laima weaves the destiny and lets you see the outcome. You can cast a vote to change it or sustain it."

"Wait a minute. You mean, I can change how people die? How?" I gasped out, unable to believe that I'd had this power the entire time.

"Ask Laima."

I plowed on, the questions flying out of me. "And it's not everyone. Why do I only see the horrible deaths?"

"Those are the only ones you can change."

"But *how*?" I pressed. "I've never been able to change anything."

"Ask Laima."

Frustration grew in me, and I exhaled. "I have. She doesn't tell me anything."

"Doesn't she?" Adelle arched a penciled eyebrow. "Hasn't she answered everything you've asked?"

"Um, no, not that I can recall. Like she never told me what Dekla is. How do you know all this, anyway?"

"I used to be Dekla," she whispered.

"Huh?" I pushed my hand through my hair, yanking when I got stuck in a curl. "You mean, you used to be me?"

She shook her head, the wig sliding slightly to the left. "No. I used to be Dekla. But I was also Adelle. And now I am dying. The power passed to another."

Her note flashed through my mind. Passing Dekla. "But why me?"

"I chose you."

"You chose me? But how? Why?"

Her light eyes pierced mine, and she held my gaze for several heartbeats of silence. Then she said, "Ask me again in a few days."

"Why not now?"

She shook her head. "I can't tell you now."

Fine. I took a deep breath and sat again, question after question tumbling through my head. "Is Laima like us, too? How long will I be Dekla? Is Dekla inside of me?"

Adelle raised a hand. "Slow down. No, Laima isn't one of us. She's immortal. We die. But Dekla is one of her sisters, and she chose to distribute her immortal soul among the human race. I had a piece. Now you do."

"I don't understand this power," I whispered. "I can't even help people. Why would she do that?"

"Your mortality makes you greater. You are compassionate. You care in a way that Dekla never could."

This was too much. But still, the million-dollar question. "How do I change their deaths?"

"Ask Laima."

I bit back a snarl. "Great, I'll just send her a text message when I get out to the car."

Adelle reached over the side of the bed and picked up an old cell phone. "Do you have her number?"

I stared at her, unbelieving. Then I pulled out my phone. "No. No, actually, I don't."

"I'll give it to you." Adelle's voice softened. "And then, my dear Dekla, I'll have to bid adieu. I'm getting quite tired."

I left Adelle's room shaken and confused. I should be contacting Laima.

I snorted. Would a goddess really answer my text?

I'd find out soon enough, because I was definitely going to text her.

I bumped into something in the hallway and turned around, an apology on my lips. "Oh!" I exclaimed. "I'm so sorry. Excuse me."

Brown leather shoes under red and yellow striped pants appeared under my eyes. "Jayne?" a familiar accented voice said. "What are you doing here?"

"Aaron?" My brow knit together in confusion. I couldn't take my eyes from his shoes. I tried to reconcile his voice with the strangely dressed person in front of me. "I'm visiting a friend. What are you doing here?"

"I work here," he replied, a bit defensively.

My eyes traveled up his pants to the red suspenders over a green shirt. A plastic flower hung out of a breast pocket. "As what? A clown?" I lifted my eyes to take in his whole ensemble. Was he wearing a curly red wig? A rubber nose?

Rubber nose, no. Red wig, yes.

"I'm a private entertainer. I do birthday parties, cheer kids up after surgeries, things like that."

My mouth dropped open and I laughed. "You really are a clown!"

"It's not funny," he growled. "The sick kids have as much right for laughter as any other child."

The tragedy behind his career struck me, and I sobered. "I'm sorry. You're right. I'm glad you're doing something so nice. I just.... wouldn't have been able to picture it if I hadn't seen it." I flashed him a smile, fighting giggles. The total absurdity of this situation struck me, and I wanted to laugh out loud. I was in the hospital, trying to learn about my curse from a dying woman, and now I'd run into my ex, dressed like a clown.

He leaned toward me, close enough that I could smell the mint gum he was chewing. "That's because you never notice me, Jayne."

I inhaled his scent. My lips part as if they were crying out in desperation, "Kiss me! Kiss me now!" Traitorous mouth. I pressed them together. "What are you talking about? I always notice you."

"You have a good way of pretending you don't, then."

His warm breath washed over my mouth, and I struggled to concentrate. Did his lips brush mine when he spoke? He was *right there*. "No, I don't," I said lamely.

"Jayne." The whisper sent tingles down my spine. "You're making me crazy." He put his hands on my shoulders.

He's going to kiss me. The thought flew through my head. *I should pull away.* But I didn't. I wanted that kiss most desperately. My pulse pounded in anticipation.

"Mr. Chambers!" A shrill voice rang down the hall, and Aaron let me go. "I don't think you're being paid to stand out in the hall when you have a birthday party to attend."

"Sorry, ma'am. You're right."

I jerked away, the spell broken. "We shouldn't be talking, anyway. It might make your girlfriend jealous. After all, it wasn't working out between us."

I threw his words back at him spitefully. I shouldered my purse and marched down the hall, keeping my head high in case he watched me leave.

ଚ

I called Dana from my car as soon as I parked at the game. "I'm here. Second row of cars."

She groaned. "Seriously? You're going to stay in there?"

"I have to!" I exclaimed. "How can I be a good spy if I'm not watching people come in?"

"Fine," she huffed. "It's your social funeral."

As long as it wasn't my real one.

A moment later Dana's yellow galoshes appeared trekking across the grass toward my car. I popped the locks and she climbed in next to me.

"Raining?" I asked, examining her matching yellow raincoat. I hadn't noticed any water hitting my windshield.

"Might," she replied, unwrapping a Dum-Dum. She stuck her purse between us and I dug through it, in the mood for a cotton candy sucker. "So. Tell me why I looked up Dekla."

Oh boy. My stomach tightened into knots at the memory of my conversation with Adelle. "Well... apparently, I'm her."

Dana squinted at me. "How's that possible? She's a thousand-year-old goddess." Her eyes narrowed even more, into tiny slits. "Wait a minute. How much have you been holding out on me? Is this, like, your seventh time through high school?"

My face burned. "No! I haven't been holding back! It's more like, I have her powers."

"So you're the goddess of fate?" Dana blinked several times. "Why can't you change things, then?"

"That's the confusing part." I shredded the candy wrapper. "There's another goddess. The woman I see."

"Laima," Dana supplied.

"Oh, you know about her?"

She shrugged. "Her name popped up on every website that Dekla's did."

I nodded. "Yeah, Laima. Anyway, she's like the actual goddess. I'm just the sidekick. And I don't know how to do anything with my powers."

Dana leaned toward me. "But you can?"

"Well, not right now. I don't know how."

"But if you learn? Then you can?" she pressed.

My head bobbed again. "Yeah. Apparently."

"Wow," Dana breathed, settling back in her chair. "That's fabulous, Jayne."

"Yeah." But I didn't feel excited. I focused on the spectators of the game. I hoped I'd figure my powers out before I ran into another lemon-scented person.

※

I didn't sleep much all weekend. The thoughts churned in my heart, emotions like frustration and hope chasing each other around. I could hardly keep my eyes open in school on Monday. We had a Spanish test, and Mr. Livingston stopped me when I turned mine in.

"You look tired, Jayne. Are you alright?"

I managed a wan smile. "I could use a break. Maybe our *Cinco de Mayo* party will be just the thing for me."

"Have the police been bugging you?"

I shook my head. "No, but I wish they would. I keep calling them. The thing is—"

He interrupted me. "Maybe the case is dying. There haven't been any more murders."

"I don't think so." I could feel myself getting fired up, wanting to lay empirical evidence at his feet. "Things have been—"

"Maybe they want you to drop it."

I stopped. I had the feeling that was true. The police didn't seem too interested in what I had to say anymore. "I have a meeting with them tonight. Then, hopefully, this will all be over."

"Why are you meeting with them?"

"Now, that's classified information." I patted the pile of exams. "Maybe I'll put an article in the school paper."

"Good luck, Jayne," he said, rubbing his eyes. He looked tired too.

My next two classes went too smoothly, and then I was headed to English. How I wished the office had let me switch classes!

Again I waited until the last minute to slip into class, and then I completely ignored Aaron and sat in the back by Drew Collins, a quiet boy with long brown hair and glasses. He sat chewing on a pencil and reading his physics book, not even sparing me a glance.

I expected Aaron to try to talk to me, to act casual and cool. But he didn't. I watched him talk to Poppy. She giggled loudly, glancing back to gauge my reaction throughout the class. I had none. Ms. Siegfried had given us a day to work on our essays, and that's exactly what I did.

When the bell rang, I took my time gathering up my things, but I needn't have bothered. Aaron's phone chirped and he answered it while he walked out, not even looking over his shoulder at me.

I got a sick pit in my stomach. It really was over. He had no interest in me at all.

Dana poked her head into the classroom. "Um, hello, Jayne? Gonna eat lunch today?"

I glanced around and realized I was the only one left. I shouldered my backpack with a sigh and stood up. "Not really hungry, Dana." I wrinkled my nose.

"Oh, Jayne." Dana joined me at my desk and gave me a hug. "Tough year, huh? Maybe Aaron's the one you should practice your powers on."

"Dana." I gave her an annoyed look. "Not now, okay?"

"But Jayne, I've been thinking about this. What if it happened because you *made* it happen?"

I rolled my eyes.

"No, serious, Jayne. Think this through with me. You see a vision of Aaron and his ex-girlfriend living unhappily ever after. So as soon as he comes along, you start pushing him away—pushing him back to her. You were *making* it come true."

I opened my mouth to argue, but then stopped. What had Aaron said? That I never noticed him? Was it possible that I made him feel like I didn't care?

"Yeah," Dana said, nodding. "You're with me. So, imagine what would've happened if you hadn't seen the future."

"I would've acted like an idiot, falling for him and thinking we were going to last forever." I lifted my chin. "At least I avoided getting my heart broken."

"Right. Looks like your heart's intact."

Tears welled up in my eyes. "I wish I'd never met him."

"You can't live trying to avoid the inevitable, Jayne. Forget what you saw. Just embrace life. And try to get Aaron back, before it's too late."

"It's too late, Dana," I said softly. "I just want to move on."

ঙ

The rest of the day went by in a blur. I could hardly wait for it to be over. Dana promised to meet me at the game, and I hurried away from the classrooms. Tonight should be a big game. Last one of the tournament, which we were doing so well in. Yet not even the thought of a championship title cheered me up.

I started up my car and headed home. I needed something dismal to match my mood. I didn't really have a good selection of depressing music, but *The Fray* could be rather melancholy. It would have to do for today.

I pulled into the driveway at home and sighed. First one home. I didn't really feel like going into an empty house right now, even though nothing spooky had happened in a few days. I opened my cell phone and sifted through contacts, wondering who I could go visit for a bit.

My thumb paused on "Laima." I had an actual number for her. Would it work? I texted out a quick message.

I need to talk to you. When you have a moment, would you mind appearing? Thx.

I read it over and laughed. This was stupid. Still, it didn't hurt anything except maybe my pride. I hit send and closed my phone.

I didn't feel like visiting anyone in my contact list. I wanted to visit Aaron.

The idea was even stupider than sending a text message to a Latvian goddess. But it fueled me, emboldened me. "I've changed my mind, Dana," I said out loud, even though she wasn't with me. "I'm going to get Aaron back." Now if I could just figure out how to change the future....

After I made myself irresistible, of course.

I ran through the scenario in my head. Put on a dress, go to Aaron's house. Make out. Or rather, make up.

One good thing about cheerleading practice after school: at least I didn't have to fight Beth for the bathroom.

I paused at the thought of my sister, wondering if Dana's philosophies applied to Beth, as well. Should I just ignore the future and treasure the time I had with her?

Half an hour later, I was in my car again. I'd done my hair, leaving it down but with more defined curls instead of just massive waves. I rolled the windows up and cranked on the A/C, willing it to cool me off enough to keep me from sweating. I had my map with me that I'd printed from the internet address search.

As for where I got Aaron's address—well, I was a journalist, after all. Now that I had his phone number again, it wasn't too hard to find.

I wasn't at all surprised when I pulled up to a large white-washed mansion, looking every bit like an English manor dropped on American soil. At least the guard had waved me through at the gate. Guess I didn't look very suspicious.

A seed of uncertainty buried itself in my heart as I stared at the house. Why had I done my hair and put on this dress? He was going to think I was silly.

You came all the way here, Jayne. Just do it. I turned my car off and started up the drive, trying to appear confident and poised even while my heart beat like a rabid drummer in my chest.

The doorbell chimed when I touched it. It didn't ring, it chimed. Who would answer, the butler?

The door opened, and Aaron stood there. The smell of musky leather permeated the air around him, and I instinctively averted my eyes. *You can look up,* I told myself, but I couldn't bring myself to meet his light blue eyes. Instead I stared at the forest green t-shirt that stretched across his shoulders.

"Jayne," he said, surprise evident in his voice. "What are you doing here?" His voice lilted upward, stressing the words musically.

No warm welcome yet. I could feel my courage slipping away. My gaze dropped to his cowhide slippers, a heat creeping up my cheeks. Chalk another one up to a stupid idea. "I just wanted to talk."

His feet squirmed. "Now's not the best time, Jayne," he all but whispered. "I'll call you tonight."

Uh-uh. I wasn't letting him dismiss me like that.

CHAPTER TWENTY-SIX

I LIFTED MY head, meeting Aaron's eyes with what I hoped was a forceful, inviting stare. "The game's in two hours, and I'm going to the pre-game set up. I thought maybe we could go together. We can talk. And I can explain. I'm sorry, Aaron."

He pressed his lips together and swallowed. "Don't, Jayne," he murmured. "Not now."

"Don't what?" I furrowed my brow. Was that sweat beading on his hairline?

"Who is it, Aaron?"

My head jerked up at the sound of a female voice. I narrowed my eyes as Libby slid into view. She wore a long lavender dress with a deep v-neck. It clung to her slender body and suddenly my short, cutesy dress looked horribly cheesy.

Libby glanced from Aaron to me, and then her voice frosted over. "Well? Were you going to invite her in?"

"Uh, no." This time it was Aaron avoiding my eyes. "Jayne just came by to... to...."

"Borrow a book for English," I finished.

"And I just told her I'll call her tonight because now's not a good time." Aaron turned to face Libby, peering into her light brown eyes.

"Good bye, then, Jayne," Libby said, not even looking at me as she closed the door.

I felt like throwing myself in front of a car.

My phone rang three times on the way home, all from Dana. I ignored them. I couldn't talk to anyone right now. She called two more times before I turned the phone to silent, ignoring the urge to hurl it across the street.

Arriving home, I pulled the shades and threw myself on my bed, burying myself beneath my blankets. I just wanted to sleep and forget everything else. Forget the game. Forget my phone. Forget Aaron and the images of him in my mind.

☯

"Jayne?"

I lifted my head groggily from my pillow, damp from my own drool. It took me a few seconds to realize my mom was at my door, knocking. The hazy sub-light of dusk filled my room, making me want to roll over and go back to sleep.

"Yeah?" I croaked from the bed.

My mom took that as an invite and popped the door open. "Jayne, are you sick?"

Yes, I wanted to say. *I'm dying.* "I'm okay."

"You're not going to the game tonight?"

I sat up and looked at my watch. Five-fifty. Dang it! The game started in ten minutes! So much for getting to the pregame. "Yes, I'm going!" I jumped up, smoothing my dress and throwing my over-done hair into a ponytail. I kicked off my heels and slipped on a pair of flats. "Bye, Mom. See you later." I hurried out the door.

I hoped we creamed the other team. That was just what I needed to vent my feelings of failure.

Dana was waiting for me in our usual spot, to the left of the baseball diamond. I slid in ten minutes after six and jerked out my tape recorder.

"Where've you been?" she hissed, her eyes scanning me from head to toe and taking in my appearance. "I've been calling for hours!"

"Which should let you know I didn't feel like talking, or I would've answered," I snapped.

She pulled her head back and blinked. "Sorry. Guess I didn't get the hint." Turning, she gave the players all of her attention.

"Dana."

She held up a hand. "Shh. I'm concentrating."

Just what I needed, for my best friend to be mad at me too. I jerked open my notepad and began jotting sentences, pressing so hard I thought the pen would break.

My phone emitted an unfamiliar ringtone, and I looked toward my bag. Curiosity got the better of me. Pulling it out, I saw that it was a calendar event. I frowned. I didn't have anything scheduled for today. Did I?

I flipped it open and groaned. *Police 6:30.* How on earth had I forgotten that I was meeting with Lieutenant Bailey tonight? I was so screwed. I'd never make it across town in half an hour. I turned to Dana. "Danes, I have to go. Can you record the game for me?"

"Uh-uh," she replied, never looking away from the field. "I don't want to miss anything. If you get my meaning."

I rolled my eyes. "Fine. I got the hint." I snatched up my bag and huffed away.

People were still arriving, and the dirt parking lot was pretty full. I had to wait a few minutes for cars to clear out of my path, but finally I peeled out of the lot, heading west.

A quick glance at my clock showed that it was twenty after six. I pressed my foot down on the gas pedal, going slightly past the maximum speed limit. I gritted my teeth, hoping I wouldn't get a ticket on my way to meet with Lieutenant Bailey. That wouldn't improve my credibility.

There weren't likely to be cops out here, though. Mostly the only nuisance on this two-lane highway would be an old grandpa who couldn't find the gas pedal.

The speed limit was fifty-five, but I was pushing sixty when all of the sudden, a loud bang sounded from outside. My car jerked sideways and then wobbled forward, a heavy thumping sound coming from my left tire.

"No!" I cried. "Not now!"

I pulled the car over to the side of the road and climbed out. My front tire had blown. Like, blown up. I winced as I examined the rim. I might have injured it slightly, as well.

"Not now!" I kicked the stupid tire as hard as I could, then cried out and grabbed my foot. "Great! I'm not at the game and I won't make it to the police department, either!" I got back in and turned on my emergency lights. The sun dipped lower in the sky, spreading purple and orange fingers across the horizon. I should still have an hour before daylight disappeared, at least. I tried to wave down a car as it sped by on my right, but it ignored me.

"Jerk!" I shouted. I grabbed my cell phone and bit my lower lip, debating whether to call the police first or my emergency assistance number. I couldn't believe this was happening. What more could go wrong?

I scrolled through my contacts and found Lieutenant Bailey's number. I sighed. He was not going to believe me. My finger hovered over the send button. I willed myself to press it.

"Jayne! You all right?"

I gasped and dropped my phone. I'd been so intent on my call that I hadn't even noticed the car pull around behind me. My face reddened when I saw Aaron. "What are you doing here?" I sputtered, my eyes darting to the paved road. "How did you find me?"

He jogged around to my side. "I was on my way to the game when I saw you standing here."

I shoved him away from me, the horrifying memory of my embarrassing debut at his house churning my stomach. "Well, keep going. I've got help on the way."

He grabbed my hand. "Jayne. Don't be angry."

Those were the wrong words to say. "Excuse me?" All my frustration and anger at the situation, at Dana, at him blew out of me. "Don't be *angry*? You break up with me through a text message. And when I go over to your house to talk to you, who do I find but your *ex* girlfriend. The one you told me you didn't like anymore. Remember?"

Aaron's eyes narrowed. "The way I recall, you didn't seem very interested. In fact, when you came over to my house, *you* were about to apologize."

"That was before!"

"Before what?"

"Before I saw that you had already replaced me!" I succeeded in getting my hand out of his grip. I trembled with emotion. "It's her you want anyway, not me! You always choose her in the end! Just get away from me!" I pushed his chest with both hands.

Aaron took two steps backward, his brows pulling together. "Jayne."

"I mean it! Go!" I closed my hands into fists, blinking hard to keep the tears at bay. Aaron still stood there, a pitiful expression on his face.

I didn't want his pity and I didn't need his help. I climbed back into my car and locked all the doors. Then I pressed my hands over my ears and sobbed. I coughed and took several breaths. Where was my phone? I needed to talk to Dana. I reached over to the passenger seat, groping for it.

Not there. I stared at the vacant seat for a moment before remembering I'd dropped the phone on the street. Had I called the police? I couldn't be certain if I'd actually hit send or not before tossing my phone on a one-way flight.

I took a deep breath and exhaled, closing my eyes. Then I hit the unlock switch and grabbed the handle just as there was a soft tap on my window.

The tears started again and I bit my lip. "Aaron, I don't want to talk," I said, opening the door and stepping into the street. "You're just delaying—" I stopped.

The man in front of me wasn't Aaron. The jagged scar cutting across his neck gave him away, and I caught my breath. It was *him*. The murderer. The expression on his face was so familiar, as if I knew him. My heart did a staccato dance in my chest. I opened my mouth to scream, but he darted behind me and pressed his hand against my lips.

"Hush, Jayne," he whispered. "Don't make this any harder than it is." He chuckled, a harsh, grating noise next to my ear. "What were you about to say? Something about delaying the inevitable?"

He had found me.

The blood pumped so hard in my chest I thought I would faint. Where was Aaron? Had he gotten away? My eyes swiveled from side to side, searching the deserted road for his car. I could only hope he'd listened to me and left.

The killer kept one hand pressed to my mouth while he fiddled with something, and then he gagged me with a piece of cloth. "There now, Jayne, I know you'll keep quiet."

That voice. My mystery caller.

He clasped my hands together and tied them up. "I hate to have to do this to you, but after all, I don't trust you. Let's walk." He moved me around my car. I stumbled under his hands, nearly falling into the ditch. We cleared it and walked into the pasture, ripe with strands of wheat. I breathed rapidly through my nose, feeling as though I couldn't get enough oxygen.

"Hush, Jayne," he soothed, one hand on my neck, pushing me forward. "You'll get your chance. I'm dying to know how you found me. Well, not really dying. Figure of speech."

The grains of wheat reached up to my armpits. Stopping, my stalker pushed on my shoulder until I sat. Then he sat down next to me. The prominent scar on his neck jumped out at me like a neon light. The grass trembled and my captor froze, eyes narrowing as he searched the field. I was shaking so hard I thought my teeth would rattle out of my mouth.

Another man stepped into the corner of our corn shelter. "You got her." The baseball cap pulled low over his face didn't mask the familiar voice. I stiffened, the fear flying right out of me as surprise and disbelief took over.

"Mr. Livingston!" I tried to scream the words through my gag, but they came out in muffled grunts. "Help me!" I flailed about the best I could.

My Spanish teacher did not look at me, and my captor kicked me in the ribs. "Shut up." He turned back to Mr. Livingston, and I realized then why he looked familiar: they had the same light blue eyes, the same high forehead and light brown hair. They had to be brothers.

The knowledge hit me harder than the kick to the ribs had. My hope sank like a lead ball in the ocean, and a feeling very much like despair flooded my limbs. I began to sob in earnest, tears flowing down my face and into my gag.

"I got her," my captor agreed. "Thanks to you. Say your goodbyes and then watch the road. She'll be dead when you see her again."

"I'm sorry, Jayne. I told you to stay out of it." Still, Mr. Livingston didn't look at me.

"I trusted you!" I tried to shout. Instead I just coughed and sputtered.

"Your silencer on?" the murderer asked.

Mr. Livingston held up a black pistol with a gloved hand.

"Keep guard, then." My captor turned back to me as Mr. Livingston strode off. "So, you've met my brother. He wasn't exactly thrilled when I decided to move home, but he's been obliging. Lucky for me, he's been keeping an eye out for anyone acting suspicious."

I'd been betrayed. Dots flashed before my vision, but I couldn't pass out now. I struggled for breath, sucking around the cloth, trying to get air. I leaned my head over, the weight of it carrying my body sideways into the dirt.

"Now, Jayne, I have a few questions for you," he said softly. He squatted next to me, his elbows level with the black boots. The last remaining sunlight glinted off the point of a knife in his hand. "If you scream, I will cut your throat. Even if someone finds you, it will be too late. Got it?"

I did. I couldn't take my eyes off the knife. How long would it take to die from a cut throat? In my vision of Hannah, it happened very quickly. Did it really happen like that? Or did the mind speed up the process to spare the victim?

He grabbed my hair and yanked my head back. "Got it?" he whispered.

I forced my head to move up and down.

"All right." He lowered my gag to my chin, then pushed me back to a sitting position. "How did you find me?"

My head swam. Salt and pepper spots floated in front of my eyes. I cleared my throat. "You won't believe me."

"Try me." He ran his fingers over the knife, the smooth edge glinting in the dying sunlight.

I knew I wouldn't live to see tomorrow. I hoped it didn't hurt too bad. I hated paper cuts. "I met Hannah."

"Hannah?"

"Short, brown hair. Black leather jacket."

"Ah, yes. So? She never met me before that night."

"I have a sort of psychic gift. And when I met her, I saw that you would kill her." How would my mother react when she found my body? Was this why Beth turned to drugs? To forget my death?

Was this why Aaron got back together with Libby? Because I was dead?

"Really." His dry, unemotional response indicated that he didn't believe me.

In spite of the situation, irritation spiked through me. What more did he want from me? "Fine. What's your explanation?"

He remained silent a moment. The grasses around us rustled as a breeze blew through, pausing to tickle the hairs on my neck as well. "No, I suppose that is the only way it makes sense. Well, that being the case, I'm sorry to have to kill such a unique talent. But you are a threat. Who else did you tell?"

Dana. My throat constricted. She was in danger. "Just the police," I whispered, trying to sound calm. As calm as I could be for this situation.

"Are you sure? Not even your pretty blond friend?"

I trembled. "No. I didn't tell her."

He leaned over and pushed me back against the corn stalks. "Any questions for me, Jayne?"

I wanted to ask how he'd found me, but it seemed so obvious now. Everything I'd told Mr. Livingston, he'd told his brother. "How did you catch me?"

"I've been following you for days. I put too much air into your tire a few days ago. I knew it was just a matter of time before it blew. You were zooming along the road back there and the tire overheated. Good fortune for me that you chose a secluded area. Anything else?"

I felt a helpless, numb feeling pervading my mind and heart, similar to the one I'd experienced during my vision of Hannah. I had plenty of questions, but suddenly they didn't really seem to matter. "Don't hurt me."

"I don't have time for games, Jayne, and I promised my brother I'd be quick. Good-bye."

I closed my eyes and felt the sharp blade slide against my throat. He grunted loudly. The pressure let up and the ground shook next to me. I jerked back from the burning pain, my scream silenced by the gag. Warm liquid flowed down my neck and a bright light blinded me.

"You wanted to talk to me, Dekla?"

I opened my eyes to see the tall blond woman floating in front of me. Her white gown drifted around her bare feet. I could see her features in sharp detail now; the high cheekbones, the pearly white skin, the stormy blue eyes.

"Laima," I said. My voice left my throat with a ringing clarity. I touched my hand to my neck, a jolt of surprise going through me as I recalled my last memory.

"Yes," Laima said, arching a pencil-thin dark eyebrow. "Your throat has been cut. In your mortal body."

"My mortal body?" Ah. That explained some things. "So I'm dead now?"

Laima smiled. The corners of her eyes crinkled up to match her lips. "No, Dekla. Not now. Don't you know who you are?"

I frowned, feeling completely confused. A moment ago I was being murdered, and now I was having a conversation with a goddess... in heaven? "Well, apparently there's some uncertainty on the issue. I tend to think of myself as Jayne. But I guess I'm also Dekla?"

"Yes." Laima took my hand. The warm softness of her skin radiated up my arm, calming my nerves. "You are my sister. There is another, Karta. Together we decide the fate of mortals."

At that moment I felt it. I felt a connection to Karta and Laima as ancient as the pyramids. A feeling of belonging and power stirred in my chest. "Where is Karta? Is she immortal?"

"No." Laima shook her head. "Like Dekla, Karta decided to give up her immortality in exchange for immortal powers. They are distributed among women of her choosing, who also help me in deciding the fates of mortals. Just like you."

Just like me. "But I don't know how to help anyone."

"All you have to do is ask, Dekla."

That's what Adelle had said, too, but it still made no sense to me. "I don't understand."

She leaned closer, so close I could only see her eyes. "From time to time you'll meet a person whose fate hasn't been decided. Each time you do, you'll see a possible fate, and you get to have your say."

"Really?" A dozen visions of various deaths flashed behind my eyes. Guilt sickened my stomach at the thought that I could've saved them and didn't. "But how?"

Laima took a step back. "You ask me to change it."

"That's it? That's all I have to do?"

She nodded. "But that doesn't mean I will change it. I will consider your request. And you only have the power to change the deaths of youth. If it's an adult, you must appeal to Karta."

My mind reeled with the concept. "So I have to find Karta? And how will I know if you change it?"

A smile again, as bright as the first rays of sunlight. "I will tell you if I approve the change."

She hadn't answered my question about Karta. But before I could ask again, her smile faded, and she continued.

"But you must be wise, Dekla. All people die eventually. You must consider their entire situation before you make a request. There is a cost that comes with each change."

A knot formed in my chest. Of course. "What is the cost?"

"Ten years of someone else's life."

I jolted. "Ten years? That's kind of a lot!"

Yes," Laima agreed. "So judge wisely."

"But whose life? Whose life will I be affecting?"

"You won't know."

"All of the deaths I See are horrible," I whispered. "I want to change all of them."

"But you cannot." She studied me. "As your powers grow stronger, Dekla, you will be given more responsibility. You will have more visions. You can change their deaths, but remember the price."

Aaron. My sister. Harold. Mr. Harris. How could I choose between these people?

Wait. Mr. Harris was an adult. I couldn't change his. "How can I find Karta?" I asked again, suddenly feeling that this was very important. I couldn't do my job properly if I didn't know where she was.

Laima let go of my hand. "You will find each other. It's time to go back, Dekla."

Back. I jerked, inhaling. "But I will die."

"No, you won't. That is not your fate." Laima took a step backwards and morphed into a swan. The bird craned its long neck toward me before the clouds faded to darkness.

CHAPTER TWENTY-SEVEN

S TATIC AND murmured voices filled the air around me. Rough hands pressed up against my cheeks, and then a face hovered in front of me, brilliant white back-lighting him. "Jayne?"

"Are you an angel?" I whispered. My neck began to burn, and I whimpered.

"Help is on the way, Jayne." The face blurred and I closed my eyes. Nothing made much sense. I'd think about it later.

I opened my eyes to a yellow room with pink and green helium balloons floating above my bed. It took me a moment to recall my last moments. My hand flew to my neck, touching a cloth bandage. A white cord dangled from my index finger, and my movement triggered an alarm.

A woman dressed in blue scrubs rushed into the room, followed by my mother.

"Jayne?" Mom cried, then she rushed to me and threw her arms around me.

"I'm alive," I croaked, surprised at the sound of my voice. Raw and scratchy, like it hadn't been used in days.

"Hello, Jayne," the nurse said, smiling down at me. "I'm Catherine. How do you feel?"

"Confused." I frowned. "I thought I was dead."

"You almost were. You had a six-inch gash across your neck, nearly slicing your carotid artery. If it had, you wouldn't be here."

I pressed a hand to my neck, horrified. My fingers brushed up against a thick bandage.

Catherine didn't notice my expression. She adjusted my I.V. and consulted a chart in her hands. "I'll let the police brief you. I know they wanted to know when you awoke. Does your head hurt?"

"A little."

"I'll bring you some ibuprofen. Let me know if you need anything else." She left the room.

I tried to turn to my mom, but the searing pain in my neck stopped me. "Mom?"

"I'm here, Jayne." She leaned over me and smoothed my hair. "We've all been so worried about you. Look, this is from Dana." She drew my attention to the balloons and a hand-drawn card. It showed a blond stick figure with a giant frown and great big blue tears.

I laughed and opened it. *I love you and I'm sorry!!! Please get better!!*

I looked at my mom. "How long have I been here?"

"Two days, honey."

Two days. Two days of which I could recall nothing. "Was I in a coma?"

"No. Just resting."

Someone knocked on the door, and then Lieutenant Bailey walked in. "Welcome back, Jayne. I'll keep this brief."

"Nice to see you too," I replied.

He nodded. "We've got the man in custody. It is, of course, the man you said it was. My question is, how did you know? Did Hannah really tell you?"

I flattened my palms on the white sheet. "Mom? Can we have a moment?"

"Of course." She shot him a look and then walked out, closing the door behind her.

I cleared my throat, wincing at the tightness. "No, Hannah didn't tell me. Not exactly."

Triumph flashed in his eyes. "Did you even know her?"

"I met her right before she died." I hesitated. "I saw her future when we met."

He blinked and stared at me.

I shrugged. "That's why I lied. I didn't want to take the time to convince you."

"You saw the future."

"Yep. It happens sometimes." I touched my throat again. "Take it or leave it. How did you find me?"

"Your boyfriend called us."

"My boyfriend?"

"Said he went back to your car to talk to you. He thought at first you'd found a ride home, but then he noticed your cell phone in the road. Your phone was beeping a message that you were late for our meeting, so he called me. While on the phone, someone in the cornfield shot your windshield out."

I gasped, immediately remembering Mr. Livingston. "Was Aaron hit?"

"No, but it was probably meant for him. He got in his car and sped out of there. I sent out a K-9 unit. Apparently we were just in time."

"You could've shown up a little sooner," I said dryly.

A fleeting smile passed over his face. "Touche. You still thought I was an angel when you saw me."

I remembered the figure hovering over me when I came to. "Oh. That was you."

"You're welcome. You'll have a scar, but at least you're alive."

"Thanks," I whispered. "What about Mr. Livingston? Did you find him?"

He frowned at me. "Who?"

"The shooter. Mr. Livingston. My high school teacher. They were brothers."

Bailey was scribbling on a notepad. "He's probably long gone by now, but we'll get someone to his place." He shifted his weight and looked at me. "Well, unless you have anything else to add, I'll be on my way."

"Nothing else."

"Are you willing to testify in a court of law?"

The thought made me shudder, but I nodded. "Of course." Heaven forbid I should experience any other visions at this man's hands.

"We'll be in touch, then." He paused. "And, for the record—if you should happen to... witness... a crime again—you can call me."

I smiled. He did believe me, then.

My mom slipped back in as soon as he left. "I just called your father. He'll be here soon."

My mind was still buzzing from Lieutenant Bailey's words. "Has a boy named Aaron been here?"

Mom hesitated, as if she'd been fearing this question. "You mean the one who called the police?"

"Yes. Looks like Superman?"

"No, honey."

My heart sank. It had been a chivalrous gesture, then, helping me. He'd done his job and now we were through. Really and truly. "Thanks, Mom." I reached over and squeezed her hand. "Thanks for being here with me."

∞

They kept me for two more days to make sure I had no permanent trauma from my injuries. The worst injury was my cut, and after the nurses showed me how to keep clean it and rebandage it, the doctor released me.

Dana came to see me four times in that two-day period, always with an offering of chocolate or candy and once with my very own bag of Dum-Dums. Aaron didn't come at all.

My mom helped clear out my room before I was discharged from the hospital. I paused in the doorway. "Mom, will you wait for me at the car? I need to say hi to someone first."

She looked at me, her aqua eyes registering surprise. But she only nodded. "Of course."

Thanks." I hurried toward the elevators.

A nurse stood over the empty bed in Adelle's room, stripping the sheets. My heart fluttered. "Excuse me."

She glanced up at me and straightened. "Yes?"

"I'm looking for Adelle. Did she switch rooms?"

Her brow knit together in a sympathetic expression, and I braced myself. "Are you family?" she asked.

"No. Just a friend." My eyes wandered around the bare room, missing all the photos and flowers from my previous visit. "She died, didn't she?"

"I'm so sorry. She died two nights ago."

I nodded, my heart wooden inside my chest. I'd just missed her. If she had just held on two more days, I could've told her my experience with Laima.

Wait a minute. Two nights ago I was brought in. Coincidence? "Do you know what time she died?"

"Not off hand. Sometime after dinner."

The hairs on my arms stood on end, and I lifted my shoulders up and down briskly. Right around the time I... didn't die. Too weird.

"What did you say your name was?" The nurse stood still, her brown eyes watching me.

"Jayne. Jayne Lockwood."

"Oh, thank goodness I remembered." She pushed past me, and I slid against the wall to let her out of the room. She grabbed up a file at the nurse's station and rifled through it. "Here." She thrust a folded piece of paper at me. "She left this for you."

I stared at it. My name danced across the top in pretty, feminine script.

"Go on." She waved it.

I need to know this, I told myself. I took the paper and moved into a small sitting room. I collapsed inside an oversized chair and opened the notebook paper.

Dear Jayne,

It's lacrosse season. I've been following the team closely and know that the tournament is almost over. Which means, very soon your life will be threatened, and mine will come to an end.

If you are reading this, I am dead, while you have faced death and survived. You might be wondering how I know this, or you may have already figured it out: I Saw you.

It was about five years ago that I met you in passing, at a grocery store. We made eye contact, and in an instant I Saw your death at the hands of the serial killer. Something about you spoke to me. I couldn't bare it, and I cast the judgment for you to live.

But Laima didn't approve it. She said the actions you would take as an investigative journalist would lead to the same fate over and over again, and she could not change you.

There was only one way for me to save you. I had to pass Dekla on to you.

Perhaps you were angry at me for choosing you, for giving you the gift of Sight. I hope now you understand. I gave my life to you. The very next day I lost my immortality and was diagnosed with cancer. I didn't mind. I have lived *more years than I should've been allowed, and I knew I could not live forever. Someday, you also will choose someone to inherit Dekla.*

You have the gift now. Use it wisely and be grateful for it. You hold power in your hands.

Your eternal sister,

Adelle

I read the letter three times, and each time it sank in a little deeper. Then I straightened, fresh resolve steeling me. I was alive, and I had a purpose.

I also had a boyfriend to win back and a sister to save. There was no way I was letting them die the way I'd Seen.

The police were kind enough to return my cell phone to me, and I called Aaron on the way home. The call went to voicemail. I hesitated, not quite sure what to say. "Aaron, it's Jayne. I wanted to thank you. And… talk, if it's not too late. Anyway. Thanks." I hung up, feeling like an idiot and not daring to glance at my mother.

What did I really want to say, anyway? That I wanted him back? That I didn't care about Libby? That I was such a fool to push him away?

Maybe.

My fingers paused over the keyboard before I sent my next message, but I couldn't be so proud that I didn't thank her. Quickly I typed out to Laima, "Thx for helping me. Ready to start. Help?" I watched the phone until we got home. No response.

Mom got me situated on my bed, fluffing up the pillows for me. My cell rang, and I grabbed it. My hope was extinguished when I saw, "JT'S." I groaned. "Hello?"

"Jayne, it's Tom." His deep voice filtered through the line, disappointment heavy in his tone. "I hate to do it, Jayne, but we're going to have to let you go. You've missed work for three days without calling in."

"Tom, I'm so sorry!" I cried. "I've been in the hospital. I wasn't conscious. I'm so sorry nobody thought to call you. You see, I--"

Tom cut me off. "That may be true, Jayne, but you are simply too unreliable. We'll have to find someone else. I'm sorry. Good luck." He hung up, obviously not caring at all why I was in the hospital. All he wanted was a reliable employee.

"Well, there goes that job," I sighed, tossing the phone off the bed.

"What?" my mom cried, incensed. "I'll go over there and talk to him. That's not right."

"No, it's fine." I had to admit I felt a certain sense of relief. "I didn't like the job anyway. I'll find another one."

Beth came into the room, dropping her eyes and shuffling her feet as if waiting for me to reprimand her for entering my domain. I smiled at her brightly. Now that I knew I might be able to help her, everything was different. "Hey, Beth. Miss me?"

Tears filled her eyes. "I thought you were going to die."

"Nope, not me." I opened my arms and she rushed to give me a hug. I exhaled, feeling dizzy with emotion. It wasn't too late to salvage my relationship with her, either.

Beth pulled back. "Does it hurt?" she asked, touching my neck.

"No. But I might have a scar."

She smiled. "You'll look like you were beheaded."

"That might be fun." My words slurred at the end, and the exhaustion hit me like a semi-truck. I closed my eyes just for a moment.

"Come on, Beth," Mom whispered. "Let her be."

༄

I slept most of Friday away also, waking up only when my mom came in with food. I checked my phone every time my eyes opened. No Aaron.

"How can I be so tired?" I complained to my mom when she brought dinner. "I wasn't even that hurt!"

"It might be emotional, honey." She smoothed my wavy hair and kissed my forehead. "You took a terrible blow."

Maybe I was depressed. I closed my eyes and hunkered down for another snooze.

The doorbell chimed and Mom closed the door to my room. A moment later she poked her head in again. "Jayne."

"Hmm?" I startled from sleep, blinking rapidly.

"There's someone here for you."

I sat up and patted my hair down. "Who?" My first thought was Dana, but my mom would've said that.

"It's a boy. He gave me his name, but I can't remember it. I think it might be that one. You know."

Aaron. "Oh!" I gasped. "Do I look okay?" I didn't wait for her to answer. I knew it would be a lie. I pushed myself to my feet, using the bed for support. My Mickey Mouse pajamas weren't going to cut it. "Help."

Mom immediately went into primping mode. "Here, put this on." She pulled a pink v-neck shirt from my closet and tossed it at me. "Don't you have any jeans anywhere, Jayne?"

I rarely wore pants except in winter, but a dress didn't feel right at the moment. "Bottom dresser drawer." I yanked the shirt on over my head, biting my lip to keep from crying out when it pulled on the bandage around my neck.

She tossed me a pair of jeans, then came over and fussed with my hair. I dabbed on lip gloss. "There."

I threw her a smile. "Thanks, Mom."

"Do you need help walking?"

"Walk behind me in case I fall." Trying to appear calm, I stepped out onto the landing and went down the stairs.

Aaron stood in the entryway studying a family portrait, his hands clasped around a thick book. Our English textbook, I noted as I got closer. I stopped a few feet from him. "Hey."

He turned around. "Oh, hey. You said you wanted to borrow my English book?"

It took me a split-second to place the conversation. The walls spun around, and I leaned my head on the railing, closing my eyes. "That's what you came over here for? I didn't really need your book, you know. I just made that up for your girlfriend."

Aaron stepped over to me and took my elbow, guiding me away from the stairs. I wanted to protest, but was too weak to do much more than follow him. "Oh. I wasn't sure." He dropped the book to his side. "I got your call."

I shrugged. He must mean the one I made three days ago. "Thanks for getting back to me." I couldn't keep the bite out of my tone.

"Didn't you want to talk?" He helped me through the entryway and down the steps to the den.

"Why didn't you come visit me at the hospital?" I blurted out.

"I didn't want to disturb you."

"Disturb me? You saved my life."

"Yes, but I thought it might distress you to see me." He hesitated. "You told me you never wanted to see me again." He settled me on the sofa and sat on the opposite end, back rigid.

Oh yeah. I'd forgotten about that. I felt the blood rush to my face. "Well, it's just that I think the way you broke up with me was really really lame." I crossed my arms over my chest and tried to glare at him. The walk took a lot out of me, though, and it was hard to glare as I panted for breath.

A hint of a smile graced his lips. "The way I broke up with you? Jayne, I wasn't even sure we were together."

"Oh? Does your girlfriend know you go around kissing random girls?" I clutched a throw pillow to my stomach and pulled my knees up. "Well?"

Aaron leaned back against the couch, putting more space between us. "Listen, I'm sorry I couldn't talk when you came over."

I shrugged, trying to push down the hurt I'd felt at seeing them together. "Obviously I was interrupting."

"Interrupting an argument."

The first of many. I bit back the words. "Is that why you're over here? Because you're fighting with Libby?"

He hesitated, his eyes wandering over the edge of the couch, giving me an opportunity to study him in profile. "You know I broke up with her a few weeks ago, right?"

"Right."

"That's because I found someone else I liked more." He turned toward me.

"Are you sure it wasn't just because you found someone local?"

"Libby thought so. She finished her senior year early and moved out here. Thought all I needed was to have her close by."

"Turns out it's true, huh?"

He touched my toe through my white sock. "What was I supposed to do, Jayne? You made it clear you didn't like me. I thought you were angry at me for kissing you. So, I let it go. Or tried to." His eyes flickered to mine before darting away. "I couldn't get you out of my head. First you show up at the hospital. Then you show up at my house. I thought it was a sign." He shrugged. "So after you left, I went out to the game to find you. The rest you know."

I pulled my knees in tighter. "Well." I took a deep breath. "I didn't mean to push you away. But—I was scared."

"Scared? Why?"

"It's hard to explain. I just..." How could I tell him that I couldn't take the ending?

But now I knew it didn't have to end that way. I might be able to change it. Whose life would I shorten when I changed his? I inhaled and turned my head, staring at the red and gold flower patterns on the couch.

Aaron's hand squeezed my shoulder, and I looked his direction, not focusing on anything. "Did you see something about me?"

I tugged on Aaron's shirt, pulling him closer. "Come here." He did, scooting next to me. I pushed my forehead against his. My heart leapt into my throat with what I was about to do, making it throb so bad I thought I'd start bleeding again. Gathering my courage, I pressed my lips to his. I felt his sharp intake of air seconds before his arms went around me. He crushed me against his body, a musky male scent intoxicating my senses. His lips moved to my jaw and I turned my head.

"Ow!" I cried out at the movement.

Aaron pulled back, his blue eyes wide. "Did I hurt you?"

I touched the bandage around my neck and laughed. "No. I'm fine."

My phone chimed, the ringtone for a text message. I pulled it out and scanned it.

Do you have a request, Dekla?

I gasped. It was from Laima. It couldn't be this simple. My thumbs flew over the buttons as I responded.

Yes. Two to begin with: Aaron Chambers and Beth Lockwood.

I paused, and then added,

More to come.

"Good news?"

"Hmm?" A silly grin spread over my face. "Great news. Changes everything. So." I shut my phone. "I take it you don't have a date for prom tomorrow night?"

He settled back on the couch, one hand resting on the rim. "See, there's this problem. The girl I wanted to go with wouldn't talk to me. So I didn't buy tickets. Instead, I'm hanging with my dog at the beach. It's probably going to be pretty lonely."

"You have a dog?" I quirked an eyebrow.

"Yes, Ma'am. Brand new."

"I was just thinking how I need a good dose of sea breeze." I tapped his hand.

He clasped my fingers, intertwining them with his. "A pretty girl would help me get over not going to my one and only prom." He pulled me forward until I reclined on his chest.

His heart thumped under my ear and I smiled, all light and fluttery inside. "Don't worry. I might invite you to my prom next year."

CHAPTER TWENTY-EIGHT

"THIS WILL be your desk, Jayne." Mr. Edwards led me around several cubicles in the Lacey-Barnegat Times upstairs floor, finally stopping at an empty one. There was a small table, a flat-screen computer, a two-drawer file cabinet, and a telephone. "Welcome to the Times."

"Thanks," I breathed, moving my chair back and sitting down. My skin tingled with excitement and I powered the computer on. My first real job. Well, technically it still wasn't a real job, since it was a summer internship. Still, if I did well, Mr. Edwards had hinted that they might take me on as a junior journalist next summer after I graduated.

A hint of lemon wafted into my cubicle seconds before the tall brunette walked over. Her green earrings danced as she tossed back her straight, long brown hair. "So you're Jayne, huh?"

I stood up, giving her a shy smile while not quite meeting her eyes. I would at some point; it was my responsibility, after all. But I would decide when. I stuck out my hand. "And you are...?"

"Kate." She shook my proffered hand. "I started here as an intern four years ago. I'm going to Seton Hall University. You're still in high school, right?"

"Right." I nodded and sat back at my desk, turning my attention to the computer. "Lacey Township High. Graduate in a year."

"Figures. Well, we'll be working a lot together, Jayne. Anytime I've got overflow, I'll pass it on to you."

Mr. Edwards had briefed me on this. I would learn from Kate by being her assistant. I nodded, watching her reflection in my screen. "Got it. I'll help however I can."

"Awesome." She flashed me a brilliant white-toothed smile. "We'll get along just smashingly."

And someday soon I'll learn how you die, I thought. That was alright. I could handle this.

I got home from my first day with a confidence that felt wrong in my body; insecurity and paranoia were my usual style. I dropped a few work assignments on my bed and picked up my phone.

"Dana?" I said the moment she answered.

"Hey beautiful!" she said, affection radiating from her voice. "Coming over?"

Warmth filled my chest, and I swallowed back the lump in my throat. Parting time. "I'll be right there." Soon she would be in college, having a blast and making new friends. And I'd be hanging out here for the summer, trying to find other people to share the joys of my senior year with.

I still had Aaron.

But there was something else I needed to do, now, while this new confidence flowed through me. Someone I owed a phone call to.

I flipped open my ghetto phone and dialed Stephen's number. I didn't have to search my contacts; I still had it memorized.

He answered on the second ring. "Jayne," he said, his voice a mixture of surprise and...happiness?

"Stephen, hey. Sorry it's been so long."

"No, no, you're fine. What's up, Jayne?" He sounded so normal that it made my heart ache. He had no idea what was coming.

I cleared my throat. "How was prom?"

"It was... great. I'm sorry you couldn't go. I hope you're feeling all right."

He knew about my run-in with the serial killer, then. Not a big surprise; most of the city knew. "Oh, don't worry about me. I'm glad you had a good time. How's your mom doing?"

"My mom?" His voice took on a defensive tone. "I mean, she's doing fine. Why?"

I searched for a good explanation for how I knew she was dying. "Aaron works at the hospital." I crossed my fingers, hoping his mom was already in and out for treatments. "He told me she is really sick."

"She's fine, Jayne."

There was a finality in his voice that worried me. I wasn't sure if Stephen was brushing me off, or if he was in denial. "Well, I know you're a great son for her. I'm sure she's proud of you. I bet your dad's having a hard time, though."

"He's doing all right." Now Stephen sounded cautious.

I cleared my throat. "I met him a couple of months ago. We talked about you for a few minutes."

I couldn't change Mr. Harris's fate; that was Karta's jurisdiction. Even if I knew how to reach her, I wasn't sure how to supplicate on his behalf. He took his own life, after all. But Stephen, I could help. "He told me something kind of personal. He said that he wished he spent more time with you, that nothing's more important than his family."

Stephen didn't say anything, and an awkward silence descended over the line. Then he cleared his throat. "Yeah, that's interesting. Thanks for telling me, Jayne. Hey, I gotta go now. But call any time, okay?"

"Sure thing." My heart sank as I hung up. He thought I was crazy, that was for sure.

Then I shrugged. I'd done what I could.

&

"This is it, huh?" Dana slammed the trunk and came around the car. She hooked her arm through mine and leaned her head on my shoulder.

"Yeah." I tried to smile but my voice wavered, giving away my true feelings. "You're all grown up and leaving me."

She squeezed my arm. "You're an amazing person. I can't believe I was your best friend for years and you never let it slip to me about your secret powers."

I pulled free and gave her a big hug. "Thanks for believing in me."

Dana stepped back and flattened her plaid button-up dress with her hands. "Careful there. I actually had to iron this."

"And now you're going to drive in a car for several hours and wrinkle it."

"Fabulous, huh?" She bit her lower lip. "You'll come visit, right?"

"I can hardly wait to see you taking that campus by storm."

"You've grown up, too, Jaynie. All ready to get out there and take chances. Look at you, a journalist!"

"Intern," I corrected, though she was right. I had changed in the past few weeks. Suddenly the future wasn't set in stone. It was pliable, and I had the power to change it. It was... empowering.

Living through my own death might have had something to do with it, too.

Mr. Sparks leaned his head out the window. "Dana, are we leaving today or should I unpack?"

I gave her another quick hug, fighting a desperate feeling in my chest. What on earth was I going to do without her? "Have fun, Danes. Love ya."

"You're the best," she breathed in my ear. "If you ever see my future through anyone else's eyes, you better call me and tell me."

I laughed and let her go. Dana climbed into the car next to her dad. As he pulled away from the curb, she leaned over and honked the horn, then waved out the window at me.

I waved until they were out of sight, and then walked slowly back to my Honda. My stomach knotted up as I thought of what I was about to do, but it was time I did it.

☙

"Beth?" I climbed the stairs with great trepidation, noticing the way each one creaked as I put my entire weight on it. "Beth, are you home?"

Beth came out of her room. She blinked wide blue-green eyes at me. I was struck by how much like me she looked. How had I missed this?

"What is it, Jayne?" Her voice was cautious, and who could blame her? Even though we rode to school together, shared a bathroom, and ate dinner at the same table, until a few weeks ago, I had done everything I could to avoid talking to her. We hadn't had a relationship in years, and that was my fault.

"Come in my room for a minute. I want to talk to you."

She followed me, clutching her hands together. "Did I do something wrong?"

"No, Beth. But I have to tell you something." Like Mr. Harris, Beth chose her death. Even when I asked Laima to change it, she said she couldn't change Beth. Only Beth could do that.

But maybe I could help her. Because the future is fluid, and I am Dekla, goddess of destiny.

ಬಾಬಾಬಾ

About the Author

Tamara Hart Heiner is a mom, wife, baker, and an author. She currently lives in Arkansas with her husband and soon-to-be-four children. Her other books include *Perilous* and *Altercation*, young adult suspense novels published by WiDo Publishing. Find her online at www.tamarahartheiner.com.

Made in the USA
Lexington, KY
17 March 2017